Praise f

LOUDER

"With *Loudermilk*, Lucy Ives weaves a wryly comic tale set in the insular, masturbatory world of a Midwest MFA program. Dissecting ideas around authenticity, status, and the chronic wish for fame or legacy that plagues or drives aspiring writers and established authors/professors alike, Ives tears down the curtain to unveil the wizard—and here all the characters are implicated in operating the clunky machinery that creates then lionizes the concept of merit or talent in the academic/literary world. The result is this wildly smart novel that hilariously exposes its characters as they try to vault or cement themselves into some literary canon and/or ivory tower, unaware that the canon/tower is an ever-vanishing mausoleum wherein living writers go to get stuck, or lost, or to scrawl their names and draw butts and boobs on the walls."

—JEN GEORGE, author of *The Babysitter at Rest*

"Lucy Ives is as deeply funny and ferocious a writer as they come. She's also humane and philosophical when it matters most. I love *Loudermilk*." —SAM LIPSYTE, author of *Hark*

"*Wonder Boys* meets Cyrano de Bergerac meets Jacques Lacan meets *Animal House*. Something for everyone."

—*Kirkus Reviews*

Praise for

Lucy Ives

"Ives . . . infuses even mundane actions with startling imagery."

—*The New York Times Book Review*

"An accomplished poet, Ives also knows how to delight sentence by sentence, with turns of phrase that cry to be underlined or Tweeted . . . a voice that is at turns deadpan and warm, shot through with a crisp irony that makes it tempting to declare it the literary equivalent of an Alex Katz painting."

—*Vogue*

"I first knew Lucy Ives's work as a poet, and to have her prose is a gift, too." —HILTON ALS, author of *White Girls*

"A deeply smart and painstakingly elegant writer."

—WAYNE KOESTENBAUM, author of *Camp Marmalade*

"A rampaging, mirthful genius."

—ELIZABETH McKENZIE, author of *The Portable Veblen*

"Like the paintings of Agnes Martin or the films of Nathaniel Dorsky, the most important character in Ives's prose is its reader. In the white space underneath these notes my own mind's wanderings take on what is not exactly an importance, but a space for reading and thinking. I move around in this writing, and become aware of my moving around within it, and consider not only the shape of the writing, but my own shape as its reader. In other words, Ives's writing encourages its readers to consider their own power and form among the reality they encounter." —*Make:* magazine

"Lucy Ives is smart in that heartbreaking way that can make a spare, suspicious, elegant work of anti-poetry out of the silent treatment between ideas and those who have them."

—ANNE BOYER, author of *A Handbook of Disappointed Fate*

"Ives's exquisite take on ellipsis as realism is a dream, as both vision and something that fully satisfies a wish."

—MÓNICA DE LA TORRE, author of *The Happy End / All Welcome*

"Ives . . . is quickly developing into a poet of sentences on par with the poem-essays of Lisa Robertson and Phil Hall for their sharp blend of lyric, thought, and wit."

—ROB McLENNAN, author of *Household Items*

"Think of the upkeep of the minotaur at the center of what can only be the labyrinthine mind of Lucy Ives. This particular creature feeds on its own enclosure. Who said time is eternity turned into a moving image? How does this work on the page? As soon as Ives allows things focus, she pulls back, revealing a small component of a larger construct, but never anything objective and irreducibly whole. Thus, effectively her subject and obsession is not the demarcation of time, but the inability of time to be properly or comparatively enacted. What if Stein and Paul Éluard were a single poet? What if Wittgenstein, Elaine Scarry, and Charles and Ray Eames collaborated on a novelization of Terry Gilliam's *Time Bandits*? What if Robbe-Grillet and Hélène Cixous were to rewrite *The Duino Elegies* as an essay? Daedalus never built anything quite like this. Good luck getting out." —NOAH ELI GORDON, author of *Is That the Sound of a Piano Coming from Several Houses Down?*

"Ives's work is certain in its undoing of certainty; it has an unforgettable voice as it strips itself of voiced identity; it summons a deeply trusted narrator in a work which cunningly challenges that trust." —JORIE GRAHAM, author of *Fast*

LOUDERMILK

ALSO BY LUCY IVES

My Thousand Novel
Anamnesis
Novel
Orange Roses
nineties
The Worldkillers
Human Events
The Hermit
Impossible Views of the World

LOUDERMILK

OR

The Real Poet

OR

The Origin of the World

A Novel

LUCY IVES

SOFT SKULL
NEW YORK

This is a work of fiction. All of the characters, organizations, and events portrayed in this novel are either products of the author's imagination or are used fictitiously.

First Soft Skull edition: 2019

Library of Congress Cataloging-in-Publication Data
Names: Ives, Lucy, 1980– author.
Title: Loudermilk, or, The real poet, or, The origin of the world : a novel / Lucy Ives.
Other titles: Loudermilk | Real poet | Origin of the world
Description: First Soft Skull edition. | New York : Soft Skull, 2019.
Identifiers: LCCN 2018055884| ISBN 9781593763909 (pbk. : alk. paper) | ISBN 9781593763923 (ebook)
Classification: LCC PS3609.V48 L68 2019 | DDC 813/.6—dc23
LC record available at https://lccn.loc.gov/2018055884

Cover design & Soft Skull art direction by salu.io
Book design by Wah-Ming Chang

Published by Soft Skull Press
1140 Broadway, Suite 704
New York, NY 10001
www.softskull.com

Soft Skull titles are distributed to the trade by
Publishers Group West
Phone: 866-400-5351

Printed in the United States of America
1 3 5 7 9 10 8 6 4 2

Rilke was a *jerk*.

JOHN BERRYMAN

CONTENTS

Personae xv

I Early Days

ONE. *Control* 3

TWO. *Doubt* 8

THREE. *Fate* 12

FOUR. *Same* 15

FIVE. *Fine Arts* 20

SIX. *In Loco Parentis* 23

SEVEN. *Settling* 31

EIGHT. *Neighbors* 35

NINE. *Prospects* 46

TEN. *The Lucky* 51

ELEVEN. *Instruction* 57

TWELVE. *Same* 60

THIRTEEN. *This Is a Pipe* 67

FOURTEEN. *This Is Not a Pipe* 71

FIFTEEN. *The Reason*......................... 78

SIXTEEN. *That Person* 97

SEVENTEEN. *Predictably*..................... 100

II Writing Teacher

EIGHTEEN. *Early Poems* 107

NINETEEN. *Motivation* 112

TWENTY. *Allegory* 116

TWENTY-ONE. *Grief* 121

TWENTY-TWO. *A Portrait*......................129

TWENTY-THREE. *Veils* 133

TWENTY-FOUR. *Soft Power* 137

TWENTY-FIVE. *Lists* 144

TWENTY-SIX. *A Break*.........................149

TWENTY-SEVEN. *Elsewhere* 152

TWENTY-EIGHT. *Custom* 156

TWENTY-NINE. *Parity*.........................169

THIRTY. *Fortune*..............................174

III Volta

THIRTY-ONE. *Images* 181

THIRTY-TWO. *A Very Interesting Young Man* ... 214

THIRTY-THREE. *Letters* 217

THIRTY-FOUR. *We Prefer to See Ourselves Living* 223

THIRTY-FIVE. *Love* 231

THIRTY-SIX. *The Iceberg* 237

IV Your Best Reader

THIRTY-SEVEN. *A Novelist* 251

THIRTY-EIGHT. *In Advance of the Broken Arm* .. 263

THIRTY-NINE. *Their Penultimate Encounter* ... 266

FORTY. *Détente* 270

FORTY-ONE. *Worlds* 277

FORTY-TWO. *Recognition* 280

FORTY-THREE. *Persistence* 283

FORTY-FOUR. *And Then* 285

FORTY-FIVE. *Mingling* 287

FORTY-SIX. *You* 290

FORTY-SEVEN. *Persona* 293

FORTY-EIGHT. Est et Non 302

FORTY-NINE. *The Author* 307

Epilogue 311

Afterword: The Libertine 327

Acknowledgments 333

PERSONAE

TROY LOUDERMILK	First-year student in the Seminars for Writing; poet
HARRY REGO	Loudermilk's companion
CLARE ELWIL	First-year student in the Seminars for Writing; fiction writer
LIZZIE HILLARY	Daughter of poets; fifteen years old
DON HILLARY	Instructor in the Seminars for Writing; poet
MARTA HILLARY	Instructor in the Seminars for Writing; poet
ANTON BEANS	Second-year poet

I

EARLY DAYS

One

Control

Troy Augustus Loudermilk has a silver 1999 Land Cruiser with tinted windows and sunroof. He claims he bought it with cash from an out-of-court settlement with the SUNY system. The civil suit stemmed from "repeated unwelcome sexual advances" allegedly made by a thirty-seven-year-old female assistant professor, an anthropologist, during office hours. Loudermilk was adept enough to preserve a number of these encounters on tape. Highlights include an afternoon of rhetorical queries—why Loudermilk "keep[s] coming back for more"; then, "what [he is] so afraid of"—followed quickly on by the professor's playful mimicry of an exotic felid. She clambers gamely onto her desk and begins to "lap cream" out of a "saucer"/course pack. She yowls and purrs. Even in audio format, it's pretty damaging stuff.

At one point on the tape, Loudermilk meekly informs his protean instructor that he is "concerned about [his] future." He says he's worried about his grades, plus his personal relationships and employment prospects. He wants to know how he can "do better." He says he's stressed out about reproducing the bullish America he grew up in. He's having trouble negotiating the unpredictable "peaks and valleys" of romantic intimacy, not to mention the color-coded shimmy of the terrorism threat advisory scale.

If you think you know Loudermilk, then you think that when he says one thing he really means something else. If you *actually* know Loudermilk, then you know that when he says something that's pretty much exactly what he means.

Overall, Harry Rego is not that inclined to pity his friend.

They've been driving now for two days.

They have traced the southern hem of Lake Erie and powered past Gary, Indiana, but here in the home stretch the Land Cruiser's CD player has at last shit the bed. They've been reduced to radio and tape deck, which, considering Loudermilk's need to micromanage the acoustic environment, has been very nearly cataclysmic. In order to maintain a sense of calm within the vehicle, Harry has been forced to shell out twenty dollars to acquire a pair of overpriced but essentially listenable cassettes, one the Breeders and the other from Ike and Tina Turner's late catalogue, at an Illinois truck-stop establishment called the Bucket. "Nutbush City Limits" is just embarking on its third consecutive rotation when a sign announcing the relative proximity of the city of Crete appears.

Harry's extremities are at least 99.9 percent zombie meat, due to extended confinement and Loudermilk's enthusiasm for AC. He should by all accounts be psyched to put this journey behind him, but instead the news of their impending arrival sends a knot of fear into his stomach—which organ commences methodically punching itself—as his tongue takes on an increasingly profound flavor of humid roadkill.

Harry boots violently into an empty Super Big Gulp.

"Dude," Loudermilk says.

"Pull over."

"Dude, we're almost there."

Harry heaves again.

Loudermilk powers down all four windows. He removes his seat belt and uses his knees to steady the wheel while he leans over and trawls the debris on the back-seat floor.

Harry gags. Something trickles up, and he spits it into the beige half liter he has already produced.

"Fuck!" Loudermilk is proclaiming. He is not having great success in his quest for whatever it is.

The Land Cruiser lists casually into oncoming traffic. Harry, cowed by nausea and dread, attempts to accept his own imminent demise, even as he regrets that someone as life-loving as Loudermilk is about to be deprived of a future, not to mention the innocents they are likely to take with them.

"You see a fucking lid over there?" Loudermilk shouts against the wind and tambourine and blasting climate control.

Harry squints. A big rig with a pale, determined-looking face inside its cab is barreling toward them.

Harry mutters, "This is the whole problem."

"What?" Loudermilk has his head down, is groping around behind the passenger seat.

Harry quietly reiterates, as the circular logo on the blue hat worn by the driver of the colossal tractor trailer becomes apparent, along with the driver's expression of baffled rage, that this, their remarkably divergent outlooks on the world, *this*, Loudermilk's blasé treatment of a scenario in which multiple tons of steel plus hundreds of gallons of igneous dinosaur juice are hurtling toward them, and they it, on a course of perfect inevitability, *THIS*, Loudermilk's insistence on placing his hand on a cup lid at this very moment, *none* of which there is time to say, is a living, breathing summation of everything that is the matter with their incomprehensibly futile, and now increasingly brief, lives.

"*What?*" Loudermilk, rifling, repeats.

The semi driver, recognizing that he is in danger of being frontally reamed by a pair of fucktards from the Empire State, deploys his horn.

"Got it!" Loudermilk exclaims, popping back up.

The semi's horn has become a deafening, uninterrupted blare. The driver's face is contorted by what looks, at two yards' distance, to be a mixture of mortal fear and the desire to commit slow, surgical murder.

The Land Cruiser leaps into its designated lane, narrowly avoiding a white Bonneville.

The rig wails by.

Loudermilk swerves to the right and punches the car onto an exit, simultaneously fitting the reclaimed lid over Harry's warm vomit. Windows rise.

Loudermilk shakes his head. "And we're in. Now what the fuck were you trying to say?"

Harry balances the Big Gulp in the Land Cruiser's cup holder and ejects the tape. He scrolls around on FM until he gets some classical. "I don't remember."

Loudermilk is like, "That is stellar, dude."

Harry examines a strip mall. It is in no way promising.

Loudermilk is saying, “I believe we have arrived.”

They overtake a cluster of field-hockey enthusiasts in shorts and shin guards who are waiting for the light to change so that they may pertly advance to a campus athletic field.

It is 2003, August, Friday the 29th.

Two

Doubt

> This isn't anyone's autobiography. What I've lost is so easy to name as to make it impossible to speak about.

These are the two terse sentences Clare Elwil has been writing for the past ten weeks. Her notebook jitters on the tray table. Even a single additional three-word phrase would be an improvement. For ten minus three is seven, which is equivalent to three plus four, and three times four equals twelve, which, one plus two equals three, again. Ten divided by three is a little more than three. Ten times three is thirty, and three plus zero is three. The plane, meanwhile, is one. It's grievously small. Clare is on the plane. It was impossible to fly direct and that of course indicates something about where she is going. It was a good day this morning, light and bright; yet, occasionally, as the plane darts and veers on its descent down the unpleasant roads of the midwestern sky, she fears loss of consciousness.

For a few months now her distress has attached itself to background noise; it is no longer "in" her. It arrives. "On catlike feet." This is someone's poem, no doubt? A book on the piano in that apartment. Her *mother's* apartment, Clare corrects herself. She is headed to the Seminars.

Slumbering beside her is a very pink man in his late fifties. His oblivion gives Clare ample opportunity, if not permission, to study the boyish short-sleeve button-down shirt he must wear in acquiescence to some regional career norm. Gray hairs curl on his speckled arms. His face has collapsed under weight of dream. He sighs. He is a machine for living, simple in conception and construction. In the right breast pocket of his button-down his boarding pass is displayed, as if to signal a belief that it might be reasonable and acceptable, a sensible business practice, that he be asked to leave the plane midflight should he be unable to produce the document at a moment's notice. Associated with him is a salty scent, a faint musk; essentially inoffensive.

Clare's body, specifically her head, rebels. Dread is taking on several recognizable shapes—like continents of the northern hemisphere of the planet Earth or, perhaps, she manages to think, these are sheep. Sheep! They lumber toward her, throbbing electrically. Or hogs. Are there three? It is possible there are three of them. Maybe four: a fourth hides behind the body of one of his fellows, seems briefly to merge stickily with the others—viscous and amorphous—before coming unabsorbed once more. "*Pigs*," Clare mutters, as the angle of descent is rendered more pronounced by the professional whose gestures control this can.

Clare is a year late. She should have been making this

bizarrely perilous short flight, like being thrown across the state of Illinois, at the end of the summer of 2002, when she was still a great writer. Admittedly, she had been a very young great writer, but all magnificently accomplished persons have had to be something before the period of universally acknowledged dominance—and Clare was evidently, tellingly being what she was then, which was very, very promising. It is in description now that Clare has a tendency to become most mired. No, *now* it is in description that Clare has a tendency to become *the* most mired. *The* tendency? Is that the word? *Mired? The?* She slides back and forth, on wheels, mobile yet unable to pass over the hump that stands between her and poised, proper articulation. What was it she was? Who was there? The very sentence is unnatural. *The sentence is very unnatural.* Who? Had anyone in fact said or believed this of her? The sense that this had happened somewhere, the naming of her, the praise of her, the walking to the home of the doughty publisher, the short man, his cobbled streets. She was to receive the award before a polished black piano. *His* piano, not her mother's. To someone, oh someone, then one Clare Elwil, these events had occurred. "You have a name for a book cover," an anemic woman in a pair of avant-garde earrings, nests of silver thread, had whispered. Clare was a stylist, a judicious narrator. She sold her story to the room. She was someone, the worthies said, who should be driving the bus, and there were daffodils jangling everywhere in Cambridge.

Here, the plane touches earth. Clare gags. A black star blooms, and she maintains herself in a kind of (obviously wishful) corporeal stillness, by force of will. The pink man stirs.

The plane bounces. There comes a smattering of applause.

Clare Elwil is in the middle of nowhere, where she will remain for the next two years, and what no one knows but they will soon discover is that she can no longer write.

Three

Fate

Loudermilk and Harry have spent Friday night at a squalid split-level rented by half a dozen rising seniors who have, or so their hosts' story goes, been lately kicked out of their sororities for various infractions. Four are currently away on a DUI-related sobriety retreat—though utilizing separate cars on separate occasions, they succumbed identically post-finals last spring—and won't be back until after the holiday.

Harry was placed downstairs on a squealing corduroy couch, while Loudermilk's non-negligible gifts were shared by the nubile pair who originally picked them up at a downtown bar. Harry cannot remember their names, though the two coeds are basically distinguishable. For ease of mental reference and to render these alien beings slightly more palatable, he has christened them "Shortstack" and "Skylar." Shortstack is short (obviously) and deeply, artificially bronzed, with prominent cone-shaped breasts, while Skylar is tall and languid and blond, her face a vivid hybrid of Christie Brinkley and Jean Seberg. Both are, however, in Harry's less than generous assessment, dumb as dirt and would willingly have mated with

Loudermilk in an actual pile of this substance they saw near a parked backhoe on the way back from the fifty-cents-a-cup piss emporium where the initial connection was made.

An attempt to set Skylar up with Harry was of course a complete failure, with Harry staring stonily past her right ear as she droned on about how awesome it must have been to go to college so close to New York City, but how scared she would be, like, if she ever went there, because she had heard that a woman had been dragged for, like, a mile once by a purse-snatcher on a moped who, no joke, literally pulled her into traffic, and she had her entire face torn off. "That is not normal!" Skylar exclaimed, as if there were some chance Harry might be so unfamiliar with the project of human existence that the sensorial implications of being separated from one's face by means of asphalt-induced abrasion might not be entirely clear.

Loudermilk knew enough not to take Harry aside and demand to know why he did not get how to act when high-quality poontang was being thrown in his general direction. Instead, Loudermilk just tapped Skylar on the shoulder mid-narrative and subtly renegotiated matters.

It is currently 7:34 a.m. by Harry's watch, and the moaning and sighing and thumping in the room next door finally ceased a little over twenty minutes ago. Harry has not really slept. He has on all of his clothes except for his shoes, and there is a large beach towel depicting a penguin in sunglasses covering him. Not only is it too hot in this room, it also stinks of something all kinds of rank that Harry peevishly identifies as pizza farts plus Vagisil. He is afraid of what he will find if he gets up to go look for the bathroom.

Harry screws his eyes shut and tries again for sleep. In his mind, images of Loudermilk blossom, fade, recur. Loudermilk glides across a lawn in Oswego, New York, nods his head in time, tells Harry to stick with him, it's going to be cool, they know more than everyone, drives Harry down to Rochester, where they contemplate the lilacs and talk about making it big one day, passes him another beer, convinces him to defer his student loans, is inexplicably but so familiarly *there*. Of course there was an era before Loudermilk, but it's only worth remembering insofar as it was a time when Harry was alone. And Harry's alone no more. What a gift, their unity. It's more than he'd hoped for. It's Harry's fate, maybe. And, as fates do, it demands things.

Four

Same

It's the morning of her first full day in Crete, and Clare, out of furnished rooms, is on her own recognizance. She has been told the name of the progressive supermarket, and now she's in it, shopping. Given the prices—like imports in Oslo—it's unlikely there will be a repeat excursion. One must invest in a membership, plus a monthly work shift, and this seems like an incredibly complex proposition given the ubiquity, at least in Clare's experience, of food.

In one aisle, Clare's perverse eye lights on a short middle-aged man, still damp from his shower, who is wrangling a chiming case of wine. Clare is momentarily baffled by the unknown man's familiarity, but is relieved to recognize him, not as a former professor or family friend inconveniently obscured by the disorienting experience of having just relocated to the center of the country, but rather as a slightly more unhinged version of a character of hers, the protagonist from her prize-winning short story, "The Lift," written now more than three years ago. It is, unmistakably, him. Or, rather, *a* him, someone further along in the process. Clare skips to two of her favorite short paragraphs in which the female villain's triumph is revealed:

> "No. It's OK. We can lend you some money." Then he says, "You aren't in trouble, are you?"
>
> Her face turns up. "No," she says. "I just need money." And very quickly, so he can't laugh with her, she laughs.

Clare smiles. Here she had done well. Clare watches the man struggle. He is only living a limited life, a life of deadly certainties, and good for him. She will never be anything like this.

She had, for example, not known that what was going to happen to her would happen and yet how had the event not been present in her life already, at all times and in all she did? It would take place. A tragedy may be well dispersed even previous to its occurrence. One learns that one could not have known and yet one also perceives in the present, with anguish, that there were certain signs, certain tells. Clare had gone to visit her father with some foreboding and had pretended that this foreboding did not exist. She had almost not traveled that June, finding Manhattan very mild and good. Only she did not want to be boring, which is to say she believed herself a promising writer and had lusted delicately after new material, and so she had gone to see her father in Paris, to see his life and learn just how disconcerting each of them would find this encounter after years of separation.

Clare's American father refused to write in English and therefore he was at once a writer of a certain interest and a writer of middling renown. His death, Clare was finding, was doing something to elevate him, but it was possible even this would pass. The query emails had of late slackened. Her father resented French but also resented something he termed, in one essay, "the Usonian," i.e., what people speak in the U.S. of A. To Clare he was a stern and distant voice, if ever he was a presence. If she could understand him now, he had been unworldly but ambitious, driven by notions of authenticity and craft that had, before the accident, seemed to Clare a fantasy designed to shelter him from the realities of the international literary market, such as it was, plus history; there was nothing for him in the country into which he had been born and little his adopted language could mean to Americans. His whole life was, in Clare's prematurely jaded opinion, an exercise in refusing to abandon what was already, and very definitively, lost. The peach tree behind his parents' Yonkers Victorian had come in for special consideration in one volume of poetry widely cited as his best in the French press. Clare had been contacted by her father's English translator several years ago while in college. The translator had wanted to meet with her. Apparently her father was—what had been the term?—not *inscrutable* or *tricky* but, oh yes, that perfect word, *elusive*. "An elusive *guy*," ugh. Clare had declined, coldly. For she wanted to be her own writer and did not wish to seed her sentences with baleful references to postwar peach trees.

On another occasion, a well-meaning scholar of comparative literature had approached her in Harvard's Barker Center and below a chandelier of bleached antlers introduced himself in order to express his affection for her father's verses and critical essays. This one was a floating worm, a scoundrel too distracted by his tenure file to recognize that he was effectively robbing Clare of her dream, which was to be anyone she pleased, rather than the daughter of an under-read poet whose crowning achievement was, in the early 1990s, to have been profiled in the *New Yorker*.

Academics like this obsequious comparatist were blissfully unaware of their lack of tact. They approached her as if she were an unusual nocturnal amphibian, glowing bluely at the edge of a poststructuralist lagoon. They were untroubled by the obvious signal of Clare's surname, which was of course her mother's, and which had been permitted to stand as a way of indicating her father's lack of participation in her early—and, then, her increasingly less early—existence. But Clare had begun to be known for her own fiction in her own sophomoric circles, among her friends, and when this began to occur more and more it was by audiences who did not read poetry and who had little French and who resembled Clare herself, linguistically at least, and who were therefore unlikely to be aware of her father's biography, much less his literary career, such as, it had to be said, it was.

These, then, were the terms on which Clare had, college diploma and acceptance into the Seminars firmly in her grasp, deigned, at the advanced age of twenty-two, to make her estival pilgrimage to an apartment in northern Paris so that she and her dad could take tea nearby and drive to a friend's country estate, where, Clare's father maintained, there was a magnificent library including several modernist first editions which would assuredly be of interest, even to his benighted offspring.

Her father, who was in his late sixties, had grown thinner rather than absolutely old. He had on a good scarf and a very good linen blazer and took her hand somewhat formally before kissing her on both cheeks. Clare knew that she was not radiantly beautiful but her father's handling of her made her feel plausibly physically accomplished. He spoke to her in a pretentious combination of English and French that was mostly comprehensible. He took her downstairs to his local café, where a younger waiter with one dead front tooth was compelled to make much of monsieur's daughter, *la vraie Newyorkaise*. When they were left alone the conversation passed from Clare's plans to her father's early life, his own time as a student in the Seminars. They were *pressés* for some reason, perhaps because the friend with the library wished to dine at a certain hour; Clare is now unsure. They must have exited the café and found her father's car, yet this memory is extremely uncertain. It takes many forms and her father seems now to have had many possible cars. It is a dream retold to Clare by someone else and she bites her tongue so as not to interrupt but alas the narrative makes little sense, there are no nouns or verbs, only prepositions, and their order will not remain clear, they keep hopping over one another, becoming tangled and messed, and she has been assured that it is normal that she can but imperfectly remember these introductory moments as well as the impact itself, which occurred as they were accessing the Périphérique and the ancient Peugeot belonging to her father in which she, Clare, was also riding was impacted by a speeding Eurovan and they went together into a concrete barrier and Clare was painfully retained while her father, beltless, flew forward to be decapitated.

Five

Fine Arts

Around 2:00 p.m. Harry is reawakened by the sensation of something stiff and damp prodding his face. His eyelids are gummy so it takes a few seconds to orient. He remembers, before he perceives, where he is.

Harry is up and on his feet with an alacrity that surprises even him. His head is pounding.

Shortstack is standing too close to him. She has one hand over her mouth, and her head is rapidly moving back and forth on her orange neck as if she is rehearsing some hyper-advanced fellatio technique, though in fact she is only giggling uncontrollably, which is much worse. Also she is holding an uncapped Sharpie in her right hand. The smell of it suffuses Harry's wrath. It's so pronounced in fact it's like he's smelling his own upper lip.

Loudermilk is somewhere and will pay for this later.

Harry stalks wordlessly back to the moldy grotto that is their restroom and spends twenty minutes scrubbing his face with a washcloth he finds wadded up behind the toilet bowl. He succeeds in dimming the elaborate spiral mustache that now adorns his right upper lip and a large portion of his right cheek. The cross with which Shortstack has seen fit to decorate his forehead is more stubborn. It's possible that she got in two or three coats there.

Harry storms back out to the front room.

Loudermilk is standing alone in the kitchen area slowly consuming a Pop-Tart. He hands Harry a plastic tumbler of water emblazoned with an image of the school's mascot, a goofy Minotaur.

"I don't know how you do it, man," Loudermilk is saying.

Harry really wants to discuss the matter of his own face, but Loudermilk is basking in some sort of postcoital reverie and is difficult to reach.

Loudermilk languidly lowers himself onto a food-spattered stool. He says, "They fuckin' loved you." He ingests the last of his postmodern strudel. "Not, of course, that they didn't love me." He blinks. "What? They had to go to work. You know they work there, right?" He means the bar.

"Handy." Harry means the location. Either the tap water or the novelty cup tastes of heavy metals. Perhaps both.

"You know, that's exactly what I was thinking? But anyways, what I'm trying to tell you is they were so into you. They were so totally into it, dude." Loudermilk gazes guilelessly at Harry. He asks to know what happened to Harry's face.

"Fuck you, Loudermilk," Harry says.

Loudermilk counters with what he deems a better activity. He says that they should go check out the lay of the land, maybe take a gander at a certain awesome apartment he's heard about, pick up their fellowship check.

This is to say, Troy Augustus Loudermilk has been

accepted into the Seminars for Writing with full funding for the next two years. It is, of course, the reason they are here. Loudermilk will receive an annual stipend of twenty-five K. In the local economy this is a pretty significant chunk of change. It's enough, even, for two people to live on, no problem. Plus, *Maxim* magazine, in its annual February "Campus Lyfe" feature, has rated this the nation's most sexually adventurous Greek community with the lowest rate of STD infection. Other undergrad communities are infinitesimally more adventurous, but none is so pure. That was really the clincher. Loudermilk had underlined the article and taken notes in the margin and taped it to his bedroom wall back at SUNY Oswego. Only one other school into whose graduate poetry-writing program Troy Augustus Loudermilk was accepted even made it onto the list, the University of Texas at Austin, which had a pretty weak showing, anyway, at number 17 overall.

This is the sense in which the Seminars was a no-brainer for them.

They've mentioned none of this to Greg, their former college roommate and unwitting chaperone in the world of graduate-level creative writing. Greg, a genuine American poet, was unsuccessful in his own applications to programs conferring the degree of Master of Fine Arts and has returned home to live with his parents and temp at a bank for the next year. They are probably going to lose touch with him.

Six

In Loco Parentis

Loudermilk and Harry wander the gelatinous Cretan afternoon.

The campus should be just a few blocks off, but they don't really know where they are. Loudermilk has donned a hot-pink trucker hat he found on the floor of the sorority-reject house. Whiteout has been used to write KEEP IT KNOCKIN! across the front of its foam dome. Loudermilk is also wearing a pair of long khaki cutoff shorts and a white T-shirt. He wears green-and-white Adidas. He is six foot three and built like a water polo champion. His face is hard to look away from. His square jaw resolves itself into a gentle cleft above which shapely lips give levity to otherwise chiseled features. His blondish hair has recently been bleached blonder. Beside Loudermilk, Harry is aware that he resembles, by comparison, a half- or subhuman, a hobbit or shaved teddy bear. He also wears shorts, T-shirt, sneakers. He has no hat, and the sun pains his sensitive eyes.

When they first met, during a sophomore-year honors course in feminist world literature at Oswego, they were the only males in the room. Harry kept to himself, deflated in a one-arm desk. Loudermilk pursued a lipstick lesbian, intermittently flicking things at her. Matters would have continued so, had it not been for the instructor's decision to turn to poetry, since, as she maintained, "You aren't doing the reading." Poems were, the professor mused, pinching her chin, mercifully short world-literary items—though it turned out she knew breathtakingly little about them. This was where Harry came in. Or, rather, where Harry's vastly solitary childhood did, since during one awkward pause he retrieved a line of Dickinson from memory before he knew what he was doing.

People stared.

Harry's pitch was a little off but not out-and-out alarming. Which is to say, better than usual. Still, he promptly shut up.

After class, Loudermilk lingered. "*Loudermilk*," he informed Harry with pastel gentleness, though Harry was already very much aware who Loudermilk was. "What was that stuff?"

Harry, vibrating in place, managed to shrug. Together they went outdoors. Loudermilk didn't seem to mind doing all the talking.

This unshy individual thus handily obtained the distinction of becoming Harry's first and only friend. It's not entirely arbitrary. Like Harry, his pal's a very, *very* only child. Loudermilk has, at this point, but one parent, and back at Oswego he talked about this impressive person a lot. Loudermilk the Elder is, as the myth goes, known to his face as Pops and, more frequently, as well as behind his back, as The Cleaner. He's an ex-military man who made good in the late 1960s and early '70s providing infrastructural triage in locales the

United States had not explicitly invaded but, you know. As his business diversified, The Cleaner found it convenient to return to the States, where he headquartered himself first in Delaware, then in the wilds of Upstate New York. His retreat to the outskirts of Ithaca when Loudermilk Jr. had attained the age of four was precipitated by the desertion of the boy's mother, a member of the Israeli secret service who (Loudermilk implies) had satisfied herself and her superiors as to The Cleaner's general corruption but lack of any real influence or intel. She decamped, leaving a brief note to the effect that it would be preferable if her son might one day learn basic hand-to-hand fighting skills as well as the use and care of a semiautomatic weapon but that the role of mother was not one she was inclined to pursue. The Cleaner, realizing at once his single-parent status and his son's previously unknown Jewishness, went into a tailspin that was only somewhat alleviated by the impulse purchase of a 150-acre ranch encompassing three lakes, a decrepit agricultural enterprise, and one small gorge. He packed his offspring up, delegated judiciously, and entered early semiretirement, a state that did not, however, prevent him from becoming alarmingly wealthy during Bill Clinton's second term.

The Cleaner of the 1990s and early '00s, having transitioned from coups to disasters, served as handmaiden to the federal government where hurricanes made land, oil tankers foundered, parking garages exploded, and, in a moment of superlative patriotic assistance, airplanes entered office buildings. The Cleaner believed in vague neoliberal tenets, which is to say that he believed that he was immune to every ideology, save that of the general goodness of goodness, a pure identity rather than a suspect value, and had seen fit to begin his son's education at a local Montessori school (unlicensed but self-professing allegiance to the movement) where he thought that Loudermilk the Younger would gain an atheistic affection for the phenomenal world unsullied by history or the more exploitative aspects of contemporary capitalism. The Cleaner was not exactly wrong on either count, though Loudermilk the Younger seems to have been more his mother's son than The Cleaner was initially willing to allow. While Loudermilk the Elder occupied himself with maintenance of a growing sideline in bird-dog breeding, Loudermilk the Younger made friends with the sons of members of the local militia and roamed the countryside, fully convinced of the unalienable rights afforded him by his American birth.

After the tree-planting ceremony that indicated the conclusion of local schooling, Loudermilk the Younger consented to continue his education at the nearest state school, more to escape his father's constant juice cleanses, plus the string of Ukrainian mail-order fiancées, all of whom were returned unwed, than because he sought deeper knowledge. Loudermilk the Younger was no fool, but he didn't really care to be book smart. The world was his preferred teacher, *action* his rhetoric and surrogate mother. And though Loudermilk the Younger was outstandingly, one might say willfully, ignorant of the ways in which money functioned, he had always had plenty of it, even as The Cleaner was perpetually offering more.

Loudermilk the Younger, at last free of unwanted parental context and thus simply "Loudermilk," and known to Harry via sophomoric *Weltliteratur*, was lucky, liberated, and on some sort of mission to amaze the world. His unsinkable poise and insatiable appetite for indelible deeds (strolling across campus at high noon wearing only a blue sock; running a competitive campaign for student-body president on a golden retriever, edibles, and Lara Croft–based platform, aka, "GRELC NOW!"; insisting on being allowed to rush several sororities, one of which offered him membership) fascinated and enraged just about everyone. Harry preferred to hover. He was at the center of things but invisible due to his friend's outsized shine. Fast-forward through eighteen months of sustained *Bildung* and by senior year Harry and Loudermilk were inseparable, which, of a crisp October morning, was when Loudermilk remarked, apropos of what seemed like nothing, that this was *it*, the last straw, that he absolutely could not and would not do it anymore, that The Cleaner had really crossed a line this time and now it was time to tee up for some hardball.

Harry wasn't exactly sure what *this* or, for that matter, *it* meant, given the mixing of sports metaphors, but inferred that The Cleaner had probably offered to pay for the rest of Loudermilk's life as a graduation gift. Loudermilk, who hadn't worked a day of his twenty-one-year existence and whose grades were only saved from complete and utter turpitude by the pronounced mediocrity of the school, fell into a deep depression the reality of which he attested to by locking himself into a room and refusing sex or recreational drugs for approximately 2.5 days. His fast concluded, Loudermilk reemerged. He was accosted on his way to debauch himself by Greg, the floater and creative writing major they'd picked up in exchange for a penthouse suite. Greg was lyrically inclined and as per usual was requesting an audience for his latest poem.

Loudermilk bowed politely. He must have been in an altered state, an odd mood brought on by his prolonged detoxifying time away from customary pursuits, because he actually lay down on the common-room floor. He shut his eyes. "Honor us, Greg," he said.

"All right, you guys." Greg stood in a doorway. He shrugged off his yellow hoodie. His hair had recently been re-dyed black and his narrow face held misty eyes over which bluish lids fluttered. "I'm going to read you a poem."

Harry loitered in his own doorway. He gazed down at the prostrate Loudermilk.

Greg took a step. "OK." He brought a paper to his nose. "The name of my poem is"—he stared up into the ceiling tiles—"'One Mind.'" This safely accomplished, Greg coughed. "The first word is crossed out, so I can't read it to you."

Loudermilk raised his head. "Who crossed it out?"

"I did." Greg blinked. "I am the author."

"Is it totally crossed out? Can you not tell us what it is?"

"If you want to know what the word is, I'll have to give you a copy of the poem."

"Can you email it to me?"

Harry stepped a little way into the common room and made like he was going to kick Loudermilk in the head.

Loudermilk seized Harry's ankle, hobbling him momentarily. "He's *emailing* it to me," Loudermilk hissed.

And so it began.

Greg started bringing home a case of Natural Light on the weekly and told Harry and Loudermilk about his advanced poetry workshop. He showed them his best poems and what he considered the best poems written by other members of his class. He loaned them his dog-eared copies of *The Best American Poetry* of 2001 and '02.

Loudermilk put the copies of *The Best American Poetry* on Harry's desk.

Loudermilk said, "Do you have any idea how many people are into this? Somebody could totally run this scene."

Harry thanked Loudermilk for the note. On the evening in question, Greg had passed out on the floor of Harry's room, so the two of them retired to a more agreeable setting.

In a take-out-container-strewn common zone, Loudermilk explained that Harry needed to listen up. He said what he was getting at was partly financial. He said there was a lot more to this whole poetry thing, that he himself had looked into some of the writing programs Greg was applying to for after college and there was significantly more lucre there than you would think in terms of fellowships and grants and waived fees and unexploited resources and what-have-you. He said that it would be stupid easy to get in and get out. He said that he had found some pretty great advocates among Oswego's older male professors who, even if he'd never exactly done proficiently in their courses, enjoyed his stunts plus his willingness to shake hands with them after their most recent meandering lecture, and he thought that he, Loudermilk, would be able to put together some pretty unimpeachable letters of rec, especially given all he'd been through with that crazy anthro chick. There was a lot of goodwill being beamed in his general direction, Loudermilk just knew it. He said all he needed now was a few poems. He said, "I mean, honestly, dude, have you even thought about what you're gonna to do after graduation?"

Harry did think. The prospect of living without Loudermilk terrified him. He pondered the hideous cover of 2001's *The Best American Poetry*, depicting what appeared, incredibly, to be a sloe-eyed contemporary odalisque. He muttered something disingenuous to the effect that he hoped Loudermilk wasn't saying he should apply, too.

Loudermilk cracked a fresh beer and handed it over. "That's *exactly* what I am saying, dude. You and me, as *me*."

Seven

Settling

They are headed up an artery named Van Veldt. Dilapidated mansions bake on brownish lawns.

Loudermilk appears happy as the proverbial clam. He keeps his eyes peeled for bunnies. He says, "This is a stellar district."

Two very blond things in white miniskirts cross a lawn. Loudermilk accords them a tiny salute.

Loudermilk pauses mid-lope. Set back from the sidewalk some fifty feet is a bungalow. It leans slightly to the east. "Yes." Loudermilk consults a scrap of paper. "Yes." He turns up the front walk.

There is an overwhelming onion reek rising from thick grass. Near the bungalow's entry is an orange plastic sled with a hole melted into its pilot's seat, and the rotting remains of what must once have been a woodpile. Loudermilk raps on the doorframe.

Harry says something about how maybe he'll just head back to the car.

Loudermilk mutters, "*Maybe*, dude." He tugs at the door.

"Hello? Hello? Wait for me, please?"

There is someone speed-walking up the path from the street. It is a female person with a wide-brimmed summer hat, dark glasses. Sizable breasts chug along on her slight frame.

Loudermilk stops what he is doing in order to inspect the boobs.

As the person comes into their midst and apologizes for her tardiness, as she is laying her dry palm into theirs and calling herself Evelyn, it gradually emerges that she is middle-aged. Her hair is long, the color of sand. It additionally becomes clear that she loves sunflowers, that her husband is her third. On occasion she acts as slumlord.

"How about we go inside?" Evelyn, glancing at Loudermilk's pink hat along with its interesting exhortation, indicates that she is ready to bring pleasantries to a close.

The kitchen has a bar. There is a main open area. At one time, a wall must have surrounded what appears to be a working bathroom. Only a faint rectangular outline on the floor remains. A toilet and a footed tub grace the center of the space.

"It doesn't have a basement, I want you to know that," says Evelyn.

"This seems like a very bona fide spot!" Loudermilk tests the flush on the toilet.

Evelyn wheels on one gardening clog. "Take it easy!" she shouts.

There is a hideous sucking sound as all the water is evacuated from the bowl. Something slithers. There is a clank, a hiss, a choked sigh. The shower comes on. The stream lands brownish.

Evelyn claps her hands. She is looking joyfully over the side of the tub. "He did fix it! That man is a genius!"

Loudermilk is wearing his 1950s corporate-circumspection face. "How's that?"

Evelyn is brisk. "Let me just show you the other two rooms."

Then, and it's not exactly clear why this happens, they end up telling Evelyn that they like the place. A lot.

Loudermilk says, "But, Evelyn, we have to be on the same page about the bathroom."

Evelyn has driven them back to her split-level. There is a plate of saltines on the table. They have Diet Coke and rum with crushed ice.

"The radical bath," Loudermilk repeats. "The lack of a *room*."

"You just tell everybody to leave!" Evelyn takes a tug on her straw and sucks her molars. She sits there like she is waiting for them to say something.

"What would you offer?" Loudermilk puts it this way.

"For rent? Oh, that's fixed. That's been fixed for a long time." Evelyn wrinkles her nose.

"What would you be asking?" Loudermilk causes his face to fall open into a tender mask.

"Five hundred is only fair."

Loudermilk is masticating a saltine, and he uses the presence of this snack in the vicinity of his epiglottis to initiate a spirited choking routine. He struggles to his feet and hacks the item up onto Evelyn's kitchen floor.

Evelyn takes this in stride, telling Loudermilk where he can find a wet rag.

Tears stream from the corners of Loudermilk's eyes. "We'll give you two-fifty," he croaks. He squats and scoops up the regurgitated cracker.

"Honey, I'm afraid that's an insult." Evelyn jiggles her ice.

"Fine. Three. But throw in a shower curtain."

Evelyn chews ice. "Ha!" she says. "Done. Wash your hands. I'll get the lease."

When she is gone, Harry tells Loudermilk that he needs to ask about the onion smell.

"*You* ask about the onion smell."

"I'm not the one who wants to live there."

"How about, dude, I don't know what smell you're referring to?"

"It's wild garlic," Evelyn calls from the other room. She comes back. "Try digging it up sometime!" She drops the lease on the table and brings her chair closer to Harry's. "You always do that to your face?"

Eight

Neighbors

Another night has expired. Crete is born muggily anew. It's a dim day, a morning for murders. Harry is on the lawn outside their newly acquired crumbling Cretan abode. He was brought out of bed and shack by sounds of life across the street—expletives, howls—and now he is pretending to putter around the lawn. He and Loudermilk are receiving someone's nationalist tabloid, *The Sentinel.* Harry scoops it up. Across the way are shirtless people. They throw beanbags into a hole in a box, their upper arms sleek with baby fat that has lately offered itself up for fraternity brands. It's 10:00 a.m.

Harry's impressed by the enthusiasm of the shirtless for beer at this hour. A person comes out of the house behind them with a BB gun. It has a bright orange muzzle and is instantly trained on everyone. "Liquor run!" the gunman bellows. He points the rifle at one person, then another, then a third. Target number 3 flinches. The barrel drops, and there is a clapping sound as its mechanism is discharged in the direction of feet in massage sandals.

"Goddamn!" the target squeals, hopping back. He's wearing a white visor and attempts to tug it down, in order that it serve as a makeshift face shield. "Goddamn it!" The visor wearer tumbles awkwardly as the gunman marches purposefully down the lawn and takes aim once more.

"It's time for a liquor run," the gunman intones.

Other beanbag participants are getting out of the way, forming a handy chorus. One of them obligingly chants, "Lick or run! Lick or run!"

"Everybody get ready," the gunman announces.

"Nooooo," the visor moans. "C'mon guys!" His breasts jiggle.

"Everybody get set," the gunman continues. "You have a count of five on my signal, bitch."

The visor gulps and moans once more, but he orients his body in the proper direction.

"Now," quoth the gunman, "GO!"

The visor takes off, rubber soles slapping desperately against the pavement. Those on the lawn begin a count: "ONE, TWO, THREE." Here the running boy's hands are lowered to cradle his balls. "FOUR." The gunman hops into the street, plants his feet, squares his shoulders: "FIVE!"

There is a popping noise, a keening yowl. The visor hobbles on. The gunman is furiously pumping his weapon. When he takes aim again Harry sees the gunman's chest heaving, from exertion or excitement, Harry is not sure which, and the visor drops, windmilling like someone on ice.

"Got him in his thigh," the gunman judges, lowering his weapon. He moves down the street toward the wounded boy, rifle slung carelessly over one shoulder, a hunter spent.

The crew on the lawn descends. They approach the trembling, desperately self-examining form in the road.

The gunman says, "Someone get him in the house. I'll take my truck." The gunman tousles the hair of the injured party, whom others bear away. The gunman crosses the street, now scratching his shoulder blades with the inverted gun barrel.

The gunman approaches Harry. He wears an undershirt and a simple necklace of wooden beads. He glistens with sweat, all the way out to the tips of his black hair. He assesses Harry.

"What are you looking at?" the gunman wants to know, and without waiting for a reply gets into a new truck, parked just a few spaces up and painted a metallic green like the head of a mallard.

Harry watches this person drive off. He recalls, from a dreary senior-year Freud survey, that the sadist is both the source of the law and the one who transgresses it.

Now Loudermilk is out. Loudermilk wants to know what the goddamn motherfuck *that* was all about.

Harry tells Loudermilk that they have neighbors, in case Loudermilk wasn't aware.

"Neighbors?" Loudermilk asks. He digs around in the back of his boxers. "That's awesome, dude." Loudermilk muses that they really need to get started thinking about their own place. He says that to tell the truth it is a fucking dump.

Harry says that whenever Loudermilk would like to make a move on that side of things that would be great.

Harry goes back indoors.

Anyway, Harry is busy. He has better things to do than observe the homosocial rituals of landlocked patriarchs.

He has already started working on the writing project for Loudermilk. He needs to find out how people write a lot of poems, because he's pretty sure that he and Loudermilk—or, rather, he—are/is going to have to write a lot of them. He's reading a book titled *Singing in the Present Tense: A Critical Anthology.* He found this volume—a poetic guidebook of sorts—in a used bookstore in Oswego before they left. "The poem is," *Singing in the Present Tense* tells him, "many things to many people. The poem is an expression of what the author of the poem is thinking or feeling, and it may even be both of these at the same time. A poem does not have to be poetic or beautiful. You may be surprised by the number of things a poem can be."

A jay outside is making a sound like a laser. Harry turns the page:

> When you are reading a poem, you may not understand it right away. There may be words or names of places and people unfamiliar to you, and sometimes a sentence may seem to go on for a very long time indeed or simply end abruptly, in a fragment. Try not to let this put you off. Use an encyclopedia or a dictionary to find the meanings of words you don't know. Read the poem through a few times to get a feel for everything on the page. Appreciate the poem as you would a piece of music or a painting or a conversation with a friend. Try to remember that the poem does not have to mean something, but it might. One way to get a feel for poetry is by thinking about the way

> that words have meaning more generally. Many words have more than one meaning. The word *seal* can refer to the wax on a letter even as it also means *large carnivorous sea mammal.* Neither of these meanings does anything to restrict or disturb the other meaning. But here we are just talking about dictionary meanings. There are also meanings that are created by the way people use words. Take the word *tall.* We might say, "She is tall," but we can also say, "That is a tall order." Even words that have only one dictionary meaning may have many metaphorical meanings when we use them in daily life. Poetry is a kind of writing that generally accepts this about words. Poetry minds neither that words may mean more than one thing, nor that they sometimes mean more than one thing at once. This is what causes some people to say that they cannot understand poems.

Harry is feeling calmer now, but also more bored. He puts the book down.

He sips instant coffee from a plastic cup, prepared with water heated in a tin can. Loudermilk, meanwhile, performs his ablutions. The shower is on.

Over the sound of the water Loudermilk shouts, "I'm taking us to the mall!"

Harry says that he will see Loudermilk when Loudermilk gets back. It's barely worth saying, and Harry doesn't really care if Loudermilk can't hear him. Harry picks up *The Sentinel* and flips past an image of a man pointing into the interior of a recently bombed shrine. He lingers on an unflattering photo of the Dixie Chicks in concert, seizes his pencil, and begins languorously redacting their sweaty, scraped-back hair and adorable faces contorted by pacifist passion, stroking the newsprint with the eraser.

Loudermilk shuts off the shower. He climbs out of the tub and displays himself naked on the floor of the living room, drying his shins with a pair of cobalt athletic shorts. "Towels," Loudermilk says. "Make a note, please, Harrison." He goes over one thigh. "And a telephone. So your moms doesn't put out a fucking APB."

Harry pretends he hasn't heard this last remark. He moves on to a photograph of Kobe Bryant.

Loudermilk is pulling on a pair of ratty, toffee-colored cargo shorts, to which he adds a white polo. He swipes Old Spice. He strokes his chin, contemplating Harry. "To the mall?"

"See you when you get back."

Loudermilk is firm. He says, "Those Orange Juliuses aren't going to drink themselves, friend."

"I don't feel like it."

"But, Harry"—Loudermilk employs humanitarian tones—"trying new things is how we *learn*."

"Thanks but no thanks."

"Remember how I'm supposed to be helping you here? Working on your little problem? Can you please just let me do that?"

Harry frowns.

Loudermilk drives.

They go by cornfields, and there is a sound from insects

like a low alarm. There looms THE REDVILLE MALL. Contractors have fixed for it a treeless, dusty plateau.

Loudermilk wants a mattress and linens and an Orange Julius and some panfried dumplings and is getting sort of manic. They move among hearty Alpines and a few Nordics whose genetic traits, Loudermilk loudly proclaims, as if in a bid to have his front teeth abruptly removed by a nearby fist, have been largely selected out of the East Coast pool.

Loudermilk buys red towels; he buys five, all the same jumbo size. Loudermilk buys navy sheets. He buys two mattresses. He makes Harry go with him to the sporting goods store, where he lights on a pair of plastic camp chairs with built-in beer cozies. They peruse the handgun options and watch as someone with acne receives a miniature duffel across the glass counter.

"You see, the mall is good," Loudermilk says. "Look how Zen you are."

Harry is pouring the last sweet kernels of a cone of kettle corn into his mouth. He does not respond. They turn into an electronics store where Loudermilk picks out a pair of midrange handheld recorders that take mini-tapes. "For when I go to class—one for recording, one for you to listen," he tells Harry, indicating that the fancier, digital recorder he already possesses will be reserved for personal use. Loudermilk picks up a cordless for the house and a Sprint PCS Picture Phone with Built-in Camera for himself. He shakes hands with the salesman.

Near a giant glass atrium that is the main point of entry and exit, on the concrete dais outside, are girls in black jeans and Doc Martens who smoke cigarettes, squatting and jumping and gesticulating all the while, as if it is a form of calisthenics. The girls are in high school and Harry supposes you could believe they have been released from their place of remedial education for the day. They wear band shirts and fistfuls of silver rings and train knowing, kohl-lined eyes on Loudermilk. One leans over and whispers something to another. The other girl laughs, levers herself off the wall. She starts speed-walking toward Harry and Loudermilk.

Harry can see what's coming and tries to start pedaling faster toward the safety of the SUV but Loudermilk glances back and is like, "Stop." Loudermilk even fakes accidentally dropping his keys and spends some time fumbling around, doing something with his wallet.

"Excuse me! Excuse me!" The girl hails them.

Harry is cursing under his breath. He pretends to find something extraordinarily fascinating to gaze at on the horizon.

"Hey!" says the girl. Out of the corner of his eye, Harry notes her Marilyn Manson T-shirt, the singer's dilated, mismatched eyes gazing balefully up from under her left tit, her chin-length ash-brown hair, her commanding hazel gaze. He gulps. It isn't even that she's jailbait. She's something way beyond that, an actress in an after-school special with genuine star power, an escape artist, a worthy fucking competitor. Harry tries unsuccessfully not to let himself get carried away.

Loudermilk is pivoting suavely.

"Hiya," the girl says. "I hope you don't think this is rude, I was just wondering, any chance you guys are in, like, the Seminars?"

Loudermilk cocks his head. "I wouldn't put it past us."

"Really?"

"It's a fact."

The girl looks back to her friends and waves her arms over her head. "Yes!" she screams. "Omigod, yes! You skanks so owe me money!"

Harry monitors the progress of a distant prop plane.

The girl has already turned back to Loudermilk. "Lizzie," she says, proffering a tiny manicured hand.

"Charmed," replies Loudermilk. He lets her know their names.

"You guys could totally give me a ride back to town if that's not a problem!"

Loudermilk says that he doesn't see why that should be a problem.

Harry doesn't comment.

Loudermilk gallantly offers Lizzie shotgun. Her marshmallow-orchid perfume expands nauseatingly to fill the vehicle's interior, and as soon as Loudermilk has the key in the ignition she begins messing with the radio.

Harry stews.

Lizzie puts on NPR. There is an interview with a nun who loves art. "Omigod," Lizzie squeals. "Terry Gross! YES!" She leans forward, chin on fists. "I love her."

Loudermilk drives studiously.

When the interview ends, Lizzie switches off the radio. She is all business. "So please pardon my asking but what are you guys up to at the moment? Are we just now settling in?"

Loudermilk says things are pretty much settled.

"That's so good!" Lizzie commends him. "Sometimes people have, you know, kind of, I don't know, culture shock? I've seen it happen before." Lizzie purses her lips.

"You seem to know a lot about the Seminars."

"Oh, I mean, like, *the area.* I'm saying, maybe you haven't realized you've come to the vortex, your blood must feed the corn and whatnot?"

"That's nice," Loudermilk maintains.

"How about you?" She means Harry.

"Harry."

"Thanks, Loudermilk. So what about Harry?"

"Dissertation," Loudermilk says. "He's writing his dissertation."

"Oh!"

"'Oh!' is right. This young brainiac studies the history of abnormal psychiatry in the U.S. I mean, it's way over my head. *Very* technical stuff. People with congenital injuries and aggravated antisocialism and that kind of thing."

Lizzie tells Harry, "I'm still in high school."

"Stay in school," Loudermilk preaches.

"Excuse me, but I am very much in school!" Lizzie sighs. They're on a street at the outskirts of town with dying trees, a vacant lot, a funeral parlor on the hill just above them, and train tracks to the left. "Now," says Lizzie, "roll the windows all the way up, pretty please."

Loudermilk obliges. He starts to want to know what Lizzie's connection to the Seminars is but she interrupts him: "Because you have been so very honorable toward me, I am going to smoke you guys out. How does that sound?"

Loudermilk shrugs. He unbuckles and settles back into his seat. Harry rolls his eyes.

Seven minutes later, Lizzie tells Loudermilk to drive them

back out into the fields to release the incriminating vapor. She says someone could rat you out, you never know.

Loudermilk offers languid thanks. His right hand drifts toward the ignition but he only caresses the leather tag dangling from the key. Everyone seems OK with nothing happening.

"So are we going to the BBQ or not?" It's Lizzie again.

"I don't know," Loudermilk says. "Are we?"

"Hello? Do you just not check your email? The *BBQ*! This is the time when you first get to see everyone? And be seen?"

Loudermilk shrugs. "Must have slipped my mind! I'm totally *so* all about the poetry. Sounds crazy, I know."

"Not especially," Lizzie tells him.

Nine

Prospects

Before them is a green. And upon the green are fifty people. And on a table near a grill, beer cans and bottles verdantly glisten. Everyone is standing at least a foot away from everyone else.

If Harry were called upon to provide some sort of formal appraisal of this gathering, a first impression, as it were, he might choose a word like *restrained* or *muted*. But this does not look like a crowd of dreamy masturbators. They may indeed be masturbators, but if so they are masturbators of a weirdly self-aware and not very physical stripe. It is like the "popular nerd" of every North American high school clique known to 1995 has been summoned to this convocation; it's a hive.

The tone of the gathering that Loudermilk and Harry are about to join is not lost on Loudermilk, who mutters, "Let's try and cultivate your ability to be normal."

Lizzie is already out of the car and, having slammed her door, skips squealing off.

Loudermilk shakes his head, produces a gentle clucking sound. He murmurs, "Ready to meet these cock-knockers?"

Harry loiters beside the Land Cruiser, contemplating the fact that the ground and the sky are two distinct entities that appear to touch each other, here in a neurotically straight Iowan line.

Loudermilk is making signs that they must progress toward the social scene. But Harry is no longer capable of comprehending his friend's suggestions. Harry hears only a high-pitched hum he assumes must be the abstract music of his own blood. Ages pass, Paleolithic eons, fossils form whitely on Harry's lips and drop softly to the earth, his eyes dry up and blow away, yet at last Harry is moving beside Loudermilk, is somehow walking.

Loudermilk has pretty much been keeping up his end of the bargain. So far, basically, so good. Few questions have been asked, and only Evelyn, their new landlord, whoever she is, native Cretan, serial monogamist, hovel mogul, has even come close to confronting Harry's odd lot. What's unusual is that Evelyn's query happened at such an early point in their acquaintance, and early on it's very much Loudermilk's responsibility to ensure that dialogue of this nature is kept to a minimum. If the person behaving in an inquisitive fashion isn't really going to become a major part of their lives, what's the point? Harry's situation is on a need-to-know.

When Harry was younger, he read the word *agoraphobe* somewhere. It, as they say, resonated with him. But Harry's not afraid of open spaces or large groups of people, at least not chiefly. He does not suffer from an overdeveloped sensitivity to human cruelty, nor does he live in constant fear of persecution by his fellow man. Rather, his sensitivity is carefully calibrated, his fear intermittent if pretty pronounced. He respects the possibility of cruelty; he largely accepts that he's destined to be persecuted by individuals bigger, richer, and stupider than he is. Agoraphobia was mainly of interest to Harry, when he first came across the term, in an existential sense, since it seemed antithetical to the very project of enduring a human life span. It was an incorrect way of thinking and feeling that was not just a mistaken opinion or species of hate. Rather, in Harry's estimation, it was a general disposition toward the future, a mode of mentally assessing what was to come that significantly limited one's prospects, which is to say, one's ability to exit a room or, maybe, bed.

Harry thinks about himself in these terms. But his problem is not, again, primarily with other people. Yes, Harry dislikes and fears most other men and women, but the central and insoluble problem for Harry is that he, in a nonmetaphorical sense, hates the sound of his own voice.

It rises in him. It enters his own ears, and after this Harry will "hear" how it sounds to others.

It's not that he can't speak. It's that he doesn't want to.

Loudermilk maintains that this is totally normal. That's the Loudermilk line and Loudermilk, since he is Loudermilk, will not be dissuaded. Loudermilk says that it's probably a phase. He says that there is nothing so remarkable about Harry's voice anyhow, once you get used to it. It's a bit unique is all, a little in between and out of bounds of normal registers.

But the thing Loudermilk does not realize, the finer detail that is somehow constantly lost on him, is that when Harry speaks what comes out of his mouth sounds nothing like what he hears in his own head. So the voice is ugly and sometimes shrill and sometimes bass and otherwise ludicrous and very incongruous and unpleasant, but the major thing about it is that it is not even *his*. And this makes all the difference.

The need to communicate on some rudimentary level necessitates a friendship of the kind he shares with Loudermilk. Things have been a lot easier, since.

However, why or how Loudermilk manages to comprehend as much of Harry's condition as he does remains something of an enigma. Loudermilk's decisions about when and where to exercise his limited capacity for empathy are cipher-like at best and often resemble the whims of an oversexed, nihilist god.

Loudermilk's own freedom is remarkable. It's brilliant, irresistible. Proprieties, doubts, fears, and so forth are simply not part of his makeup. If Loudermilk is constrained by anything, it's by the lack of any sense of limit on his agency. Loudermilk believes that he is capable of anything and that, pursuantly, anything he is capable of is pretty much permitted.

Given his looks plus blinding self-regard, Loudermilk has to actively choose and/or struggle not to glide along the path of least resistance. As a person with a surfeit of emancipation, he has no fear of being labeled lazy and will only consent to make any kind of effort at all if he can be sure that the whole endeavor will take the form of an enormous obscene joke *cum* high school science experiment.

"Hello?" Loudermilk is demanding.

Harry stares at Loudermilk, taking in for a moment his friend's inhumanly symmetrical features, shaded by the hot-pink novelty trucker hat.

"Dude, can you please not go in your weird hidey-hole? Remember what I just told our adolescent friend: You, Harry, are studying something no one else can understand and you're the fucking boss of that. If anyone wants to have a problem with you or anything associated with you, they can take that up with yours truly, which, trust me, nobody in this weak scene is going to have the *cojones* to even think about. And pardon my asking so soon but, riddle me this, has everything not totally worked out thus far?"

Harry lets Loudermilk know that he plans to reevaluate their lifestyle come winter but for now, sure, living in a two-bedroom shit house seems fine.

Loudermilk sighs. He says that if the bunch in Harry's panties were to get any bunchier they'd have to get him a wheelbarrow to roll it around in.

Harry in no way agrees with Loudermilk's assessment but begins walking. He is only putting one foot in front of the other; this, at least, is what he tells himself. The lawn area is evident before them. There is a shelter and a violet cloud of grill smoke.

Harry lets himself fall behind. The sun is very bright, a dull blade poised against the earth. Harry follows his friend.

It's like, he'd really like to believe it's just his voice.

Ten

The Lucky

It is the first introductory BBQ of the fall workshop season, a time of new beginnings. The younger bard Anton Beans, emerging conceptual lyricist, the, who is he kidding, *heir apparent to the poem-based sector of the American humanities multiverse*, hovering beside the condiment table, is finally about to get across to Marta Hillary, award-winning poet and faculty member, the central conceit of his second, as-yet-unpromised manuscript, *The Noise of Noise*. Beans, who has been in the program for a year, arrived already under contract. His first collection, *Distillation Metrics*, will be published in May by a small but extraordinarily reputable press. Beans is all but guaranteed to secure academic tenure within the next five years, and he knows it. The only reason Beans temporarily abandoned San Francisco for the Midwest was to study under Marta, who is not just renowned but quite possibly the greatest poet of her generation. If she were not at the Seminars, he's not sure what the point of his malingering here among so many reactionaries would be, although perhaps the degree itself is worth something.

Beans is twenty-eight years young. He has a PhD in linguistics and, before he left the Bay Area, was toiling very lucratively in consultation with certain IT interests, though he says nothing of this to his Seminars cohort. Beans is not a great fan of his fellow poetry students, in particular, nor is he a great fan of the arts, in general. As a toddler, he was pushed into show business. Beans appeared in a string of camera commercials before the onset of a stubborn form of childhood irritable bowel syndrome made his, albeit glowing and cherubic, face, due to its relative proximity to said bowels, unemployable.

From this early career loss, Beans learned the importance of a plan B. In his last year of grad school at Stanford, Anton Beans used some of his consulting fees (he, for the most part, was able to steer clear of options) to invest in real estate back in the city, buying a building on 24th and Mission. He knows exactly what he is sitting on, where it's going in the next couple of decades.

Anton Beans is in some ways fairly unconcerned about his future. His ambitious mother, meanwhile, is pondering a second marriage to a cunning contractor.

What keeps Beans up at night is his own historical significance. He is not an academic, though he was happy enough to follow through with his degree. He isn't really even a writer.

What it means not to "really" be a writer: It's not that Beans can't write, because he definitely can, but that he does not exactly see the point, if you see *his* point, which it is unlikely that you do. If you understand anything at all about mankind these days then you know that the entire race has a rapidly approaching expiration date stamped on its forehead.

All this business about symbolism and getting something or other eternal across to the sensitive souls who choose to buy your puny book is just so much outdated twaddle as far as he's concerned. It's a pipe dream of pre-network Romanticism.

All the same, Beans can't quite rule out the importance of reading. And the fact that he can't convince himself that the work of reading has no power and no allure and no gravitas suggests to him that there's something he, Anton Beans, can and should do with the rest of his time on earth as far as literature is concerned.

Poems are good for Beans's purposes because they're short, because he can engineer a poem exhaustively, can attempt to determine its semantic capacity in a complete sense. His favorite writers are Gertrude Stein and Ezra Pound, individuals who, interestingly, did not seem to particularly care for each other.

Beans likes to dress as his own personal approximation of an anti-retinal, postwar American artist, basking in the soft power that comes of eschewing figurative content and, later, objects altogether. He would never bother living in inflation-struck New York City at this point, but he thinks Sol LeWitt's appearance in the Cold War gallery system was pretty neat. He enjoys the utter primacy accorded the "concept" by this exalted man. Beans stands with LeWitt, against rhetoric, against expression. Long live "the square and the cube as . . . syntax"! Long live logical sequence. Long live the beauty of evacuated form.

For the BBQ, Beans is wearing a pair of studiously, delicately paint-soiled white jeans, a white T-shirt, and white canvas sneakers from which he has painstakingly removed the logos using an X-ACTO knife. He began shaving his head bald several years ago and compensates for this elective scarcity by encouraging a pleasingly thick, wiry black beard of anarchic proportions to obscure his neck.

Beans is pretty sure that Marta does not know what to make of him, but that her refined and at least partially unconscious powers of pattern recognition have convinced her of his intelligence. He, for his part, would like: First, to secure a letter of recommendation from her, and, then, with this out of the way, to attempt to understand what makes her tick. If he were not currently practicing celibacy as a form of mental and spiritual self-discipline, it is likely that the two of them would be making love on a daily basis.

Marta is drinking white wine from a small green glass she must have brought for herself from home. Beans hovers at her side. Marta smells—he thinks, uncharacteristically employing simile—like an ocean breeze traveling along the tip of a rosebud. In fact, she is sex on a stick. Her face is small with a long, straight nose. Her jewelry makes elegant sounds.

"So my procedure," Beans begins to explain, but here something very, very unpleasant occurs.

An enormous male-model type in a hot-pink hat inscribed with an obscene slogan appears at the condiment station. Beans's fragile web is disturbed as Marta's interest shifts. The bro has a pair of plump dogs over which he deploys nauseating quantities of ketchup, nodding approvingly to himself. A couple yards off, a weird, undersized person who looks a lot like a fraternity torture victim due to fading permanent marker drawings on his face, and who must be the wingman of the philistine, is miserably peeling the label from his beer bottle.

Marta turns away from Beans.

It is like this scumbag thinks Marta is another student, albeit one aging gracefully into her mid-forties via a budget that permits investment in Prada and the occasional foray into Comme des Garçons. And the truly frightening thing is that Marta seems to like it! She smiles that slow, dreamy smile of hers and offers the goon her hand. She greets him as if she remembers him from somewhere, which, if Anton Beans permits his worst fears momentary realization, must be his application to the program.

"Troy Loudermilk," Marta says. "Welcome."

The piece of shit is saying, "Welcome to you, too."

"Yes," Marta tells him. She makes no effort to introduce herself, rather examining the face of Troy Loudermilk. "You look so different?"

"That's funny," this most complacent of oafs replies. He is fussing with a pickle jar.

"I meant, from how I'd *imagined* you," Marta finishes. "I never look at the photographs. It's barbaric the university even makes us ask our students for them. The unaccountable needs of bureaucrats!" Some stronger sentiment seems to flit across her face but is quickly dissolved under another indolent smile. "Lovely to see you."

The kid with the cross on his forehead is staring at the ground so hard he may burn a hole into it. Beans likes him, if this is possible, even less than he likes Troy Loudermilk. Why someone like Loudermilk would put up with a specimen like that is a curious case. Probably has something to do with needing to seem plausibly human while you walk around looking like a boxer-briefs commercial.

Troy Loudermilk is saluting Marta. "Bye!" he says, grinning moronically. He bears his submerged wieners away.

Marta watches Loudermilk go. "That is a very great poet, or so I believe." Marta eyes Beans. "We'll have to see if he can live up to his potential."

Beans forces himself to smile, he hopes enigmatically. "Anyway, about the manuscript," Beans recommences, "what you were saying was so—" But he stops.

Marta has glided off. Beans is incensed to see her standing now in the company of Troy Loudermilk, Loudermilk's presumably foot-long schlong, and Loudermilk's bizarre minion, the last of the trio having already succeeded in smearing the entire lower half of his face in Heinz.

Beans watches Marta nod, watches her rest her shapely hand on Loudermilk's shoulder and leave it there. More than anything else, Anton Beans hates the lucky. Not only do they absorb all the top prizes in life's insipid games, but they have the habit of doing very little work in the process. Anton Beans abhors the lucky. They are the cherry on the top of humanity's miscreation.

Beans turns to the cooler, roots furiously for a seltzer.

Eleven

Instruction

Clare Elwil has made the decision not to attend any of the Seminars' much-touted seminars, classes on the theory of composition that have allegedly defined the American literary landscape for decades now. She pretends to herself that she is apathetic—that she has no head for ahistorical formalism, the wages of New Critical disinterest in all but professional politics, the cult of style, etc., the Seminars' celebrated and overweening interest in mechanics—but the real problem is the other students. Because she herself cannot write, she has little concern for the writing of others, and all the others ever seem to want to talk about is their own writing. By way of substitute, Clare will double-count a graduate course she took in college. She has been apprised by administrators that this is not merely possible but even usual. "You want," they say, "time to write." She will just need to come in and touch pen to form.

Clare is in her trio of furnished rooms north of campus, late afternoon. She stands—as in the second paragraph of a sentimental novel—before the mirror that is screwed to the back of the door between her apartment and the landing of the building's central stair. She wears a black turtleneck and gray corduroy jeans that used to belong to her mother. She will shortly don an anorak she purchased three falls ago from a Boston Army-Navy.

Her face is big. It's a soft oval. She has large hands and feet but spindly limbs, a long and narrow rib cage. Her hair is black, shoulder-length, straight. Her eyes are a weird lemon color, like a cat's. Her small lips form a flat-bottomed heart. Currently her lips are chapped. She grimaces. She is five foot eight.

Clare contains her hair in a rubber band from the carrots.

Clare leaves, walks toward Building 109. The building is at the crest of a hill and the wind picks up at Clare's approach. Clare enters. Now she is mounting stairs to the second floor; now she is making a left and then a right and is walking down the hall to the office past an open room, its door with diamond of wire-reinforced glass ajar and the beige edge of the seminar table, and she does not turn her head to look inside. She hears a voice, a man, say, "Now you're here we can make an accommodation and try, at last, to begin. As I was saying—" and Clare turns. She sees a short man. He is with his class, standing. His eyes touch hers. He does a quick probe of her face plus lingering swipe over breasts but does not stop speaking.

Clare recognizes him from the progressive supermarket, the man with wine bottles, a late version of her protagonist Dr. Lehren, who in Clare's story becomes the butt of an unfathomable and even sordid joke that rises in the mind of the young antihero, Eloise. And Eloise laughs. And Clare is not sure what this means but is glad to find herself successfully mapping her own previous traversal of time and space and literature.

The man is saying, "I don't give one donkey *fuck* what you do while you're here. I honest to god do not. This is not a contest and I do not give out prizes. And the first of you knuckleheads gets that through his or her skull will be the lucky recipient—"

But Clare does not hear what anyone may expect to receive from the man because she has come to the office and the noise of another sort of commerce blots out instruction.

It is only later, when she is walking down the hill again, form in hand, that she recalls the man who does not willingly distribute donkey fucks. Could one imagine that his pronouncements herald a really excellent form of meritocracy, somehow? That his is, paradoxically, the most sublime of pedagogical metrics—since incomprehensible, profane, and therefore absolute?

Clare thinks that this has got to be a poetry teacher, and perhaps this is the look and sound and style of today's poetry.

She also puzzles over the fact that certain kinds of information are produced ex nihilo, just by way of the presence of more than one person in a given room.

Twelve

Same

"You remember," Loudermilk yells, apropos of nothing, as the screen door slams shut behind him, "when we were at the mall?"

Harry jerks up in his chair. It is 5:00 p.m.

Loudermilk is back from class—from *workshop*, Harry specifies.

Loudermilk strides into the main room and wants to know if Harry remembers the girl.

Harry has been napping. He has lately returned from the university library stacks with a selection of award-winning poetry titles from the past year. These are sitting in a plastic bag near the front door. Harry mutters something about nice to see you, too.

"The one in high school, right? Lizzie? Likes to get into cars with strange men?"

"Speak for yourself."

"Yeah, yeah, yeah," says Loudermilk. He quotes Marisa Tomei in her Oscar-winning turn as Mona Lisa Vito: "*You blend.*" He rolls the papers he's carrying into a cone and brings it to his mouth like a megaphone. He intones, "Her dad is my instructor!"

Harry is sitting in one of the beer-cozy camping chairs, staring out of one of the back windows of their hut into the overgrown backyard. He squints, transforming the view into blobs of brown and green. "That's nice," he says.

"It's annoying, is what it is. I didn't realize who we were dealing with. That's the kind of deception that really gets to me. Anyways, this is what you have to read." He drops a few pages onto Harry's lap. "Sample poems. Fresh from the recycling bin. At some point T. A. Loudermilk must make his own contribution."

"I'll try to write something!"

"Yes, Harrison, as in, a poem!"

Harry sighs.

"Jesus, you goddamn cum-dumpster, stop pretending you're not totally psyched to do this. And, uh, have it ready for, like, this Wednesday." Loudermilk pauses. "*Please*."

Harry begins flipping through the printouts. He wants to know if he's supposed to write crap like this.

"It's supposed to be really good, is what it's supposed to be! Like everything you write! How you think we got in here?"

Harry claims not to be in possession of this info.

"No, dude, you *will* admit that you know. *Own* thy poetry. By the way, have you even left the house today?"

Harry wishes Loudermilk would notice things, like the open book on his lap, the new kettle on the stove, the miniature cactus in neon gravel on the windowsill, things which were not transferred to this building by magic.

Loudermilk is stalking back to the kitchen. He asks if Harry wants a beer.

Harry gives a thumbs-up behind his head. He's obediently reading.

Loudermilk returns. "Find anything?"

Harry accepts a PBR. He clears his throat and forces himself to declaim:

vivisepulture

fly-eyed flickers eventime and i wake you
tunis pheromone shallow lucency
should stop shunts fujiflex and i do not
not

Harry drinks.

Loudermilk grabs the paper out of Harry's hand. "Shit!" He is laughing. "I knew it!" Loudermilk crows.

Harry asks what the celebration is about.

"You see this?" Loudermilk indicates a signature at the bottom of the page, *A. Beans.* "Anton motherfucking Beans. This homo sapiens was *way*, way up in my grill."

"This person's name is 'ant on beans'?"

Loudermilk whips his recorder out of his shorts pocket, pops out the tape. He is trembling slightly, whether with rage or joy Harry does not know. "First, Harry, *friend*, you need to have a wee listen to what's on here. However, let me offer you a preview: This dick-munch is not capable of writing! Not that I know anything about poetry, but I'm guaranteeing you that right now. He's a liability."

Harry informs Loudermilk that this disquisition, while certainly dramatic, is not very helpful on the fact front. He testily accepts the mini-tape.

Loudermilk frowns. "I'm trying to tell you, he's onto me—onto *us*. It takes one to know one! What a mother-loving hack!"

"Guess I'll try not to imitate him."

Loudermilk drops into the chair next to Harry's. "I'm just saying, dude, I happen to know how good you are, so let's take advantage of that, am I right? Let's mess with this cum-guzzler. How's that for a mandate?" Loudermilk hands the xeroxed poetry back to Harry. He raises his beer. "Anyhow, cheers, dude."

"Likewise," Harry mutters.

Harry wonders exactly whose cum Beans is meant to be guzzling—is it, for example, the cum also contained in Harry's "dumpster," or is it more diversely sourced?—but decides he will reserve this question for a later juncture. He puts the poetry facedown on the floor under his seat, along with the mini-tape.

He and Loudermilk touch cans.

"By the way, so I went to the bank, dude?" Loudermilk takes out his wallet. "And I was thinking, after expenses, I give you like five hundred, first of the month? How's that?"

Harry slowly nods.

Loudermilk extracts a roll of twenties. "God, did I mention I fucking love this fellowship? Jesus Christ!" Here Loudermilk cannot resist a brief imitation of Jim Carrey in 1994's *The Mask*. "'*Somebody stop me!*' Anyway, don't spend it all in one place, yo." He peels a random portion off the roll and drops it in Harry's lap.

Harry drags himself out of his chair and goes into his room and, without counting, hides all but two of the bills in a sock. "By the way," he asks, returning, "do you know what *vivisepulture* means?"

"That's an actual word?"

"Yup."

"Amazing! He *is* a genius."

Harry's adolescence included an after-school program at a Catholic school. He knows some Latin. "Live burial," he says.

Loudermilk employs an approximation of a British accent. "*Burying alive, you say?*"

Harry nods.

"He's a nice young chap, the Beans!"

Harry doesn't think this is particularly funny.

Loudermilk lets the accent drop. "So, tonight, right, I was thinking, if you're not too busy, which, let me check, yeah, you're probably not, we should head over to *le bar*."

Harry doesn't say anything.

"With the Seminars people. Show some face."

Harry informs Loudermilk that from now on maybe he should be satisfied with his own face.

Loudermilk is like, "But, dude. I pretty much am?"

"You know what I mean."

"I just happen to think, dearest Harrison, that we should maybe consider trying to, like, you know, mix a little, go with the flow? Like make you one of the gang? I think it will be good, at the very least, for yours truly's *poésie*."

This annoys Harry, who says that he hopes that he didn't spend half the morning today listening to the reverberating labors of Loudermilk's sphincter for nothing. He tells Loudermilk that in truth he's pretty flowed.

"Dude," Loudermilk intones with mock solemnity, "I'm so impressed you remembered. Did I not totally finesse that?"

Harry is helping himself to another beer. "I'm still traumatized."

Loudermilk continues, "Anyway! You need to see what I'm—what we're—up against. I don't think it's exactly gonna work, like, otherwise."

Harry isn't sure what Loudermilk is referring to.

"This! Everything! I need you to really feel it, live it, be it, eat it, drink it! OK?"

Harry gulps beer. Sometimes Loudermilk is insufferable.

Loudermilk grins. He indicates his own face and torso. "I mean this. This! This fucking hard body, dude. This face. This physical being! You have to write the poems that, like, emerge, no, *explode* from the pen of this beautiful man. The artists don't make art, man—the art makes itself *through* us. I'm not the doer, you know? I'm just along for the ride. It's like you always said about the power of literature, like you can just fall into a book. We've got to get into that, like, harness it for real. We really have to hone our act. You and I, we're gonna take over poetry! My face, your brains. My ideas, your, um, spirit or whatever. If it's just you hermitting out in here, sniffing your stale jizz rags and contemplating your fart crumbs, that's not really gonna happen, if you catch my drift. Those are not the true immortal themes, bro! Plus, you, for once in your existence, need to have a social life. Let's win the war on mediocre mashing at least one geek lust object at a time."

There's a weird logic.

"Have another beer and stop with the I'm-pining-away-for-my-dorm-at-clown-college look," Loudermilk advises. "I'm actually trying to help you. By the way, I just remembered something."

Harry would like to know what this something is.

"OK, so, maybe you can tell me. What's the difference between a vitamin and a hormone?"

Harry says nothing.

"Dude, as in, you can't *hear* a vitamin?"

Thirteen

This Is a Pipe

Loudermilk and Harry wander over to a place called the Common Lot, one block off the main boulevard dedicated to the inculcation of a new generation with the time-honored practice of alcoholism. Happy hour in the college town is in full effect. Girls stagger around in nothing but underwear: satin strings and miniature triangles. Males are wearing shirts that read CO-ED NAKED PANTIES '03. They are falling down and dragging females with them.

Loudermilk is appreciative, but mainly he just steps stiffly around bodies. He seems preoccupied, keeping his eyes fixed in front of him. A team of three young women in tasseled pasties surround Loudermilk, but he brushes them off. Harry is wasted from the five beers he shot-gunned before they left.

They enter the Common Lot. Most of what is inside the bar is painted black, and it is a long, narrow establishment. Adding character of a kind is a female mannequin wrapped in dusty ACE bandages to resemble a mummy. She is propped in a corner behind the bar. There is a HELLO MY NAME IS sticker affixed to her left breast; the sticker has been completed with

LUSCIOUS, in cramped Sharpie. The only other decorative accent is a television screen above Luscious showing the evening news: a farmer in a local field whose comb-over a breeze lazily perturbs as he speaks into a microphone. The name MONSANTO appears in the upper right-hand corner of the screen. Harry wonders if he should look this up later.

They score a booth and Loudermilk orders lagers. "Something gentle," he comments.

The drinks come. Harry sips. Harry's head spins.

Harry knows what to expect of himself in situations like this. He knows that the sugar from the beer will make him hyper. He knows he will want to speak. He knows he may or may not be able to stop himself from speaking to strangers when the impulse strikes. He knows that if he does speak, he'll have to drink harder to forget what just happened. He knows that the harder he drinks to forget what just happened, the more he'll want to say stuff and the worse it's going to sound. So it is going to be bad tonight, probably very.

Loudermilk is asking Harry if Harry wants another.

Harry nods. Harry swills lager.

Additional people climb into the booth. These must be Loudermilk's classmates. Harry has been given a sidecar containing Jäger and currently the shot glass is empty.

Harry squints at the unfamiliar faces of Loudermilk's cohort. These are two females and a male. One of the females has glasses and the other a T-shirt advertising the doubtful sobriquet WEAPON OF MASS AFFECTION. The one with glasses will not stop talking, which is OK by Harry, totally fucking great. Let her take care of things for the moment! There is also this guy, who is sitting opposite Loudermilk, and the guy has his legs sticking out the side of the booth, straight out, and people keep almost tripping or having to walk around the guy's legs and it's obviously not a good idea, but the guy does not ever move the legs. The guy is bald, bearded, and weirdly he resembles, like, a giant baby? Harry is having difficulty understanding this. It seems like the guy can't decide whether to stare at Harry or at Loudermilk. The guy keeps going back and forth. Harry suddenly really wants to help this poor guy out.

The glasses person is saying something now about how she and her boyfriend enjoy driving around the state. She says they enjoy looking at things that are authentic.

"You," Harry suddenly starts to say, "you just want to look at him, right?" The words come out, if Harry himself can be any judge, pretty slurred and battered.

The glasses person ends her disquisition.

Harry is so drunk he can't remember what he's just said. Anyway, has he just said something? Probably not. He decides it's crucial to point at the bald guy's fetal face to ensure his overture is properly received. "You like him?"

"*What?*" The infant frowns. The infant is sipping something clear with ice in it that is probably water.

"Ha ha ha! I'm saying"—Harry bobs his head sympathetically—"you know and whatever and stuff? He's interesting guy?"

It's not evident where Loudermilk is in all this.

Harry converts the pointing hand to an open palm. He keeps this palm bobbing in the air. For some reason he says, not without a certain optimism, "Yeah?"

"What?" This is the baby man again.

The infinitesimal sobering that has gone on during the

course of Harry's outburst allows one corner of Harry's brain to function. Realization dawns. He wants to destroy himself.

Now Loudermilk is here, dragging Harry out of the booth. Loudermilk is like, "That's such a good story, Maya!"

Maya, the glasses person, is saying something about how Loudermilk should really come with them on one of their jaunts sometime. It sounds a little like she is saying that Loudermilk should really come on her face sometime, but Harry is too preoccupied by his own catastrophic flaws to pay much attention.

Loudermilk is hustling Harry out. "That was hilarious!"

Harry is abruptly, dramatically sober.

"You're a comedic genius, dude." Loudermilk is slightly out of breath. Screams of inebriated college students can be heard a block over. "You know who that was?"

Harry doesn't care.

"Fucking *vivisepulture*? Dude is a new breed of fuck."

Harry doesn't say anything.

"When are you going to get over yourself? Trust me, it was fine. You can say whatever you want to these summa cum laude nerf herders. Life to them is one eternal underwater tea party. Anyways, I'm starving. Let's get a slice."

Harry says maybe he would prefer home. He doesn't feel so good.

Loudermilk surveys the bacchanal that surrounds them. "Harry, when are you going to realize nobody fucking feels good?"

Fourteen

This Is Not a Pipe

But it doesn't end.

The reason it doesn't end is that there is, outside the Common Lot, on one of Crete's municipal benches, a person sitting cross-legged smoking a cigarette. This person raises one of her bare arms and begins to wave. "Hey-ey!" she yells.

The person gets up and jogs over. "It's *me*!" the person announces. She comes to a standstill before Loudermilk.

Harry looks Lizzie over. Tonight she is only subtly goth, veering toward neo-hippie.

"Hiya," says Loudermilk.

"At least you're willing to say hello."

"Been a long day," Loudermilk says.

"Where ya goin'?"

"Somewhere."

"Where's that?"

"Have you ever heard," Loudermilk airily brings about, "of something called a hint?"

"You're totally welcome and it's so not a problem! I'd love to hang out." Lizzie releases a perfect smoke ring.

"Sorry, we're indisposed."

"Come on, please? You guys seem cool! I *like* you!"

"Lots of people like us."

Lizzie smiles. "Are you sure?"

"Does the pope shit in the woods?"

"Hi, Harry," Lizzie says.

Harry nods.

"Don't encourage her!" Loudermilk snaps.

Harry recalls the agitation with which Loudermilk had informed him that Lizzie was the spawn of his poetry teacher. Of course this had been earlier, in the afternoon, previous to Harry's complete and utter divestment of self-respect while inside the Common Lot.

"Listen, guess what and surprise! You're in my dad's poetry class! A, sorry I didn't mention that, and B, he already talked about you."

"I'm not surprised," Loudermilk tells her.

"Will you please just listen to me for one half a second? I'm trying to tell you he was telling my mom you have some kind of crazy oversized ego and they fucked up the funding again. You really must have done something to piss him off!"

"What? That's insane."

"Um, it's really not."

It occurs to Harry that he may in fact like this Lizzie person, in spite of her extremely sensuous mouth. Though somehow it's someone else who's seeing this mouth. He should write this down, he reflects.

"Hello, he's the director? He can take your funding away if he wants to. You know that, right?"

"We signed a contract. That's impossible."

"We? Who is 'we'?"

"*I*, OK, I signed a contract! They can't just take the money away."

"Not this year, they can't." Lizzie takes out a fresh cigarette. She taps it contemplatively against the top of the pack. "But you weren't at orientation, were you, Loudermilk, so, like, I guess you would have missed out on that little fact of life. Like, it's pretty lucky for you we're having this chat now? Too bad you're not interested."

"Did I say that?" Loudermilk is gearing himself up for contrition. He has rearranged his face.

"My dad hates to reward jackasses, by the way. *Totally* his pet peeve."

"I would have expected nothing less from a towering giant of the poetry world."

Lizzie ignores him. "You want to go someplace or not?"

Loudermilk looks at Harry. Harry just stares right back.

"I'm saying, it's so gross around here? So plebeian? Let's go to the park. Harry's invited, of course."

"Whatever." Loudermilk sighs.

They start walking.

Lizzie is persistent. "Like a few days ago you were so nice? What happened?"

"Is it that you have no friends? Is that what it is?"

"Omigod, I'm just curious, so sue me! Like, for example, you're at the mall, and there's this, like, underage girl, right, and she comes up to you, all sweet and innocent, right, starts talking, and you just let her into your car, just like that! So crazy! But it turns out you're really nice guys, not molesters or anything."

"That's a great story," Loudermilk says, "but you're leaving out the part where this fetching young skank asks two strange males for a ride. What about that?"

"Oh, that's easy. I read the files on all the new students. I knew exactly who you were before I even talked to you. It's not like I have a death wish."

Loudermilk makes it known he'd appreciate being let in on what "exactly" Lizzie knows.

"Like, what do *I* know? Well, I'm so sorry but I know that you nearly flunked out of college but at least three of your professors were willing to swear up and down that you were the best student they ever had. That was kind of intriguing. And you're a Gemini, emotionally unavailable but always ready for fun. And you write really good poems. Also, you're totally photogenic but way hotter in person."

"Thank you," Loudermilk says. "It's funny how that's true."

They come to a small park, the scene of the introductory BBQ.

"It's weird, though," Lizzie is saying, "when I read your file I kind of wanted to, like, get to know you? But you're actually so different from how I thought you'd be. Anyway!" Lizzie lowers herself onto a swing with a blue plastic seat. She kicks dirt.

"Your parents know you do that?" Loudermilk selects a swing.

"Do what?"

"Read files, sniff out persons of interest, humiliate yourself publicly?"

"Ew! I *never* humiliated myself! Harry, is he always this rude?"

Harry shrugs.

Lizzie says, "Loudermilk, I know you're not always this rude! But since you ask, they could probably care less what I do."

"Pray they care less," advises Loudermilk.

Harry selects a spot on a nearby jungle gym. He leans back and observes the stars.

"Your folks always lived here?" Loudermilk wants to know.

"Us?" Lizzie asks. "I have, mostly. I was born here. My dad actually was married before, when he, um, started teaching? He has two other kids. We're not really that close—I mean, to his other family. My mom's sixteen years younger. She was his student."

"But now your mom teaches?"

"She sure does." It's hard to see Lizzie in the dark, though it sounds like she is frowning. "I mean, you probably already knew that." She laughs.

Loudermilk sits up a little straighter. "I just meant, I didn't know about the whole story, you know?"

"Oh, *right*, you mean about their marriage and everything! Because I was about to say."

"Totally."

"I know! I mean, my dad is kind of famous, but my mom is, like, *so* famous." She laughs again. "Everyone's always so curious about that! I mean, actually, I was just thinking how it would be really funny if someone got into the program but they didn't even know who she was!"

"Wow," says Loudermilk. "That would be very funny."

"It would, wouldn't it? It would be so hysterical!"

Harry knows that Loudermilk has done it. He put way too

much shit on that last one. Harry awaits the descent of the other shoe.

Lizzie is like, "Hey, hey, hey, so by the way, I was wondering, which of my mom's books do you like the best? Because I know that can get really contentious among the first-years!"

"Gosh," Loudermilk says, "it's so hard to choose."

"I bet!" Lizzie is swinging. She puts her back into it. The set whistles and caws.

Loudermilk doesn't say anything.

"I'm waiting!" Lizzie yells.

"Don't know if I have a favorite!"

"OK!" Lizzie pumps higher and higher. Her words are choppy: "So here's—question—mom's—name?"

Loudermilk doesn't say anything.

"Come—! Easy—pie!"

"What?" Loudermilk yells.

"NAME!"

Loudermilk, who never remembers anything, says something about Mrs. Hillary.

"Shit!" Lizzie is laughing maniacally, and at the highest point in her journey she launches herself from the seat of the swing, screaming, "I SO KNEW!"

There is a thud, then silence.

Loudermilk and Harry disengage from the equipment. They stumble over the black grass and find Lizzie in a ball. Her shoulders move rhythmically.

Harry hears himself say, "You all right?" His voice breaks on the second word, and it comes out as an unintelligible croak.

Loudermilk translates. "He's asking if you're OK."

Lizzie peers up at her interrogators.

Harry can taste blood in his mouth.

"They don't love each other anymore, by the way, in case that's what you were wondering? They actually talk about it in front of me, like I don't exist."

Fifteen

The Reason

Everyone knows it's hard being a writer, but what they don't know is that it's hard being a writer most of all because inevitably you have a past. As a writer, you will have used this past to write things and now, in the present, it's difficult not to think about what you've done. The unfortunate things you wrote silence you, but, unfortunately, the successful things can do the same. Not that any of this matters for Clare, who can't write at all, at least not in the present. Clare's prize-winning short story, composed approximately three years ago, published in late 2000, and officially lauded in the spring of 2001, is titled "The Lift." She submitted it as her writing sample with her application to the Seminars.

Clare wrote this in a single night, in one sitting. It was a magic event, and she still does not fully understand what she was writing. She does not, for example, know anyone in the story in real life. Or, she *used* to not know anyone in the story. Now, of course, for whatever reason, given the existence of the small man who seems to teach poetry, she does.

Clare calls up the Word document for the draft she

turned in to the undergraduate literary magazine where the fiction editor was an ex-boyfriend. He had ended the relationship summarily but said he would like to "keep reading [her]." Clare is basically glad she obliged, though the two of them don't keep in touch. Then again, Clare doesn't really keep in touch with anyone.

She tries thinking now about what this ex-boyfriend, the editor, might have seen in these words, which is to say, what anyone might have seen; who she had been to all of them, then, at school. The sentences feel so odd under her eyes, because she will never write something like this again, and also because it is extremely unlikely that she will write anything at all, ever again:

The Lift
By Clare Elwil

> This woman his wife gave him two daughters, Amy with thick hair and Jenny who has been slightly bald all her life. Both of them smart, both of them in college now. His wife was squatting to get under the sink and find him the Joy. He was overweight, and he was a cardiologist. He caressed his belly.
>
> He was supposed to wash a dish, but instead he set down the Joy and picked up an apple. We did it last night, he thought at the moment he bit. He wandered into the living room where he could see the field that stretched from their deck to the trees and what was going to be a highway on the

other side of the trees. It was October, and during this month it always felt like riding in an airplane to stand in the living room of their summer home. He had never done this before. He wasn't living in New York anymore, and he was not a cardiologist. The sale of the apartment had gone through. Massachusetts was full-time.

Except for Florida in the winter. The phone rang.

"Richard, sweetheart," his wife calls him.

The phone is still ringing. She has not picked it up, and this house might be a universe long. Why did they decide that the living room needed to be two stories tall? The fireplace is holding up the ceiling, but something seems to be making the room rock as Richard goes to the phone. He is wearing sock slippers with pasted-on treads. The socks are too small. They are for children. "Hello?" he asks.

"Hello?" says a girl with a voice like dust.

"Hello, who is this, please?" Richard keeps his distance. Quiet now, it is Eloise.

"It's Eloise. Is Jen there?"

"No, Eloise. She's at school."

"Oh. Is Amy there?"

"No, she's not."

"Can I leave a message?"

"Do you expect them to be coming here soon?"

"I didn't know."

"What?"

"Well, actually I thought they might."

"No, they're not here." Richard is trying to decide if something is wrong with Eloise. "I think that the best thing to do would be to call them at school." A triumphant hunter-green plaid flashes before his eyes. The pattern of the upholstery on his chair.

"I need to talk."

"Oh. I'm not sure I understand."

"That's a long-distance phone call. I'm calling from work now."

"Oh. And where is that, Eloise?"

"At the basin."

Richard has the extra flesh that covers his right haunch in one hand. When he is idle, he will sometimes attempt to manually measure whether or not he has gained weight in the past few days. His wife is washing a dish. She has her face down over the sink. He can see the dark star along her scalp where her dyed hair parts. It might be that she is pretending not to listen to him, smiling, with the water on hard. But she is probably just not listening. She has always had the idea that because he loves comfort he can do no wrong.

"Well, gee, Eloise, I don't suppose I can interest you in making this phone call from our house?"

"Well, you might."

"Because, you see, we also have to communicate with our children sometime. Is it Jen you're interested in speaking to? That would be good, because it's been a few days since we've talked to her."

"Yeah, well, it really doesn't matter that much."

"Yeah, well, OK then." He can't quite place what's in her voice.

"When are you going to call her?"

"Whenever you want. I don't think she leaves her dorm room except late, late at night."

Eloise does not react. There is no further acknowledgment of either Amy or Jen. "So I don't know if you're really busy or what, but if you wouldn't mind driving over here, I'd really appreciate it. Something happened to my car two weeks ago, and now I'm basically stranded except for when my brother can spare his. It would be a big, um, really *help*, Dr. Lehren."

She's not working very hard at persuading him, but Richard would like to go for a drive, so he pretends that he is somebody's father. "Sure then, Eloise. Where shall I pick you up?"

"I can stand in the lower lot."

"Sounds good to me. See you in twenty minutes?"

"Yeah, you should know I also changed my hair. It's short and I darkened it."

"Well, then I'll know which one you are."

"Yeah, well, the place is pretty much empty today, but I just thought I'd let you know."

"Well, OK. I'll see you in a little while, Eloise."

"Bye, Dr. Lehren."

"Goodbye, Eloise."

They both hang up, and Richard is sure now that he's put on some weight. His wife shuts off the water. Perhaps she has washed some of her own dishes as well. They look at each other for a minute, smiling, heads tilted to the same side.

Richard put on shoes; he stepped into his loafers; he tucked in his shirt. "Hey, so Eloise is coming over. I hope you don't mind."

His wife is moving dishes around in the sink and then comes to the door of their bedroom. "I'm sorry, did you say something?" Her hands are wet. She is holding them away from her body. Her shoulders are raised.

"I said Eloise is coming over and I hoped you didn't mind."

"No, I don't mind." She turns back to the kitchen. "Everything's all right?"

"I have no idea."

"Oh?"

"She wants to use our phone."

"What was wrong with the one she was calling you from?"

"I think she wants to talk to Jen."

"Glad to be of service, I guess."

"Apparently she can't call from work."

"Right. Well, you don't have anything in

particular to do." She isn't only trying to tease him. She is giving him permission, and Richard moves after her into the kitchen. He likes how she dries her hands on a towel before putting them back in the sink and turning the water back on and washing more. "I'll see you in a little while," she says.

"Bye."

He goes into the garage. The cave smell makes him start whistling. He knows it will be close to rain outside. He likes the weather when it is like this, unpleasant. He believes he can be happy in a dull climate. He swings himself into the Jeep and powers down all the windows before backing out.

The basin, the tiny ski resort where both of his daughters worked on the weekends during the winter when they turned fifteen, is less than twenty minutes away. The sky is a sheet. At the other house across the road they are moving boxes. A woman comes after two men, carrying a vacuum cleaner across her shoulders like a big gun. Richard opens his mouth and waves his arm at them. The woman turns toward him and watches him as his car gets up to thirty-five and goes around the bend. The men, he sees in the rearview mirror, do not pause and are putting their boxes in the bed of a truck. Lots of brown trees shoot into his line of sight.

There was one year when he drove Amy to work on Saturday mornings, and then sometimes on Sundays, when they needed her. His wife and

Jenny would come along, and they would ski together when Amy got off work. They would shout things up and down the mountain. His wife is very slow. She favors one-piece suits, makes perfect turns. The custom is to line up at the bottom of a run and comment as she comes down. And then Amy had her license, and she drove herself alone early in the mornings, and he knew that sometimes she was skiing at seven before the slopes were open, and that she had friends who also worked. He and his wife got another car for Amy to drive, because soon she was driving Jen, too, and the girls had friends who were locals, and they went to parties. Eloise was a local. He did not know whether she was Amy's friend or if she was Jen's friend. She was probably a little younger than Amy, but she was definitely not as young as Jenny. She was around their house often, and she called often, and when she called, she would ask for Amy, and when she was over, he always saw her talking to Jen. But she was part of a group of kids who came to his house and were attractive and polite and sometimes ate a meal with them. He never met her parents, but once she told a story about how they had let her brother name her when she was a baby, which he remembered, so he knew that they existed. The other thing that he can think of is that one time he saw Eloise kissing a boy on their deck under the light. The boy was leaving early; she had gone out with him to say goodbye. It had been a surprise to see that kids did that, the way she was formal with him, and he saw her mouth, "Good night," after.

He turned into the huge muddy lot, past the pond that never froze, dug for skating, and the green cross-country trails. A small blue car with white racing stripes and rust hooding one of its taillights, a gray van, and a black truck were lined up at the fence at the end of the lot. This is really part-time, thought Richard, and he pulled in next to the blue car. There was an empty box of Ritz crackers torn open in the back and a white T-shirt pulled over the passenger-side front seat of the blue car. He turned off his engine but kept looking inside the blue car. Eloise wasn't waiting for him. Richard got out into the mud, locked the Jeep, and walked toward the lifts through one of the ticket booths.

Around the lifts there was still some grass. The mountain started the second you passed the ticket booth: the ground shot up, no trees except between trails. There were rocks Richard had not been able to see in winter, when they made snow. The main chairlift was running. Yellow benches sailed up and down and swung out around the giant engine in a metal house at the base. There was a man in a red shirt on the roof of the engine. He had his head down and was adjusting something Richard could not see. The lift made more noise now than in the winter.

"Hey." A man in a black windbreaker with wet hair walks toward Richard. The man has a very broad face, so Richard sees his features before he is near. This is a man Richard has seen working the lifts before. The man says, "Can I do something for you?"

"Yes." Richard's voice is raised. "I'm looking for a young woman. Her name is Eloise. She works here."

"Yeah. El is at the top right now."

"Do you know when she'll be down?"

"Hold this." The man gives Richard the car battery he was carrying. His thumb in a thick glove presses the button of a walkie-talkie he has produced. He brings the device to his mouth. His eyes roll up to get the words. "Yeah, can you get me Eloise." There is a crack and a whir. Someone says, "Sure," and then there are scratches. Eloise says, "Hey."

"Here," the man says, passing Richard the walkie-talkie. Richard puts the battery on the ground and takes the walkie-talkie in both hands. "You press that," says the man, indicating.

"Thank you," Richard tells him, and patiently puts the lower half of the walkie-talkie near his mouth. "Eloise?"

"Yeah?"

"This is Dr. Lehren. I just came in my car."

"Yeah?"

"You still want to use the phone?" Richard

feels like he is in a storm. The man in gloves has squatted down to do something with the battery on the ground, and the man on the roof begins motioning for Richard to come toward the lift.

"Yeah, I do. Things just got kind of busy around here."

"Oh yes?" Richard shouts. "There's a guy on the roof of the lift motioning to me. I'm going to walk over there now. Are you at the top of the main lift?"

"Yeah."

Richard is standing underneath the lift now, and the man on the roof comes to the edge and leans off.

"Do you want to come up?" Eloise asks him.

The man on the roof has a brown beard. He is young and smiling, and it seems to Richard that one of the man's eyes might be slow, but he can't really tell from this angle. "Are you gonna ride?" the man asks him, one finger indicating the chairs running underneath the eaves.

"Yeah, Eloise? I'll come up." Richard takes his right hand off the button. "Just a second," he says to the man on the roof. The other man in the gloves is still crouching over his battery. Richard hurries back to him and touches his shoulder. When the man turns, Richard holds out the walkie-talkie and says, "Thank you."

"No problem," the man tells him. "You going up?"

"If that's all right. I don't want to get in the way of your repairs."

"No, no, nothing's broke. We're just making some adjustments. Yeah, really my car's fucked and no one needs what's in the sheds out here. It's supposed to be for the ski patrol. We're just, well, Wallace is fine-tuning it, but yeah, you should ride up there. See Eloise."

"You're sure?"

"It's a great view. Oh hey." Now the man is concerned, looking at Richard's chest. "You're gonna be cold. Here, you take this." The man pulls his windbreaker over his head and sticks his arm out to Richard. The windbreaker is in his fist, and it swings from side to side, and the man's comb-over rolls away from his head. "C'mon. Take it. I'm going inside."

Richard takes the windbreaker from the man in the gloves. It is much thicker than he had expected, almost like rubber. Richard gathers it into a doughnut and sticks it over his head. "Thanks again. Where can I give this back to you?"

"You leave it with Wallace when you come back down. Have a good ride."

"I will," says Richard. The man looks down at his battery, and Richard begins the process of convincing the windbreaker over his upper body. It is an anorak. It cannot be parted in the front. Then Wallace starts calling him, "Hey, hey!" Wallace stops the lift and smiles and waits for Richard.

*

The ground bobbed, and the sky was white. When Richard reached mid-station, rain began to fall. Whatever Wallace was doing to the motor, it was not making things run more smoothly. Over the birch trees, on the trail to the left of the trail below his feet, Richard espied the yellow body of the old school bus they had dragged out of the woods for the kids who rode snowboards. In the winter he had seen them sitting on the roof, boys and girls, some asleep and some eating and laughing. And then there were laurels under his legs. He thought he was breathing a lake. Water fell from the sky, and it fell from the crossbar over his head, and it fell from the cables that were slinging his chair up the mountain. The laurel covered the steepest place, where there was no trail, and Richard seemed to be face-to-face with the hillside. And he could see the top, with a cabin and a metal house, partner to the one at the base where Wallace was changing things. Then the lift stopped.

Richard sat in the rain. He was trying to imagine what he would say to Eloise when he got to the top. He could not say why he had left his house, or why he had gotten on the chairlift. The black jacket the man had given him was cutting off his circulation at the wrists. His glasses had fogged up. He swung and wondered, Does Eloise know that once I saw her give a kiss under our deck light? Then the cables gasped, and the chair started again.

Eloise was outside the cabin. She had on her instructor's coat, which was dark purple, nearly black with rain, and came down to her knees. You bought these coats from the owners of the resort if they offered you a job as an instructor. He had paid for two of them: two hundred and fifty dollars each. And Eloise did have short dark hair. She looked strange, her face not more complete now than it had been when he was trying to picture her. "Hey, Dr. Lehren."

She sounds good to him. "Hello, Eloise." He gets off the chairlift awkwardly, taking too many steps. He comes obediently to a stop in front of her and wipes the water from his face, pulling it down and shaking it off his hand in one motion. "Well, I'm here."

She doesn't smile at him. She tells him, "I'd like to talk for a second if that's OK."

"I've come all the way up the mountain, Eloise. Let's talk."

She looks past his shoulder, then back at him. "OK. Come with me." But she doesn't take him into the cabin. She walks back toward the thin woods where the two trails begin. "Someone's in there." She nods at the cabin. Water rolls down her nose and over her mouth.

"Oh," he says.

"But it's raining." She drags out the *rain* of *raining*. "It's raining. And you came all the way up here."

"It wasn't raining before," he says stupidly.

"No, this is no good." She's looking around her. The trees are small and far apart. "There's no place comfortable. Shit," she says, and pulls at her coat.

"Look, Eloise, maybe we should just go back down the mountain."

"No. I have to do this here."

"Oh," he says.

"Look, I need to ask you something. That's why I called." The woods are shaking. The sound of weight on paper is everywhere.

"But you couldn't ask me over the phone?" he tries.

"No. Your wife hates me and you would have been too surprised."

"Yes?"

"Shit," she says. "Yeah. I need money. No, this is the wrong way to do this. Shit. This was my brother's idea. Dr. Lehren, please, I need a loan. I'm sorry. I'm so worried about things right now, I can't do anything right."

"No. It's OK. We can lend you some money." Then he says, "You aren't in trouble, are you?"

Her face turns up. "No," she says. "I just need money." And very quickly, so he can't laugh with her, she laughs.

She is angry, and he walks toward her. "We're happy to help out. We've known you for nearly eight years now. We'll talk about this."

"OK," she says. "I guess I'm acting crazy," and she turns and starts walking out of the trees, back to the lift.

"It's just like for one of our own daughters. We'll help you out." But it's not like for one of his daughters, and rain has made him a necklace at the tight neck of the other man's coat.

Clare closes the document. As she remembers it, it had been an exercise in style: How precise could she be in her descriptions, how flat a protagonist could she get away with, what sorts of interventions could she make into this most American form. And then, unrelated to style, at least not directly: Whether she could manage to say something about class. Most unusual among her formal "touches" here is a mix of present- and past-tense narration. Clare knows she had a reason for indulging the whim, that it wasn't a whim, but she cannot recall that reason now. Kafka had somewhere done something similar. Perhaps that was it, a man with five letters in each of his names, just like her, a mirror image: Franz Kafka, Clare Elwil, one, two, three, four, five, six, seven, eight, nine, ten, one, two, three, four, five, six, seven, eight, nine, ten, yes. His matching letters: *f* times two, *a* times three. Her matching letters: *l* times three, *e* times two. Chiasmus, Christmas, etc.! Clare wins the game! But never mind.

Because this is not a story about her life. At least, she doesn't think so.

At any rate, her father never had any money. He was from New York, born in the Bronx on the eve of the Second World War. Before he became a poet, he was a Marine. And before he was a Marine he was a petty thief. And before that, he had been a child, presumably. Clare's father's name is John Dariush. As he recounts in his early book-length poem, *Of Thee*, written when he still deigned to employ the English language, he has a mother of uncertain Polish extraction and a father who as a preadolescent during the second decade of the twentieth century fled the persecution of Christian villagers in a remote eastern pocket of the Ottoman Empire, to settle first in Melbourne and then, as a teen, in the Big Apple. Clare has never met her paternal grandparents and doubts they are alive, given the date of her father's birth. Her mother seems to know nothing about them.

Clare's father attended the Seminars, starting in 1960, on a fellowship for vets. In 1963 he returned to New York City, where he hovered around St. Marks and became briefly attached to Warhol, appearing in a screen test that flatters his pale eyes. Later, scholars associate him with Ted Berrigan, so-called magus of the LES poetry scene. There is a passage in one of Berrigan's journals in which he and "Johnny" steal steaks from a deli, mashing them into their pockets and sauntering bloodily out. A nominally more established Dariush met Trudy Elwil a decade later at a gallery opening when he offered her a fresh apricot from a pint he had recently lifted. Trudy saw her chance and proceeded to offend her family. Clare, born in 1980 and brought home to a Spring Street loft, is proof of these activities. It is no nominal piece of luck that Trudy is as talented a paramour and general social being as she is. Dariush's presence waned in direct proportion to the accrual of years and memory on the part of his daughter, until he was permanently residing in a *chambre de bonne* within striking distance of the

Buttes-Chaumont, somewhat famously and very perversely composing all his work in French, and, in a final twist, dead.

Though Clare remembers little enough of the writing of "The Lift," she does recall thinking something like, This is what happens to girls who don't have fathers. All the same, even as she knows that she at one point thought this was *her* story, a story about her, she now disagrees with herself. Because this isn't what happens to "girls who don't have fathers"; it's what happens to girls who have *too many fathers*. And the story isn't in fact about that, about Eloise, the girl. Eloise doesn't really matter. It's a story about Richard Lehren, about reading Richard, about how we cannot really determine Richard's motivations, because Richard's own comprehension of himself is so paltry. He is led forward by fantasy; grasps at soft things and believes the world is a smile turned in his direction. Richard could be one of Trudy Elwil's various husbands, lovers, and associates, but he might also be a version of Clare. Indeed, he is perhaps the embodiment of Clare's own weird existential virginity, if not that of almost everybody. He is Clare before anything happened.

"Goodbye, Richard," Clare thinks, exiting the document. Today she is managing to feel less sad than usual about her lack of production. She's amused to have discovered herself here in her own story, for she is more and more convinced that it is, indeed, she. It's a curious self-portrait her past self seems to have hidden on behalf of her present self, in plain sight.

Clare is supposed to write while she is here and decides, for this reason, to pretend to try. She knows that, as usual, nothing will happen and so doesn't feel concerned. It's been like this for months now. Clare opens a new document and observes the cursor at the top of the page, how it appears and drops out of view again like a pulse. Clare has had an idea for a story. Or: it's not so much an idea as a memory, a short vision of being in the Musée d'Orsay her last year of college when she had gone to Paris for a few days on a whim and had not informed her father of her presence there. She'd wondered once during those days whether she might see him by chance but never did. She remembers this. At least, she remembers walking through the Orsay and viewing Gustave Courbet's small canvas *L'Origine du monde, The Origin of the World.* She remembers thinking—as she now also thinks—that this painting looks nothing like anyone's cunt.

She is unsure, at this moment, what the story is in this, but she can feel the tension that once indicated to her a beginning. She isn't sure if this familiar feeling is only imagined by her. She hopes she's just imagining it. Nevertheless, she begins making a list of possible elements for the story. It feels fine to do this because she knows she will never manage to turn this into anything, find the reason for these clues. It's too hard to begin.

- *Paris*
- *College*
- *Father*
- *Courbet*
- *Lie by omission*

Clare pauses, adds a sixth bullet:

- *About recognition*

Sixteen

That Person

Sometimes it seems to Harry that there is someone else. Who the person is doesn't matter.

It's just, someone else is here. The person, that person—mythic and free, an indefinite being—sifts through experience alongside Harry. You wouldn't see that person, like, in real life, but Harry knows that person is there. The reason Harry knows is that often Harry thinks, or even *sees*, things that he couldn't possibly think and see, or, for that matter, hear. Knowing this, about that other person who is there, *that person*, explains how Harry can sometimes be capable of acts of perception obviously beyond him.

Take, for example, today's issue of *The Sentinel*. Harry has been underlining phrases that interest him. Sometimes when he finds a phrase, he writes it down on an index card. He then files the card away in a metal box with a hinged lid that he recently acquired via a tub of FREE STUFF (CLEAN) on the nicer residential block between here and the library.

Harry creates a card for *civilian status*, derived from an

article on overseas deployment. Are there, he wonders, other statuses?

There are. Harry is living in America.

Harry knows, based on his limited poetical reading, but whatever, that he's supposed to be using language that might "mean more than one thing" when he's creating a poem. But it's confusing to him how exactly this should work, from the point of view of production. For this reason, he's developing a work-around. He's decided to find language that definitely means one thing and then to try his best to use it in another way, so that it definitely *cannot* mean the very thing it usually means—which is to say, exclusively.

On one level, this seems complicated, but in practice it's been simple. It's like switching price tags in the grocery store. It's so satisfying to remove that fragile gummy fragment. To place it on a different can.

Harry sighs.

He closes the top of his tin box and shakes. The cards make a sound.

There is some pressure to make a poem.

Harry flips to the crossword.

The Great Communicator is a nice clue, 23 across, so he writes that down on a card.

Harry stands, stares at the door, sits.

There's this feeling he's been having, like the feeling of wanting to tell a story, but that's not the word for it. The thing about stories is, you do need quite a lot of confidence about the way things come to pass in the actual world to write one. You need to be pretty sure that the world contains humans, along with these other discrete entities, aka, events.

Harry thinks about going into an imaginary grocery store and peeling all the labels off everything, prices and names and bar codes, images of kittens and blond children and delicately sweating grapes. It is late—in the human project, but additionally the store would probably need to be closed—and perhaps all the signs will have fallen off the walls, too.

Yes: Harry wades to a display window and begins culling from the linguistic, numerical, symbolical heap. Truth be told, the torn paper is so copious it comes up over his ankles.

After the deluge, he thinks, *me*. He wets his fingers in his mouth, turns the page of the tabloid. He turns the radio back on, picks up a pen.

But it isn't, he thinks, me.

Seventeen

Predictably

Anton Beans is not having the best of all possible semesters. Tuesday's introductory workshop was trash, and for the past four days he's barely been able to squeeze out a single coherent line, not to speak of a full-on poem. Beans has put pen to paper but the energies are in no way flowing. He's tried cutting up and collaging a few paragraphs from the Patriot Act but to no effect. His chakras are hermetically sealed, his mojo pathetically quiescent, his lower intestine acting up again. He has reorganized his bookshelves and updated his wall chart of outstanding poetry journal submissions: one acceptance, four rejections; five down and one hundred sixteen more to go.

On top of this, his meeting an hour ago with Don Hillary was total shit. All Hillary would say about Beans's work was that he thinks Beans's stuff is "very advanced," that Beans is definitely onto some "high-level concepts." He is looking forward to Beans's "perspective." Beans knows this is just code for Don Hillary hating everything he does, but for whatever reason Hillary didn't find it convenient to come out and say so, perhaps because he's checking to make sure Beans isn't going to report him for fueling his office hours with gin conveyed via Sprite can. Instead of providing any sort of usable feedback, Hillary launched into one of his down-home routines about how he, Hillary, is but a poetry simpleton who can't get beyond the basic themes of love and death and war. Hillary went off on a tear about the finesse of Frost, the aplomb of Lowell, the swagger of Berryman. He told Beans he just wished he could tune into that erudite postmodern frequency Beans has locked as the permanent station on his "poem radio." That was literally, no joke, Hillary's metaphor. *Poem radio.*

Hillary owns a ranch in Colorado and knows how to ride a horse and shoot a gun. But everyone knows that Don Hillary hails from a wealthy Connecticut clan and was a legacy at Princeton, like both his grandfather and father, pioneering psychiatrists. People will, as they say, talk. And while it's not entirely clear how the heavy drinking fits in with the true-blue cowboy routine, whether the former excuses the latter or it's the other way around, any kind of proximity to Hillary's person will let you know that he is either slowly embalming himself as a source of obdurate patrician fun or is unaware that suicide is best accomplished by more direct means.

Because Marta Hillary and Donald Hillary, as everyone knows, have gone well beyond being on the rocks. To further mix the metaphor, they're straight out of the bottle, paper-bagging it. Or, at least, they would be, if Marta hadn't so clearly moved on. As things stand, these days only Don seems to indulge on the job.

There is speculation among the students about what will happen to the poetry program if their marriage collapses this academic year, in medias res, for example. Would one of them leave town? Who would take the hatchet?

Anton Beans is slouching his way to Building 109. He has to pick up the packet for next Tuesday's class. This would be a dramatically less irksome task if it weren't for some of the other individuals Beans will have to confront across the seminar table once the weekend has come to a close. Foremost in Beans's mind is, of course, the newcomer, Loudermilk. This person isn't a real writer, and Beans would like very much to know what Loudermilk is doing in the Seminars, besides, for example, living a subsidized oversexed lifestyle that it's better not to even begin to visualize.

Just so Loudermilk keeps his distance from Marta: If he can do that, then Beans doesn't care. But let him start currying favor with Marta Hillary, then Beans and Loudermilk will have words.

Beans grinds his teeth crossing the threshold of Building 109. He glowers at the oversized oil portrait of Rainer Dodds, founder of the Seminars, encountering Henry Ford amid rolling fields. The two giants clasp hands beneath a candied sun.

Beans pauses before the cubbies where the new packets appear once they have been photocopied by the all-female administrative staff. He searches the labels and finds his workshop. He selects one packet from the center of the warm pile.

Flipping through, Beans exits. He's hot and his shoulders are too tight. On the first square of sidewalk he reads something that stops him in his tracks.

II

WRITING TEACHER

Writing Teacher

The person was a civilian status.
He had no part in the creation
Of a mass grave near his home.

Like being in a cool, dim Easter
Basket, a gift for the unblinking self,
A one-way mirror was produced

And held up to the soul.
In an age of collapsed distances
There's no such thing as might

Or day. He orchestrated
Their emotional surrender
With roving satellites

And hoods. The person was
Advised to disappear
And he has said he would—

To live among the best
Communicators, in a crackling
Mural of persuasion.

—T. A. LOUDERMILK

Eighteen

Early Poems

When Harry was younger by a lot, very young, there was a woman living next door, and whenever she would knock on the wall, Harry had to knock right back. Harry had been staying with his grandmother, but his mother said she couldn't stand it anymore, she had to have him with her. So Harry was alone while his mother went to work at Tops.

When Harry was a kid, he often thought about Tops, the word and the name. He was always alone, then, in the first apartment. He imagined one day his mother would come home and say, "Harry, it's Tops time!" And together they would climb into the air.

They were living in a former mill town (mill now defunct), and they did not have a television, an anomaly that would become apparent to Harry only much later. Harry was four when he learned to read.

"Thank you for being my good boy!" Harry's mother always said when she came home. She threw her arms around his back and cradled his head with one hand. Harry clung to her neck, the perfume of which (fabric softener) was the sweetest of all scents, or so he believed.

Harry's mother made Harry Chef Boyardee, and she smoked out the window. He liked to pierce the raviolis, to divide them into perfect quarters before he consumed them. He examined the brown meat inside, the white edge of the pasta envelope. He read the label on the can.

Harry's mother would get on the phone with Harry's grandmother.

Harry didn't know what his grandmother was saying, but Harry's mother seemed to talk a lot about how well Harry was doing. Sometimes Harry's mother said Harry was asleep when Harry was not asleep. Harry's mother regretted her inability to bring Harry to visit his grandmother.

At this time, they had a sofa bed they shared. Harry's mother was a quiet sleeper. In the morning, Harry's mother made corned beef hash that, once cooked, she divided in half. She placed half of the corned beef hash in the refrigerator for Harry's lunch. He remembers it as a beautiful time. There was ketchup and milk.

One of Harry's favorite games was to lie on his back and look at the molding on the ceiling. He imagined how it would be if the ceiling were the floor of a room, if the ceiling were somehow made available to him as a floor upon which he alone could walk, and which he alone could furnish. The lamp suspended on a dust-bearded chain from a filigreed lozenge at the center of the ceiling would be a blazing flower. He'd put a chair nearby so that he could sit and gaze into it.

Harry stared out the window at telephone wires. He

imagined himself leaping through the air from post to post. He'd spring from a post onto the eave of a building.

He'd ascend a distant church spire.

Harry sometimes spent twenty minutes imagining that the glass top of the side table in the second room was a frozen surface beneath which Paleolithic fish were swimming. He gazed down onto their black, spiny bodies. Harry set himself tasks. He placed books in a stack and he placed the radio with a pen and a notepaper block on the kitchen table. He copied down the words he heard on the radio, and sometimes he wrote other things.

Harry was six. His mother said that he could go to school the next year but then this never happened. It seemed like they went outside about once a week. Sometimes they went to the library.

Harry read a children's book about a young girl who goes driving with her mother, and they pack chicken in newspaper to eat along the way. The mother wears a scarf in her hair.

Harry listened to the radio because it was a fun game to write down the words. There was an advertisement about fur storage in Albany.

Harry felt, when he was writing down the words, that he was doing something that brought him closer to people, not to the people on the radio but to the idea of people. It was like a secret about human living that he was whispering to himself over and over as he formed each letter, as he devoted each letter to a complete word.

There was a crumbling paperback dictionary and Harry knew how to use it.

Harry drew words from the sound. He pulled the words from the extent of sound, from sound's event, someone speaking.

When Harry was seven, Harry's mother started asking him to tell her about what he was reading. She brought him paperbacks from Tops to read and tell her about.

Harry's mother did not like to read. She said that Harry's talent was a testament to what a trick it is anybody makes anyone feel that school is the answer. She said that she was glad that she could do something for her son. She found Harry some old copies of *Reader's Digest* at the Salvation Army.

When Harry was eight, Harry's grandmother showed up for a surprise visit. She looked exactly the way she looked in a certain photograph, but for some reason Harry did not know her on sight. It took her over an hour's cajolement to convince him to let her in the front door. When she did come inside she started crying. Harry was afraid and went into the other room. His grandmother followed him and sat beside him and told him that the only reason she was crying was that he was so handsome. Harry's grandmother said that Harry had grown into such a handsome boy. That he was so handsome on the outside must mean that he was handsome on the inside, too. Harry was still afraid, but he did not say anything or try to move away from her again. After this, Harry had to go to school. It was not that he avoided the other children so much as he was so satisfied by the act of observing them from a distance that actually speaking to them seemed somehow wrong.

The teachers at the school moved Harry into the fourth grade, then the seventh grade.

Someone threw yogurt at the back of Harry's head and he stopped going to the cafeteria. During recess and lunch he sat in a locked bathroom stall and read.

Things were worse at the next school. Harry saw boys trap a girl under the bleachers beside the running track. A messenger from a central clique approached him and informed him that he should begin praying to god every night in hopes that, for his own sake, he would die soon.

A woman came to the house to make sure Harry was going to school. Her hair was coarse and crimped.

Harry began to cultivate unobtrusiveness in himself. The school was the kind of place where discipline was in such short supply that Harry's absence from certain nonacademic classes and occasions of assembly was not just overlooked but privately condoned by a quorum of the better-seasoned staff. They knew what was waiting for him at the area high.

The woman with the crimped hair retired. A new, stout woman came.

Harry's mother got another job and they moved to a small house. Harry had his own room.

Early on, the stout woman suggested the idea of community college classes. Harry was bagging groceries at Tops. He could afford one class a semester. In the summer he did lawn work, and he could afford two classes. He got his GED his sophomore year after someone stomped on his foot in the hall between classes and broke two of his toes.

The stout woman helped Harry apply for a scholarship. Harry took out a small loan, which he has since deferred.

Harry was fifteen the year he went to college. Harry's mother was thirty-one.

Nineteen

Motivation

Harry mentally replays a conversation of earlier in the week, when he requested to know if Loudermilk had ever read *Tristes tropiques* by Claude Lévi-Strauss. Harry pointed out that if Loudermilk hadn't yet laid eyes on this classic he probably should, because the book contains some pretty relevant notes for their project, to which Loudermilk was like, "What, dude?"

Harry repeated, *Tristes tropiques*, englishing for Loudermilk's benefit. He cited a paragraph in which Lévi-Strauss contends that the main function of writing in human history has been as a tool of enslavement. Harry said, "It makes you think." Harry wonders now just exactly what he'd meant by this.

Harry's also been—here literally—replaying the remarkable documentary tapes Loudermilk brings back from workshop, how on week one you hear Loudermilk come into the class and the first thing he says is, "Apologies, sir."

He's late.

"I don't usually let in stragglers," a man, the instructor, rumbles.

"Completely." Loudermilk moves into the room. "Understood."

"But I guess now you're here we can make an accommodation and try, at last, to begin. As I was saying," the meticulously hungover individual who is apparently the poet Don Hillary pursues, "I don't give one donkey *fuck* what you do while you're here. I honest to god do not. This is not a contest and I do not give out prizes. And the first of you knuckleheads gets that through his or her skull will be the lucky recipient of absolutely nothing." Don Hillary pauses. He has to acknowledge someone. "Yes? You already have something you need to tell me?"

It's Loudermilk. "Hi, everyone. I'm Loudermilk."

There comes a deafening stillness.

"*Dear Class*," Don Hillary finally hisses, "please meet Loudermilk. He's new here."

No one says a donkey-fucking thing.

"Oh, I'm so sorry," the remarkably expressive Hillary continues. "How rude of me. And this is everyone else. Loudermilk, please meet every fucking body in your brand-new class." Harry can tell that Hillary is about to ram it home. "Here, by the way, is every fucking person who is going to make your life a goddamn living hell for the next four months, did I mention that? But don't worry, they're all going to be your bestest little cuddle buddies, too. That's the irony of this province and its charming customs. Remember how you used to write to get away from it all? To be alone and at peace? Well, you can forget about that now, because it's time to start writing by committee. Every time you sit down to write any bloody effing thing, these idiots are going to be up there in your brain all over it, offering anodyne suggestions. See Kari over here? I had her in this same impotent time-suck last semester. She doesn't like pigeons. God forbid you might put a pigeon in your poem because she will dig that thing out like a terrier. I'm not even kidding you. And, by the way, I'm Don. Though you must already know that. And, by the way, I don't care about you. You are not my responsibility. Only thing I have the time or, I should add, inclination to care about is the work. Period. End of story." Hillary's chair creaks.

This is for starters.

In class number two, Loudermilk's first poem, aka Harry's first poem, aka "Writing Teacher," is up for discussion.

On the tape, the students ponder "Writing Teacher." They labor to describe it. They say it seems at once familiar to them and unlike anything they've read. They admit that they don't know what it means but that they like it. It feels mysterious. They think it's a poem about America, recent imperial foibles. They treasure the part about the "cool, dim Easter / Basket," whatever that is.

Harry smiles at that.

Harry knows, intuitively, that this is the right kind of response to be getting—that this means something, he's done well—and he wants to dig further into this effect. He wants to solicit pleasure and this other thing, which is kind of like some form of fear. He has mixed his registers and included some ominous references to historical violence as well as contemporary war. He's been thinking a lot about men. He worked in a few neologisms as well, which, his listening has informed him, is a thing that really gets his audience going.

Even Don Hillary, *grumpus numero uno*, special agent of

the fugue state, was not entirely without respect for Harry's, which is to say Loudermilk's, debut effort, and seemed willing to forget about the first session's rancorous exchange. Hillary murmurs, "There's something kinda . . . *mystic* about this thing." It's not the most original observation, but it also isn't Hillary telling Loudermilk to go frig himself in the dick with a freshly sharpened number 2 pencil. This is a pensive Don, slowly licking drooping literary chops, savoring the pedagogical present, wondering aloud about Loudermilk's motivations. "Who is this 'Writing Teacher'?" Hillary asks no one in particular. "What does this guy *want*?"

Twenty

Allegory

L'Origine du monde, The Origin of the World was painted by Gustave Courbet at the commission of Khalil-Bey, a Turkish-Egyptian diplomat and playboy, in 1866, probably from a pornographic photograph. Small, approximately twenty-one by eighteen inches, the painting was, as per various accounts in the prose of local decadents and critics, reputed to have hung in Khalil-Bey's vast pink bathroom, veiled by a green curtain that might be drawn aside to amaze the eyes of the fashionable and wicked. Khalil-Bey, who was reported to spend fourteen thousand francs per day on his own wicked lifestyle, fell out of fashion and cash in late 1867, departing Paris for Constantinople.

Sold privately during the latter part of the intervening decade, *The Origin* was masked with a specially constructed cabinet, topped by another Courbet painting of 1875, *The Château de Blonay*, a likable picture of a castle in snow. When next traceable, *The Origin* had come, cabinet and all, into the possession of the Baron Ferenc Hatvany, of Budapest. It was now the early twentieth century. Something—no one is sure what—happened to the painting during the Second World War. It was seized by the Red Army from the depths of a Budapest bank in 1945, and/or Baron Hatvany, who was Jewish and who benefited from a passport provided by Raoul Wallenberg, escaped with the painting concealed in the false bottom of a suitcase two years earlier, and/or the baron simply escaped at some time or another, perhaps as late as 1950, from behind the Iron Curtain, bringing the painting with him. What *is* known is that after the war Hatvany set up house on the rue de Rivoli in Paris, where he concluded his days writing a study of the influence of photography on nineteenth-century painting. *The Origin* appears in this learned text as an exemplary canvas; strangely, the baron misremembered its name, retitling it *The Creation of the World*. In 1958, he passed away.

The Origin had in fact resurfaced in polite French society some years earlier, in 1954, having been purchased, as if in a novel, by the celebrated psychoanalyst Jacques Lacan. The painting took up residence in Lacan's country home at Guitrancourt, a space he shared with his second wife, Sylvia Bataille, née Maklès, the film actress and former spouse of Georges Bataille, author of *Histoire de l'oeil*, that major literary blossom of the slow death of French cultural dominance. At Sylvia's request, the painting was masked again, now with a vaguely vaginal landscape daubed on wood by André Masson.

After Lacan's death in 1981—he had suffered a car accident on the peripheral highway in 1978 and gone into decline—the painting disappeared again, or nearly. Lacan was rich and his two wives, along with their respective children, were at odds. Sylvia Lacan, formerly Bataille, would claim that it was she who had first noticed Courbet's canvas in the 1950s, that it was she who had asked her husband to acquire it on her behalf, that perhaps they had split the cost. Sylvia—who had apparently removed *The Origin* from Guitrancourt in secret—was only discovered to be the clandestine owner by another woman, the perspicacious American curator Linda Nochlin. In 1988, after the painting traveled to the Brooklyn Museum, where it was exhibited before the public for the first time, it was also properly reproduced in color. As the catalogue, *Courbet Reconsidered*, circulated, the painting at last entered into general notoriety. In 1995, in a final burst of glory, it was collected by the Orsay.

This is, at least, Clare's understanding.

When she thought about all this before, it was *before*, then, truly. It was before the accident, and she had truly been in Paris.

She had not told her father she was coming to his city. She had had the idea that she would wait and see. What, she thought, if I see him, just by accident? What if he spontaneously appears?

She does not know now if that idea is what inspired the trip, or if the idea came to her later, after she was there, crunching through the Jardin des Plantes, etc. What had come first? Clare cannot now remember.

Also—and this is the greater problem, perhaps—Clare cannot remember if she did see her father when she was standing there, in Room 19, in the Orsay. She tries to go back to the moment, but the moment is already a story. She tries to go back to the time before the accident and know what she knew then, when things hung together in an order, but she is unable.

What had she known then and there, in her last year of college? Had she really seen her father, or was it all a convenient ruse for plot?

She had planned to visit Paris in the spring. In Paris, she had been inspired with an idea for a story while staring into a mysterious and often (as research informed her) veiled painting. She had returned to the U.S., yes. This might be what had happened.

But it might also be the case that she had planned to visit Paris *in order* to write a story, and then what she had planned to write had in fact occurred. That she had thought she might wish to write this scene, in which her estranged father appears, and her wish had summoned him. Or, her wish was no different from the writing. Thus was she able, as in a realist painting, to write from life, because there was no difference between writing and life. Thus did she encounter what Courbet might have termed "real allegory," a portrait of the world that is completely accurate yet not devoid of symbolism. The allegory is real, because there is allegory in the world.

Clare had graduated. She had returned to Paris. It was summer. She returned to the scene of a nonencounter—because she needed to know, which is to say, what had happened. She called her father and they met.

Clare wants to force herself to tell an ending. She wants to get there fast. But in the search for ending, the beginning disappears. It is sucked up into a pale void.

She remembers researching the Courbet painting in spring, after she got back the first time, before the second trip. She remembers realizing that she couldn't write the story, not without her father, because she did not know where it begins.

At least, this is what she thinks she remembers.

But which time was it? Which was the penultimate? Had he actually been present on that day with the painting, flashing through that secure room?

Clare had read, too, Lacan's 1957 lecture on veils.

By 1957, the painting would have been hanging, for at least three years, on the wall in the study where Lacan retired each Sunday to plan his classes. Three years of staring at it masked or unmasked, as the analyst liked. Headless, legless, armless, a sort of globe, this pelvis in creams and pinks and browns.

Lacan says, meanwhile, in the text derived from his 1957 seminar, that it does not matter. He's talking about love. He says that what is instructive is to think about veils. He says if you put a veil in front of something that does not exist, you create an image of something that is there, only hidden. And if you put a veil in front of something that *does* exist, you create an image of something that is there, only hidden. The crucial thing is not whether it is there. Real presence does not matter. The thing is, whether we can imagine it—and at the same time imagine its absence. This is what the veil permits: it is a screen on which loss and gain mix, in which something that is not there and something that is become equivalent. The veil is the image of a loss, an image we cannot otherwise picture. We give ourselves this veil. We give ourselves this image. We put it in the world. This is how we love.

Twenty-One

Grief

In the recordings, Loudermilk experiments with various styles of self-presentation. For the third session, he's a provocateur, which is to say, an ass. Admittedly, he is abetted in this project by his instructor, Professor Hillary. In a repeat performance of the affective stylings of class number one, Hillary makes no attempt to conceal his rage. If anyone asks Harry, which no one does, Hillary's ire is caused not by anything in particular Loudermilk happens to do or say. And not even Loudermilk's loudness, which may be a contributing factor, is sufficient as irritant, as it were. Nor can Hillary's explosion be entirely explained by his combination of possible hangover plus definite renewed drunkenness, the slur under half of what he says, the growl of dehydration. No, there is something more. Hillary is imagining Loudermilk having sex with his wife, Harry is sure of it. It's the first thing on Hillary's mind the minute Loudermilk walks through the door and it remains Hillary's primary thought until the last second of the day's lesson, such as this lesson is.

Hillary, on this day, eclipses everyone else. The chemistry between him and Loudermilk is classic; they are a Western with slapstick overtones and a real possibility for serious gore, ketchup splashing, a violent situation tragedy. It's a weird example of straight men in love and gives Harry a shot of vicarious joy: the passion, the histrionics. But Harry is simultaneously glad he didn't have to be in the actual room for it, that he, personally, is protected by media.

"You think I'm scared of a preppy shit like you?" Hillary wails. "I'm the guy who spent the last decade and a half interpreting crayon cave paintings someone thinks is poetry! You think I haven't been here twenty times before? You're a goddamn cliché and your daddy paid for your last lap dance."

Loudermilk opts for cruel whimsy. "I'll have to go back and check my credit-card bill to see if that's true. *Like*"—Loudermilk stage-whispers—"*because I'm pretty sure I'm not the one who has to pay for ass.*"

In the fourth session, Loudermilk is a bit slyer, biding his time. He's silent, which means he essentially cedes Anton Beans the floor. He gives Beans just enough rope to hang himself with, in other words. Beans struts; he preens. He has a few notes to disseminate regarding the production of poetry in America today, its tired norms, its naïve credence in the transparent referential capacity of language. Up for workshop is a sentimental piece about someone's grandmother's attic. It's a vision of middle-class nostalgia for the postwar era, when continuity and unionized employment were assured, and all of life could be reliably archived in one's home. The attic is a place in which the smell and feel of the grandmother's body, her crepey limbs, is transferred, in what even Harry comprehends is a poorly scaled metaphor, onto the storage space. Chelsea, the poet, reads out loud.

When Chelsea's performance is complete, Beans thanks her for sharing her middlebrow creation. He remarks on how interesting it is that we think of certain topics as being best suited to poems. So, for example, Chelsea has elected to write about matrilineal matters of the heart, plus the twentieth century. It's not, Beans observes, a poem about romantic love. Rather, it's a poem about memory loss, decay, the vagaries of intergenerational succession. It's also a poem, Beans maintains, about how bodies and objects signify, about how and where language exists, outside/beyond language, as such. This said, Beans continues, even if the poem (as if the poem might be somehow alive or sentient in itself) gestures or nods at enlivening possibilities for its own meaning, it is not in itself fully inhabiting these gestures. The poem does not appear to fully know what it is doing, and in conclusion—Beans sighs and there is a popping sound as of knuckles cracking (these may well be Beansian knuckles)—this effort at walking amnesia fails to make good on its own possibility and lands as a debased platitude.

Beans's disquisition is greeted with what to Harry sounds like shock. But maybe it's silence of another type. Harry is not sure if Beans is psychotically convinced that everyone around him is in awe of his skills of literary observation or if he is convinced that he is altruistically disrupting everyone's tacit misting-over of their true identities as mediocrities, hacks. There are, one must admit—and see Don Hillary's own class-time speeches—way, way too many individuals accepted into the Seminars, selective as it is, for even a small majority to become acknowledged, award-winning writers. Beans is, however, not about to let even small offenses slide, not when they have broader implications, and moreover he seems to have some sort of crypto-critical agenda. Beans, for all his pessimism, really seems to believe in the process! Of course, perhaps this is just a way of delaying his own realization that he is among the ranks of the talent-free . . .

Others weigh in. A few are, like, “This poem feels so utterly familiar. I like it for that. It reminds me of home.” Hooray, they say.

Harry ponders this notion: it is not beyond the realm of possibility that a poem—or any other piece of writing, for that matter—could have value because it reminds a reader of home.

This tame rejoinder sets Anton Beans off. Now Beans is well-nigh unstoppable; he is locked into a track and can no longer be reached for negotiation.

“*Home*”—Anton Beans pronounces the word as if it is coated in multiple layers of aspic, bile, and perhaps petroleum jelly—“is a construct. It has also, if we recall anything of history, been used to justify so many atrocities across the regrettable creep of the last hundred years, not to mention the current colonial escapade being waged in ‘our’ name. I would be surprised if any one among us even knows what that really is, what *home* really means. I’m sorry but of course Chelsea loves her grandmother. ‘Cry me a river,’ as Justin Timberlake says. However, Chelsea’s grandmother—fortunately, for so many reasons—is not equivalent, even metaphorically, to the house she lives in! She’s a person who had a *life*, who was a subject of American sovereignty and capitalism, and this poem wants to reduce her to a piece of ideology, a symptom of the Cold War, now reheating in the era of peak oil in the Middle East. I doubt that I need to remind everyone that we are currently living in a surveillance state, a *homeland*, not a home, and to me it matters, *deeply*, whether or not the poems I read seem aware of that. I'd like to add that I don't think we've survived the poetics of modernism for nothing and I would like it very much if this poem reflected the history of its own form just a smidgen."

Stillness.

Now the question is, Harry thinks, who's the most dangerous man in the room: Loudermilk or Anton Beans? Are the two of them in competition for this title? And has this contest already gone beyond being an event Harry can participate in? Maybe Harry's locked out and he'll observe their emotional affair from afar, *Beans + Loudermilk 4EVA*. Harry feels slightly ill.

But on the tape Loudermilk does not respond, does not make a play for the limelight. And it's as if this reticence on his part is a message to Harry, as if he's speaking to Harry through the recording, telling Harry: "Just listen in. It's all here for you, man. I wanna make sure you're intuiting the ripeness of these whimpering IQ voids." And as Harry listens on, he hears the message all the more strongly: *It is here for him.*

The fifth session begins in the midst of the fourth. Harry is not sure what Loudermilk did with the recorder, whether the cut is intentional. Where the fourth leaves off, you can tell Hillary is about to take the floor. Harry wonders if Loudermilk interrupts Hillary on purpose, if he stops the tape because he does not want Harry to know what Hillary is about to say. Or maybe it's that Hillary is so predictable: You have to assume he's about to defend Chelsea's exploration of her grandma's crawl space, even if he'll do so through semi-gritted teeth. He has to do this, because this is the basis of Hillary's "poetics," if Harry has that term right. Hillary has certain values, has shown himself over time to be an adherent of certain schools (Harry is aware, due to his poetic research), and now Hillary is obliged to set the table such that only those who can eat of the particular meat on special shall be served, recognized. It is a competition—the thing of poetry—if not an all-out war. If Hillary has an actual job—other than continuing to breathe and sit upright in his chair and utter whatever unfiltered industry juice courses into his cranium—it is to continue to purvey and promote a brand of sentimentality, a sentimentality branded and also promoted by certain institutional-poet ancestors of Hillary's, like the renowned regionalist Timothy Flower and, previous to Flower, the celebrated formalist Jan Batman. Hillary is a straw man, a vacant effigy, not just because he is an alcoholic whose second marriage is about to dehisce, but because it *is his job,* quite literally, to be an alcoholic whose second marriage is about to dehisce, because he is *exactly*—and not one iota more or one iota less than—who he is paid to be. If he were a better teacher, or even a slightly better human being, he would surely have been fired from this position long ago.

Never let it be said, Harry should tell someone, that he, Harry Rego, pulls any punches. He may be trapped inside this pathetic physique, gagged by his own ungainly voice, but never let it be said that Harry Rego ignores the world around him. Harry's eye is limpid, unimpeded by the distorting influence of a viable body or social life. Harry's mind can, to some extent, be thrown from the corpse it inhabits, and this is why he is of such extraordinary use to Loudermilk, who is, in truth, disadvantaged since sapped by the presence of his own magnificent frame in the world. Anyone who really knows Loudermilk, as Harry knows him, has to feel a certain pity for the guy. It's a mystery how Loudermilk finds the necessary blood and/or synapses to think at all, given the other needs of his physical form.

But the fifth session: Here Loudermilk returns, and it's a new Loudermilk, a more refined and sportive Loudermilk, a Loudermilk who arrives at the seminar table with his recorder switched gamely on, who wants to glad-hand and crack jokes, who manifests an appropriately robust sympathy for Hillary when Hillary arrives, Hillary who—judging from the slurring of his monosyllables and reluctance to even attempt sentences—is not merely nursing a hangover or even tipsy, but in the midst of a full-on bender.

So easy, Harry thinks, to get caught up in the bacchic aspect of the creation of poetry, whatever poetry is. It likely takes a strong person not to get carried away, not to rage or swoon or ride off on the proverbial cawing dolphin. Harry, at any rate, can understand people wanting to escape. He gets the thing of wanting to be overtaken by an aspect of yourself that seems larger and stranger than the everyday, with its petty harms and disappointments. If Hillary weren't so privileged within the bizarre milieu in which he practices his lifestyle, Harry might have it in him to feel sorry for the guy. But that's difficult given the fact that Hillary is, by Harry's standards, rich, and his wife looks a lot like an aging model.

Session five does not really take off. In fact, "does not really take off" is a dramatic understatement. A better description might be *founders, implodes*. Hillary can't seem to begin, in spite of Loudermilk's hearty maieutic gestures toward collective bro psyche. The class is obviously supposed to start, and it's gotten to the point where by all rights Hillary should be inaugurating things, but no one is talking and everyone's waiting and even Loudermilk, stalwart that he is, newly minted Hillary adherent, can't seem to find a thing to kid about.

There is a muffled sound, then a couple of gasps, and Harry recognizes that this new repetitive noise he's picking up, this pattern of breaths and sighs, must be weeping, Don Hillary's real, live, late-middle-aged weeping.

Harry shuts off the tape. He has to write a poem.

Twenty-Two

A Portrait

Strictly speaking, Lizzie Hillary does not read the poetry packets. She does not concern herself much with those she thinks of as her parents' "other," optative children. Or, at least, she used not to, before she met Troy Loudermilk. Something is going to happen this year with the poets, Lizzie can tell. It's standing right there, in the person of this exquisite criminal, who isn't actually a poet at all, though it's possible he brought someone who is a real poet with him, just to liven things up, as it were.

Lizzie doubts that her parents are going to crack the code. They're too excited about having some sort of superstar on their hands. It's even possible they'll delay their divorce another few years.

The difference between Lizzie and all the Seminars people—the male students who are keeping score, the female students in various accoutrements bespeaking liberal-arts educations in the time of free trade: vintage T-shirts promoting now-inoperative airlines, ethical sandals, MP3 players loaded with Rufus Wainwright and Manu Chao—aside from the fact that Lizzie is biologically related to her parents, the fully mature adult poets, is that Lizzie knows that her parents, the adult poets, are just human beings, mere mortals. They don't have supernatural capabilities, nor do they have some sort of grand scheme they're slowly and deliberately unfurling. They're living day to day. They're not even all that great at writing.

What no one knows is that the only person with any sort of a grand scheme and/or supernatural flair is Lizzie. And part of the reason they do not get this about her is they do not realize that Lizzie is an artist.

Of course, as her mother constantly reminds Lizzie, it's going to be a lot better in the long run if Lizzie understands that making art is something you do on the weekends, in your barricaded sound-proof garage with painted windows, while during the week you pursue a real job, raking in a respectable salary. Sure, Marta may have lucked into something in her day, but that's also because Marta has a calling and once looked like a young Aphrodite minus half shell and Reagan had only just been elected, and, oh, by the way, does Lizzie understand that she is definitely not going to art school?

Even her mother's latest "friend," a cozy Swiss-American neurologist with whom Marta has allegedly been conducting some cutting-edge interdisciplinary research into facial mimicry and poetic address, toes the line. He insists on calling Lizzie by her full name, with pretentious inflection, "Eh-LEEZ-a." He brings her tins of aquarelle pencils, with which *Eh-LEEZ-a* is evidently meant to generate neoclassical studies of birds' heads, fallen leaves, and cornfields—and which her mother will quietly consign to the recycling bin once Lizzie reaches the age of majority.

This is why Lizzie has needed to have a plan. Because she needs to make some really big art now, so that she can use it to get some really big scholarship, so that she can get the right education, so that she can get, she doesn't know exactly what, but so she can get out there and out of here and start becoming a visual artist pronto, at which point she will be living in New York.

Lizzie likes to go over to Building 109 late on Fridays. She has her father's keycard, which, to be honest, he wouldn't notice was missing even if he noticed it. He'd just convince himself that it had basically always been lost, that he'd never *actually* had access to the place where he teaches. This fatalism would earn him a drink, which is, of course, why he'd engage in it in the first place.

Lizzie swipes herself in after hours and lounges. She pages through any remaining packets, hunts for inspiration and gossip. She sprawls on the floor in the front room and glares up at that hideous painting, with its fart browns and fart greens. The land smiles obediently as two dildos in suits commend each other on some precious shit related to new civilization.

Someday, Lizzie will create her own foundational masterpiece. Until that time, she needs to scheme. And that's what she's working on right now, sitting here in this evacuated institution. If she's feeling particularly bitchy, she'll go around and pee in a few of the office plants, though so far they seem immortal or possibly plastic.

More recently, prowling the premises, specifically the mailbox area, Lizzie came across a copy of *Playboy*. It was shoved into some second-year dude's slot, presumably by some other overwhelmingly gifted and subtle second-year, and Lizzie fished it out, thinking it might make an accessory for a genius prank. On the cover were a blonde and a brunette, crotch deep in swirling greenish waters, their undergarments fashioned from cargo-shorts scraps and athletic mesh. Both appeared to have been shaved and starved within an inch of their lives, though they still had the hair on their heads plus breast fat. They were former *Survivor* contestants and, as the cover maintained, with vaguely genocidal wit, "Their Clothes Got Voted Off!" Also available: "CASUAL SEX 2003," "COP TEASE," "THE AMAZING TOBEY MAGUIRE." Lizzie wasn't that interested in the reality stars, and most of the interior was stale and heavy on the lip liner. Carnie Wilson made a cameo, post weight loss, in a dour corset.

Everything here is like looking into a ghost's flaccid face, Lizzie thought, flipping to the centerfold. This model, with apple tits and tiny features, did not do much for Lizzie, except that there was one shot where all her crotch was visible, demurely shut like a walnut, with a decorative sprig of fur. Lizzie didn't know why, but it moved her, this mound.

She ripped out the page and rammed the artifact back into so-and-so's cubby, rumpling a Xerox. Let them wonder, Lizzie thought.

She went home, thinking of Loudermilk's no-doubt ropy arms, gilded with an appropriate amount of hair.

I so love him, she mused, even as she hurried indoors and upstairs to gaze again at the walnut, which she would, for reasons still unclear to her, frame in an elaborate craft-paper theater/altarpiece, placing it in the farthest regions of her desk drawer.

Twenty-Three

Veils

In 2003 Halloween in the U.S. of A. falls on a Friday. Which means that all of Crete is giddy with notionally sublimated homicidal lust.

The most popular costume is the university mascot—in various iterations. A few feckless dweebs have on full-fur suits, but the ideal ensemble has to be: 1. freshly shaved pecs, preferably greased or dusted in some sort of glitter; 2. loincloth; 3. lace-up gladiator sandals; 4. bull's head, or just the horns if you really have a great face; 5. short, thick sword.

Among female undergrads, the reigning look is prostitute, though other paths are explored: sexy nurse, sexy surgeon (for the ambitious), sexy CIA operative, sexy nun, sexy postal worker (with or without death-dealing firearm), sexy houseplant, along with an assortment of sexy animals and extremely sexy babies.

Loudermilk has elected to dress as sexy Groucho Marx. In Loudermilk's conception, this disguise demands a bathrobe, wool socks, bedroom slippers, boxer shorts, glasses (with attached nose and mustache), fake eyebrows, and a six-inch fake cigar.

Harry says something about, Didn't Groucho usually have some pajamas? Or maybe a three-piece suit plus tie? He seemed to have been fairly modest?

"Sack up, dude, because this is his behind-the-scenes look," says Loudermilk. He is affixing the dark costume eyebrows to his blond eyebrows. "This is Groucho letting you know what Groucho is really all about." Loudermilk is done with his toilette. He turns. "Because I know you're still down to be Harpo?"

Harry retreats to the common area. "No thanks."

"What?" Loudermilk is doing an overly nasal approximation of Groucho's voice. "This is unacceptable. I'm having a beer and you're having one, too, or should I say, three?"

Harry sinks into a chair, points to himself. "Working."

Loudermilk continues, "With that kind of a show, who needs an audience! Fuck me," he says, breaking character. "I sound like Looney Tunes Al Capone." He goes into the fridge.

Harry reluctantly accepts a beer. "It's not too late."

"What, dude, for *Al Capone*? I don't think so! This is much better. Better for conversation." Loudermilk finishes his beer in one long draw. "So, Harrison, since you refuse my offer of relatable wingman, what, pray tell, are we going to do with ye?"

Harry blinks. "We're not doing anything."

"You keep saying that, but I really don't think that's what you're saying, dude."

"No, that's what I'm saying."

"Right, except that you're not!" Loudermilk shakes his head. "Because no means yes, Harrison."

Harry says that no definitely means exactly what it sounds like.

"With you, maybe. But you don't see the bigger picture."

Harry sips his beer. Dread is a lead bib. Loudermilk is a gas-happy dental technician. They have been playing this modified game of *fort/da* on and off for the past month. Harry tries a different tack. He asks, Has he not been writing the poems? Has he not graciously upheld his end of the bargain?

Loudermilk, behind glassless glasses, grins. "That's very touching, Harrison. And, to remind you, it's so far been just one poem. Which went over very well, spank you very much, and by the way I know you've been trying to milk that shit for all it's worth. However, you and I both know there's another side to this project, which involves me getting you up off of your veal-like caboose from time to time."

"Not interested."

"Harry, dude, I know you're not, as you put it, 'interested.' That is the whole mother-loving point. Your lack of 'interest,' as you call it. It's worrisome. It's abnormal. It's going to ruin your life. We've been through this."

Harry's stomach is beginning to bother him.

"I am trying to help you. You comprehend that, right?" Loudermilk withdraws and returns in seconds with a white sheet. "Here, for you, you fucking crazy diamond," he says, flourishing the bedding. He goes into the kitchen and gets a steak knife and rips a pair of crude holes in the material. He drops the sheet over Harry's head. "Shine on."

"This is a joke, right?"

"I find zero humor in your predicament, Harrison. Thus I'm one-hundred-percent honest-to-god serious, and *non, non,*

non this is not my idea of *une très funny joke*, as the Frenchies like to say, right before they go off to do something esoteric and cowardly. This is, like, *the ideal.* I'm a fucking genius and I'm cooking with lava. Now, let's get a move on. Party's at butter-face Christy's, and I want to be drinking her liquor before I'm back around here having"—Loudermilk pauses—"whatever I'm having."

Harry doesn't say anything.

Loudermilk, in a mechanical rage, drags Harry outdoors.

Only on the street does Harry cease resisting. It's dark out, very dark, and Harry realizes that this is because the streetlamps in the area have been covered with heavy-duty black contractor's bags and duct tape. The lawn of the neighboring frat has blazing tiki torches in it.

As Loudermilk and Harry come to the end of the block they hear behind them the unmistakable smacking, popping sound of Evelyn's shack-shaped source of retirement mad money being mercilessly egged.

Loudermilk speeds up. "Don't look back," he says out of the side of his mouth. He pulls Harry around the corner. "Biblical, right? I'm saying, *see*, dude, aren't you glad I didn't leave you in there without supervision? I mean, home invasion much? Would you really put that past these shitcanned hyenas? Trust me that you're way better off out here with me."

Harry has to hold the eyeholes in place, otherwise they have a tendency to be tugged up to the top of his head when he walks. He lets Loudermilk steer him downtown.

Twenty-Four

Soft Power

Christy's house, it turns out, is a pink affair. She has the whole bottom floor of a 1960s split-level, and wherever the walls are not covered with fake wood paneling, they've been painted a bright, labial blush. There are a couple of white-shag area rugs and, somehow, a crystal chandelier. A stuffed black squirrel with a head like a rotten chestnut clings quirkily to a stick atop one bookshelf.

The house is full of Seminars people. Loudermilk pats Harry on the head. "This is going to be fun for you, little Casper."

Harry fusses with his eyeholes.

Christy makes them. "Oh my god, Big L? Is that you? Oh my god, Groucho? How funny! How adorable! You are so brilliant."

"Thanks, babe." Loudermilk takes it in stride. "Love that new haiku series, by the way. Been all over it this afternoon. Gotta email you later."

Christy is posing. She is wearing sexy dead-person makeup, a vintage housedress with strategic scorching, and has the outer casing of what was once a toaster oven over her head. Harry doesn't need to read the crazily inked extra-large title on the extra-large "book" in Christy's left hand to know that it says *Ariel*. "C'mon, Loudermilk." Christy pouts, admitting zero interest in the presence of Harry. "This should be easy for you!"

"Nice appliance!" Loudermilk fudges, rolling his eyes and wiggling the brows.

Christy giggles.

Loudermilk bangs Christy on the top of her oven several times with his cigar, saying, "I hope to see you again shortly."

"Sure," Christy replies, perhaps even wistfully, though it is difficult to be certain in the crush.

Loudermilk pilots Harry before him until they come to a table decorated with hard stuff of many shapes and shades. "Now, who the hell is she supposed to be, dude, because I know you fucking know."

Harry shrugs.

"Oh, no, no, no! You need to let me in on this one. This is about our *careers*." Loudermilk is reaching around among the bottles, checking labels.

"If I tell you who she is, then can I leave?"

Loudermilk is dumping quantities of tequila over an ice cube. "Stick that under your shroud."

Harry receives the drink.

"Drink up and consider what you just said." Loudermilk is fixing himself a double. "You're stressing me out, you know that?"

Given the lack of an immediate escape route, Harry decides to halfway acquiesce. The tequila splashes pleasantly against the front of his brain. "Anne Sexton," he mutters. "Pretty obvious." He uncovers his cup for seconds.

Loudermilk holds the bottle poised. "And who is that?"

Harry says that Anne Sexton is an American poet. This, at any rate, is true.

The cup is filled.

Harry adds that she was an incredible cook.

"Kinky," Loudermilk muses.

"I guess."

"No, I mean the girl, that Christy. She's quite the kinkster. I wonder what she's trying to tell me?"

Harry is drinking tequila.

"With a name like that—*Sex*-ton. I mean, like you say, you can't get much more obvious! But seriously though, dude." Loudermilk sets down the bottle. "I've been thinking about it. A lot of these people like I could just kind of do without them or whatever, right? But some of them, I mean, like, at least one of them? Must be kind of smart or whatever and maybe they would, you know, get *you*? You know?" Loudermilk attempts to gaze penetratingly into Harry's sheet. "Fuck, that thing is uncanny."

"It was your idea."

"You see what I'm saying?" Loudermilk refills Harry's cup.

"I can't really see anything."

Loudermilk is gazing around the room. "They like what you *do*, dude. You realize that, right? I mean, they *think* they like what *I* do, but you know what I'm saying. They fucking loved 'Writing Teacher.' These are probably, like, your people or something. I mean, maybe if all were right with the world you'd just be out here on your own, being a poet or something. Happy and whatnot. I do kind of think about that at times. I'm not a total craven douche."

Harry thanks Loudermilk for his solicitude.

"What?"

"Your kindness."

"Sorry, dude. Sheet."

"Thanks for caring."

"So listen," Loudermilk is saying, "I'm gonna go back and check in with Christy and so forth, make sure she's enjoying her party, compliment her on her look, shoot the shit, testify to my knowledge of sexy *Sex*-ton? I'm not going to promise you I'm gonna return right away, but I will be back. Main thing is, you can handle this. You're ready for a solo mission if ever anyone was, and I can't keep holding you back, see, killing you with my kindness?"

It's not that Loudermilk is suddenly successfully doing the Groucho voice or moving his eyebrows or anything like that, but he seems momentarily so much more convincingly Groucho-esque than ever before. It's as if he's leaning, like, a mile out of the fake glasses. It's as if he, too, is experiencing this weird plane of private mental ecstasy along which all of Groucho's characters seem, magnetically and maniacally, to float. Or: the analogy holds for a second, but then it's gone, because Loudermilk is off, bobbing through the party like he is the best friend a party ever had.

Other revelers seek comfort at the bar. They are reaching around and muttering and giggling. There is a black cat with grease-paint whiskers, an Olympic gymnast, a dude with a potbelly dressed as a bumblebee. Harry shuts his eyes and backs away from the table.

Harry's not paying very good attention, obviously he's not, there's just a lot going on that he could process if he cared to, that he could make sense of, perceive, if he wanted to, if he cared to involve himself in any of it. But all of this, the party and its din, its chatter, has no use for him. It has never understood a word that Harry's said, so why should Harry, in a room full of strangers, suddenly want to tamper with it? This—this floaty and vaguely inebriated misery that Harry's currently in—is just the way things work.

Harry is still moving backward when his head contacts a wall with a painful crack Harry is certain must be audible throughout the room. He stays standing exactly where he is, skull throbbing, and prays that everyone else is so wasted plus self-absorbed that they are either going to be uninterested in the event that produced this noise or assume that it is a result of their own Seminars-approved imaginations.

Harry groans, as waves of pain slosh ominously up the back of his skull. Stillness, he reasons, may be the only first aid available. There's the additional unpleasant fact that Loudermilk's university health insurance will cover only the body of Loudermilk, no matter what happens to this body's rather more compound mind, a significant portion of which is housed in Harry's dome.

This is when Harry hears, at his left, a low voice, a female voice: "That had to hurt."

Cautiously, Harry nods. He feels tears form at the corners of his eyes.

"Wow. I bet." The speaker is not exactly sympathetic, but at least her assessment is accurate.

Harry wants to turn and examine the source of these words, but he knows that motion will lead to additional cascading signals of trauma, so he stays put.

"Don't move. Maybe I can get you ice," the voice says.

The next thing that there is in front of Harry's face is the face of Bill Clinton. The forty-second president is, with astonishing gentleness, lifting Harry's head away from the wall just enough to slide a bag of cold substance behind it. Harry is not able to see much inside the mask's eyeholes. The Bill Clinton appears to smile.

Harry swallows.

"You should say something. That would be my recommendation." The Bill Clinton reassumes its earlier position to Harry's left.

Harry nods.

"How do you feel?"

"OK," he whispers. It is like someone else has uttered the two letters. Harry waits.

The Bill Clinton is speaking. "I'm glad you're OK. Anyway. Not to dwell."

"No." It's like there's someone completely normal saying these things, someone with an unremarkable, working voice, someone Harry doesn't know, someone Harry can control.

"I'm not condoning this party, by the way." The Bill Clinton laughs. Its hair is painted white. "I'm just here."

"Cool," says Harry. This comes out perfectly noncommittal, just a word anyone would have heard a million times.

"I thought it was more normal than staying home. Anyway, I have *this.*" The Bill Clinton points at its/her head. "I was thinking, you know, it's difficult, kind of, to find a use for this kind of thing?"

Harry knows there is something called for here, some quip or whatever, something to let her know he's hearing what she's saying, what she, specifically is saying, that he has some idea who she is, but now he's, more characteristically, mute.

"You a writer?" She makes an effort.

"Am *I*?" There's a squeak at the end, some of the old, true Harry. He presses his lips together.

She laughs again. "I mean, it's totally possible that you could be a writer, right?"

"Anything is."

The Bill Clinton nods. She folds her arms across her chest. "So, uh, what do you write?"

"Whatever they tell me to."

"Really? That's too bad."

"Not really." Harry is starting to enjoy himself. "I pretend." His head hurts less, almost not at all. There's just this infinitesimal, dull worry.

"You do fiction? Poetry?"

"Poetry."

"What kind?"

"I don't really know."

"Oh, yeah. Of course." The Bill Clinton seems to be looking around the room.

"I'm *Troy*," Harry for some reason volunteers.

"Cool. Hi, *Troy*," the Bill Clinton is telling him. Her tone suggests a frown. "Hey, it was nice talking." She pushes herself off the wall and fixes him with what would probably be a human smile if there were not a smiling mask obscuring it. She slips back into the crush of bodies just as House of Pain's mammoth single, "Jump Around," begins working its nostalgic enticement upon the well-lubricated crowd.

Twenty-Five

Lists

Harry is home, planning his day. His notebook is open and he has drawn the face of a watch, a wristwatch. Maybe it's a little crude but it helps him to see. He puts in hours, 1 through 12. It is approximately 10:00 a.m. now, and he circles the 10. He draws a line from the 10 and writes, *Focus in on time, lists.* Then he goes around the watch and adds activities for the day's remaining hours. For 11 he appends, *More lists.* For 12, *Lists again but turn on radio.* For 1, *Radio transcription.* For 2, *I'll read the newspaper.* For 3, *New thoughts.* For 4 and 5 he writes, *Composing a poem* and *Composing a poem more.* For 6, *Beer.* For 7, *Books/reading.* For 8, *Look at poem again.* And 9, *Contemplate sleep.*

Harry glances at 10. He crosses it out and feels ready. He begins a list:

Questions

- *Do I want something to eat?*
- *Yes or no?*
- *Can I just sit here?*

- *Yes or no?*
- *Does it matter what I do?*
- *Yes or no?*
- *Can I avoid easy questions?*
- *Do I know what I am doing?*
- *Do I know what I will do?*
- *If I know what I will do, will I do it?*
- *Yes or no?*
- *How to act?*
- *How can I act?*
- *Am I writing?*
- *Yes or no?*
- *Am I writing now?*
- *Who is writing?*
- *Who are all the people?*
- *What is the origin of the world?*

Harry pauses. It's early but he's thinking about turning on the radio.

He decides, with a small ache, that he will attempt to maintain the schedule for now. He turns to a fresh page:

New Questions

- *Am I the one who is writing these words?*
- *Can I be sure of this?*
- *Who is the one who is writing?*
- *Who's he?*
- *Does he sound like this?*
- *Do I sound like this?*
- *Does he like this?*

- *What is behind what he is doing?*
- *What inspires his poems?*
- *Does he do this for me?*
- *Does he exist for me?*
- *How does he exist?*
- *Why does he exist?*
- *Why do I know him?*
- *Why do I know he is here?*
- *Will he always be here?*
- *Yes or no?*
- *Will he always be with me?*
- *How will I know he is writing a poem?*

Harry can still hear street noises, the vague natural sounds of what's left of an area woodland, formerly prairie; insects sawing the cool-ish air, cars.

Harry tries to think about it. Also, he tries not to think about it. He has to write. There is something flickering in him, but maybe *flickering* is not the right word. Maybe it shifts, twitches, yes or no. *Natural things*, Harry writes. It could be the title of a new list. But a poem, Harry thinks, is not a list.

Harry has the feeling he wants to walk backward. Of course, he is sitting down, but he can make out some kind of music. The music seems to be behind him. It's not exactly a song, but that does not prevent Harry from wanting to hear it. The challenge is to get himself to fall. He can't walk where he needs to go. It has to be an accident. Meaning is stale in every realm known to woman or man, and Harry cannot be where stale meaning is. He needs to sink back into that greenish-reddish veil through which he can see the gently pulsing backs of words, the frilled edges of sentences. The only way to get to the poem is to drop into a perfectly Harry-shaped shadow. Which is where he is, he sees, right now.

The paper is nearby and there is the radio.

Natural Bush

In the god-drenched eras of the past
He applied to seven schools, got into none.

He wrote so charmingly about the cunning
of underage girls, salads, heart-on-leotard
    emotion . . .

There was nothing crabbed about his
    declaration.
He was buying a country newspaper.

He would call and go, "Oh look, they're breaking
bones! Oh gosh!

Feels like a lottery we're running,
but the charity is (an) illusion."

His dovish views, his catbird seat; he was
quick to apologize to veterans' groups.

Gaze into his background.
He comes to us from Maryland.

—T. A. LOUDERMILK

Twenty-Six

A Break

"Harrison!" Loudermilk yells. "You're making me proud! This is some good, weird shit." It's late afternoon and Loudermilk is back from wherever he has been for the past three days.

Harry had left the new poem, neatly printed out, on the kitchen bar. He was hoping, though he is not eager to admit it, for just such a response. Now he emerges from his cave and greets his long-lost comrade in literary treachery. "Hey," he says.

"Only thing is"—Loudermilk is bending over the page with the Groucho robe slung around his shoulders, though underneath he wears what appears to be standard attire, no doubt obtained at some point in his travels (Are those women's jeans?)—"this title? Like, maybe a tad much?" Loudermilk strokes his chin and ponders the ceiling. "Yeah," he murmurs, "I just can't tell! There's something kinda eerie here, you know? I can feel it. Like, think about it, 'Natural Bush,' like, really, what the fuck *is* that? When has a person like me ever seen that? I'm saying"—Loudermilk stares at Harry—"you're *onto* something, like, effing with them, jamming the old poetry radar! You're challenging their god, you know?"

"All in a day's work."

"Only you would say that, Harrison. So what do you want me to do with it? I should submit it so these assmasters can scrape and grovel at your genius?"

"It's not *mine*."

"Oh, right," Loudermilk says. There is something light and odd in his tone. "I almost forgot! These are *my* poems."

"To a certain extent."

Loudermilk isn't listening. "For I am the genius and master of all ass! Sometimes I forget! Like, going about my day-to-day, I have cause to ask myself, 'Who is *Troy*, I mean, *Loudermilk*, anyway?'" Loudermilk purses his lips. "Can it be that I am really he? Do I not sometimes sense that *he* is someone else? And, thus, who am *I*? What if I were to lose my identity altogether? What would I *do* with myself, then?" Loudermilk, as if lit from within by a glutinous nineteenth-century feeling, drifts toward a window.

Harry suggests, "Maybe you would just be whoever you were?"

"But I do not really think so, Harrison! I *like* who I am."

Harry asks what that is supposed to mean.

Loudermilk shifts back into his normal register. "Whatever, dude. I'm sure a systems nerdalingus like yourself can figure that out. Now, would you mind getting out of my way because I need to shower?"

Harry, before he can stop himself, blurts out his surprise that Loudermilk is going out again so soon. Because he can tell that's what Loudermilk's planning.

"Yes, Harry, I am indeed going out and boldly so. I have a life. I have things to see, people to do. You know the drill.

Anyway, if I'm going to hand this poem in this week, we're going to need a few more of them coming up. So you'd probably better head back to the old drawing board."

Harry is trembling.

"I'm going out," Loudermilk repeats.

"Where?"

"I'm making friends," says the real poet.

Twenty-Seven

Elsewhere

Harry is dreaming.

He stands in a white space. Rectangles seem important here. There are screens, about the size of chalkboards. They are made of translucent white gauze. Harry walks among them. The problem, he can intuit, is less that he has no authority here than that he has neglected to find protectors. It's all his fault.

Harry peers around corners. Also, inexorably, behind him there is a wind. The wind has a sound; it's not just a feeling. One of Harry's ears gets hot.

Harry is in a small room.

Someone is kneeling in a corner, a man.

At first Harry thinks this thin man is naked, but when the man stands up, Harry can see that he is wearing a tight beige suit the same shade as his face and hands. The man is wearing a tall hat. The hat is conical and pointed, like a witch's hat. The hat is made of clear glass and its tip glints ominously, like a piece of medical equipment.

"Hello," says the man.

Harry doesn't know what to say.

"I am the Glass Hat Man," the man says. "Otherwise known as Neutral Man."

Harry realizes that the Glass Hat Man, aka Neutral Man, looks a lot like Loudermilk, except thinner and much older, as if Harry is seeing a faded, shrunken version of Loudermilk at a distance.

"I live here," the Glass Hat Man, aka Neutral Man, says. "This is where I work." The Glass Hat Man twirls a luxuriant white mustache that Harry has somehow neglected to notice. The mustache is like cotton or snow, the fur of a rabbit, pure and filled with blue light. The Glass Hat Man's mustache must be made of glass.

"You want to move," the Glass Hat Man tells Harry.

Harry feels himself nodding. Behind Harry's head, the wind picks up. Harry can see that the Glass Hat Man's lips are forming words, but the rushing sound blots out everything else. The Glass Hat Man is raising his arms. He is pointing with both of his index fingers. Harry follows the gesture.

Harry is moving. The Glass Hat Man becomes a voice. Harry can no longer see the Glass Hat Man. Harry is in the hallway again and the hallway extends to another space. Harry can make it out before him, an arched entry.

Harry can't stop shivering.

The wind blows.

"They are hunting," the Glass Hat Man says.

Harry notes that although the wind seems to be coming from behind him, it actually originates at a point in front of his body, possibly the entrance before him. Harry is beginning to hear a clamor, too. It's the sound of metal pots being struck by metal spoons, dogs barking, paper shaking, car engines turning over, the low horns of ships, intermittent explosions.

"It's the hunt," Harry hears the Glass Hat Man, somewhere, remark.

"I'm not supposed to be here," Harry says.

"Your name is Hearry," the Glass Hat Man says.

"What?"

"Heeerrrry. Heeerrrrry! That's your name!"

"OK," says Harry.

The Glass Hat Man does not reply, but Harry's ears precipitously become unclogged and he is inside. It's blue here, a sky just before evening, when space begins to blacken at its edges. There are flashes. The flashes occur in the shapes of stars. The ceiling is domed, veined with red. Before Harry is an immense gold ladder. The ladder sways. Harry can feel the Glass Hat Man, Neutral Man, aged, shrunken Loudermilk, whoever he is, at his side. The Glass Hat Man shoves Harry toward the ladder with warm little shoves, sighing with what seems like a kind of ecstasy each time he touches him.

"Look!" the Glass Hat Man exclaims, and Harry is compelled to gaze up, up to the top of the ladder, where he can perceive a large, bright entity.

Somehow the wind is also—or, rather—emerging, originating from this being. The being becomes bigger and bigger. Harry can make out details of her form. She is a monkey or a cat, he thinks, but covered in feathers. Harry can see that the feathers are composed of extremely fine frosted glass. She has the bladelike wings of a swan or other large waterfowl, affixed to her back upside down.

"*Madame Singe*," hisses the Glass Hat Man.

Now Harry sees the face. He begins to hear trumpets, the sound of hundreds of columns in a hall. Madame Singe's face is doors, not a face. It is a gate that shudders as the ladder rocks—

Harry wakes with a jerk, soaked in sweat.

He listens, grateful, to a passing car.

Twenty-Eight

Custom

Harry is trying to believe that it is a good idea. He wants to give Loudermilk a chance to make up for his increasingly numerous and protracted absences.

Loudermilk has appeared out of nowhere with a bottle of scotch. Loudermilk is in the house again and is not even listening to Harry's concerns.

"We're going," Loudermilk says.

"Unwise," Harry repeats.

"No, no." Loudermilk shakes his head. "No, no, no! You're not getting what I'm saying, little one. I wasn't looking for clarification. I'm pretty much sure it's been almost a month since you went outdoors. What was the last time? All Hallows' Eve? I'm telling you, this is not even a fucking conversation. Plus, you accompanying me is still the best strategy of all time. We're hiding you in plain sight! P.S.: Is that what you are wearing?"

"I am physically wearing these clothes."

"Again with the attitude, dude. Switch that up and make it some *gratitude*! I'm asking, Harrison, you want to wear *that*? You look, seriously, like shit, dude."

"Thanks."

"You're welcome. Now change."

Harry says that he does not feel like changing.

Loudermilk takes a lap. He is walking without bending his knees. "It's always like this with you these days, dude."

It is 11:00 a.m. on Thanksgiving. There has been a frost. Clouds loom, and an odd, saffron-colored light hovers over the front lawn.

Loudermilk says that perhaps Harry does not comprehend the progress that he, Loudermilk, has recently made with his instructor Don Hillary, his amazing incursion into the man's good graces. Loudermilk says that he, for all intents and purposes, has everything sewn up for next year as far as stipend money is concerned if Harry would just come make nice with these hamsters. "Please help me seem humble, dude!"

Harry asks to know how exactly his presence will contribute to Loudermilk's humility.

"Because I told them about you! I mean, not *told* told, but I, you know, told them something, about how I have this stellar friend who's, like, this complete surreal genius although he has these pretty severe emotional handicaps, and now, believe it or not, they want to meet you. You're expressly invited. I can't fucking go without you."

Harry reminds Loudermilk that he's been introduced to Marta once before. He also reminds Loudermilk, in case he's forgotten, that what he's telling these people is complete and utter bullshit?

Loudermilk counters with something about how this is a hazard of their current working conditions. Or, he says, he means their current free-money, nonworking conditions! He says it would be greatly appreciated if Harry would for one hot millisecond stop obsessing over minor details and gaze at the grand scheme. He asks Harry if he, Loudermilk, needs to remind him, Harry, that today is Thanksgiving, the American day of thankful giving, and from where he, Loudermilk, stands, the two of them have a lot to be thankful for, Harry in particular.

Harry doesn't reply. He would like to be removed from the present by any possible means. He dislikes Loudermilk so much in this moment! But he also feels very keenly the lack of any alternative. For the true problem isn't Loudermilk. The true problem is that Harry doesn't care enough about the generally social project of living. Harry knows this now. Unlike Loudermilk—who, for all his vile habits, is really quite committed to humanity—Harry can't involve himself. He can't work himself up the way Loudermilk does. In fact, Harry mostly doesn't care at all.

It's a typical mood and a natural predilection of Harry's. It's a way he wants to be—an idea he has about how he'd like to spend his day, which is to say, in punishing solitude. Nothing about life, for Harry, is integrally informed by the fact of the presence of others and all their difficulties and the need to deal. It's not some kind of far-reaching machination as it is for Loudermilk. It's just not how Harry sees things, because Harry doesn't, in fact, "see."

Anyway, Loudermilk knows this. Loudermilk says, "You see my point."

Harry tells him, "Fuck your point," but he gets up and goes into his room and puts on his one nice shirt and comes back out.

"Stellar," observes Loudermilk.

They walk over to the Hillary residence. The campus is a tomb.

Harry wants to know if Loudermilk has any idea who else will be there.

"Dude, I really do not know. Do the math. It was enough for me that we got the invite."

They are approaching the front door. Loudermilk does this little neurotic touch of his hair that informs Harry that Loudermilk is in some way excited about what is about to transpire.

Loudermilk makes use of a brass knocker.

Now there are footsteps. The door is opened by Marta Hillary.

"Marta," Marta Hillary says, extending her hand to Harry. She has either actually forgotten their initial meeting or is letting him know she will be willing to.

Harry allows his hand to be held, stroked by small fingers.

"You must be Harry. Troy has told us so much about you. Your work sounds absolutely fascinating."

Harry blinks. "Yup," he mutters.

Marta laughs. "Don's just in the kitchen. He's dying to see you, Troy. He says you're going to keep up with him. I know you'll do your best."

Loudermilk hefts the bottle of scotch. "Apologies!" He mugs regret.

Marta Hillary laughs again. This time Harry thinks he catches something, a part of the laugh that is not really laughter. Harry tries to hear this part of the laugh more clearly, but as soon as his mind inclines toward Marta Hillary the unusual part of the laugh dissipates, and the laugh is nothing more than the most generic of cues, some sawdust.

Marta Hillary is looking at Harry. "Why don't you go ahead?" she says. A hand flicks up. Marta indicates a hallway.

Now Marta Hillary is gone. They're alone.

The house is not modest. It's in the colonial style, as if to spite its midwestern setting. The floors are a light wood, bare and highly polished. The walls are eggshell. A formal stair ascends to a second-floor landing. The look is Americana, updated for the now-vanished 1990s: Shaker chairs, Hudson-school scene, plus brushed-aluminum side table. Harry thinks they pass a priceless abstract expressionist silkscreen on their way into the kitchen.

Here they find Don Hillary tied into a red apron, ministering to the stovetop. There is an open bottle of port to his left and below him sputtering gravy. Hillary's face is purple from heat and inebriation.

"You're here!" Hillary bellows.

Loudermilk does introductions.

"Good! Yes! Great!" Hillary exclaims. Today he is in high spirits. He springs across the room and pulls down a pair of jelly jars that he fills with several fingers' worth of amber fluid. "There!" He hands the jars out. "*Salud!*"

Loudermilk sets the gift scotch on a counter. "This is already an unbelievable improvement on Thanksgivings past. I just want you to know that, Don." He downs some port. He is doing this face loaded with legible appreciation.

"And you brought your old 'writing teacher' a gift!" Hillary dances belatedly over to the bottle. "I can guarantee you *this* won't go to waste."

"I would never have believed it would." Loudermilk grins mildly.

Harry is standing silent in the center of the kitchen floor. He has not touched his drink.

"You know me too well!" Hillary hops back over to the stovetop. He sniffs his gravy. In fact, Don Hillary is an unusually slight man, a frog. His narrow legs are bowed inside his creased blue jeans. He wears a striped oxford shirt, the back yoke of which he has sweated through already. The outlines of a white undershirt show. Hillary hums a few lines to himself: "La da dee, la da da. La da dee, la da da." He taps his metal spoon against a pot edge. He guzzles port. "She's homeless, she's homeless," Hillary yodels in falsetto.

"This is a great place," Loudermilk is saying, ignoring Hillary's unexpected rendering of Crystal Waters's club favorite. "You and Marta have a truly extraordinary home!"

Now Hillary applies an electric can opener to the rim of a can of condensed mushroom soup. He yells, "She has her spots and I have mine! It's pretty civilized, or should I say, civil! I'm Catalonia and she's Spain."

"Ha!" is the sound Loudermilk makes. He leans against a counter. It's obvious to Harry, at least, that Loudermilk has no idea what Hillary is getting at. Foreign affairs are not his strong suit.

"If you ask her, she'd probably say something about the Balkans. She's so fucking tragic!" Hillary consults his port once more. "Anyway, I bet you already want to get in her class next semester. Am I right? Find out what all the *buzz buzz buzz* is about?" Hillary is now laying the mushroom sludge over a glass casserole containing green beans. He admires his handiwork.

"I don't know!"

"I like you, Loudermilk." Hillary is doing something with a container of bread crumbs.

"But, I mean, what's really tragic is we can't repeat—" Loudermilk is beginning to say.

Harry is edging toward the door.

"No, I'm saying, for lying to me, right here"—Hillary snorts—"in my own house! You fit right in!"

Harry steps out into the hall.

Harry is in the downstairs hall of Don and Marta Hillary's residence.

He thinks, I really need to figure out what to do.

Harry wishes he were not thinking this or anything else, for that matter. Often he wishes that he did not have to think, but now his prayer is somewhat more fervent. He has no idea where to go. He feels hot and unclean. He thinks that a logical impulse would be to go find Lizzie and say something to her about something and then leave or just leave without saying anything to anyone, but instead he goes down the hall in the direction opposite from the one they originally came. It's like his body belongs to someone else. His legs move stiffly, automatically. He sees to his right a staircase, carpeted in white. He sees that it leads up, and Harry for some reason makes the decision to climb this stair.

On his way Harry convinces himself that he is looking for a bathroom, and he tells himself that if anyone sees him he or she will surely infer that he is simply in search of a bathroom. He's looking for a bathroom, and this, then, is the reason for his presence on the second floor of the Hillarys' home. Harry tries to make a face that could conceivably be worn by a person headed in search of a bathroom. It's a face of innocence, a quiet and modest, small face. The effort required for the formulation of this face gives Harry a modicum of confidence, even if he has no idea why he does not, at the moment, feel particularly innocent. It's as if there's something he wants to find.

The stairway leads to a hall, also carpeted in white, with white walls. Harry goes down this hall. Here, photos of the Hillary family are in evidence. Marta, topless in the ocean (presumably the beginning of the relationship), waves joyfully. There's a garish Polaroid of a grinning, plastered Don. He's in a tie and shirtsleeves at a Christmas party bearing toddler Lizzie. A later iteration of Lizzie Hillary, age eleven or so, in a Bulls cap, slouches beside a tractor. Marta and Don on horseback. Marta reading at a podium with what looks like a presidential seal affixed to it. A black-and-white shot of Don as a ravishing teen in dungarees with movie-star smile, squatting in the Y of a birch tree.

There are no pictures from the earlier marriage.

Harry recalls his narrative about a search for the bathroom and begins trying doors. He gets a linen closet with a sweet, soapy odor. He tries another, which is locked. He tries another door.

This door is locked, too.

Harry feels an eerie, unwonted boldness. He doesn't really know where he is. And here, in this quiet, dim hallway, in this big, clean, expensive house, no one knows him. Nobody knows him in this whole town, except for Loudermilk, and, maybe, in some sense, the girl Lizzie. Lizzie, at least, has seen him—which is possibly more than Harry can say for Loudermilk.

Harry wants to laugh. He feels suddenly so alert, awake; the air is spiced by cooking.

Harry stalks the white carpet of the second-floor hall admiring Marta Hillary's framing and arrangement of her own memories. He laughs, lightly, dryly. Who is it who does these things so carelessly—even with a sense of entitlement? It's "Troy." Not Loudermilk, but Troy. Troy does this. T. A. Loudermilk, even. And it is for this reason that it is Troy, aka T. A. Loudermilk, who comes to a door that sits just slightly ajar, and Troy who lingers, listening to the voice on the other side.

Troy lingers near the door. There's no Harry.

Troy hears someone say, "It's none of your business!" This is Marta Hillary. Troy waits. Marta Hillary exclaims, "Well, but what if I still think it isn't?" Marta Hillary is speaking to someone over the phone. "Yes, I know," Marta says conspiratorially. There is a pause. "Well, I don't care. At any rate," Marta is saying, "I'm going to have a new student soon. A good one. I know! Yes. No, he's already here. Yes, yes, I know. Yes, next week is still good. It's all I can think about. Well, we wouldn't have to. As you *know*."

Troy can hear Marta moving around the room.

"I'm getting changed. Yes, obviously we're having people over. The masses. You know us. Oh? Well, now that you remind me of it! No, he's been entirely acceptable." Hangers squeal. Marta seems to be struggling to extract a garment. "Yes, Dieter, darling," she tells her interlocutor, somewhat breathlessly, "I got them. I *love* them." Here she adds a phrase or two in what Troy determines is lilting German.

"Hey!" Someone pokes Troy in the back.

Troy half jumps and turns and is nonplussed to discover

Lizzie Hillary shaking her head in insouciant censure. "Harry, Harry, Harry," she is saying. "Way to be way lewd, dude."

Troy/Harry blinks.

Lizzie tugs at his sleeve. "Hello?" she whispers with a certain amount of force. She drags Troy/Harry away from the doorway. "They barely know you and you're going to act like a total freaking perv? Do you just love to hate your boy Loudie so much? Because I feel like you don't want him to get any money next year?" Lizzie wears a pale pink cardigan and her cheeks shimmer with copper pigment. Her hair is ironed and she's edgy and clean. "Like my outfit?" she wants to know.

Harry nods.

"Thanks, man." She is pulling him down the hall. Words tumble out of her. "I mean, you shouldn't have been looking at my mom like that, but everybody has, you know, their *days*? I know I totally do. Anyways, I want to show you my room? I think I might feel like that's a good idea. I do really like you, Harry, did you know that?"

Lizzie opens another door. "Ta da!" Lizzie is saying.

The room Harry is now looking into is an unremarkable girl's room, the room of a normal, if privileged, teenager. The walls are white, the carpet pink. The bed is white, the comforter a white-and-pink trellis. Embellishments born of more mature tastes hang on the walls. There are images of early R.E.M. and Smashing Pumpkins and Charles Bukowski and a poster version of Odilon Redon's dancing spider, a Jenny Holzer truism, Tyra Banks in profile. Near a mirrored closet, clothing sits in a heap.

"Here is my desk!" Lizzie trills, hopping over to another

white item with intricate legs. "My workspace, I mean. I have some mock-ups for my newest art project, if you want to see?"

Harry, silent, hovers near the door.

Lizzie seems disappointed. "I have this whole concept. It's about copying. But whatever, I get it, time is money and so forth. Want to smoke?" She is smiling hard in Harry's general direction.

Harry does not know what to do. He feels worse about himself than he has in a long time, and this is genuinely saying something. He can perceive something, an idea, a plan that has formed in Lizzie's mind, and now he can't seem to keep it out of his own mind. Lizzie thinks that she caught Harry peeping at her mom. She thinks that she has seen something about Harry, who he is. Lizzie thinks that he, Harry, wants something. That he has an agenda, is concerned with her mom's extracurricular activities. Lizzie—Lizzie wants to let Harry know—has an agenda, too.

Harry would like to say something now about how really it was "Troy" who'd been eavesdropping on Lizzie's mom, not spying, but the way Lizzie is looking at him makes it impossible for Harry to conceive of his ever having been anybody but Harry. Maybe it actually was Harry who was eavesdropping on Lizzie's mom, Marta Hillary, and maybe he did do more than eavesdrop. But suddenly Lizzie is standing only about a foot away from him, and Harry doesn't know how she got so close.

"Hi, Harry," says Lizzie in a weird, deep voice.

Harry almost manages to say hi in reply.

"I'm really glad you're here." Lizzie continues with the intent gazing. "I have a joke for you."

"OK."

"Why should the Pilgrims have killed cats instead of turkeys?"

"I don't know."

Lizzie smiles. "Because then every Thanksgiving we could eat pussy!"

Harry begins analyzing the carpet.

"It's a joke! It's kind of feminist, or whatever?"

The carpet in here is the color of ham.

"Harry, I just meant to, like, break the ice? See, thing is, I kind of really need, like, some feedback. Maybe you can help me."

Lizzie smells like summer.

Lizzie says, "Anyway." She takes a deep breath. "I also need to ask you something about your friend Loudermilk."

Harry does not say anything. He looks up at Lizzie, whose eyes are closed. Her lashes twitch. "I might be in love, Harry." Lizzie's eyes are still closed. "How does that sound?"

Harry takes advantage of Lizzie's self-inflicted blindness to back quietly from the room and hustle down the hall. Harry descends the soft stairs. In the hall below he encounters Marta Hillary.

"Oh!" is what Marta, like an echo, exclaims. She is standing just outside the door to her own kitchen. She wears black pants and a loose black blouse, pearls.

It is apparent, to Harry at least, that he has interrupted Marta while she was attempting to listen, unnoticed, to a conversation transpiring in her kitchen. She has abruptly made her face delightful and fascinated in Harry's general direction. Now she blinks at him as if he is a unicorn come to offer fealty.

Her face offers a mixture of mild awe and gentle enthusiasm. She is quick to say, "There you are."

Harry nods.

The forced expression on Marta Hillary's face begins to fade. It is replaced by a wistful smile. "We were just about to ask where you *were*," she is saying, as if this makes any sense.

The doorbell rings.

"I hear you study psychology."

Harry nods again.

Marta is gazing intently at Harry. "It's so *interesting*."

Harry thinks he can feel a weird, persistent pressure at the rear of his skull, as if a thin, sharp instrument were slowly, dreamily poking around in the back of his brain.

"How interesting," Marta Hillary repeats.

The doorbell reiterates its call.

Now Marta Hillary does as her dual role as wife and professional intellectual ordains, which is to say she floats away.

More and more people begin to enter the house. Harry can hear them and he moves to where they are because this is what is appropriate, and when Harry next notices where he is, he is beside the refrigerator nursing a beer. He nurses several beers. It isn't a dinner so much as it is a long party, an eventually very drunken party. Harry doesn't talk to anyone and remains in the kitchen. Occasionally, as the night scrolls by, he catches the eye of Lizzie Hillary, who always somehow seems to be looking right at him.

Twenty-Nine

Parity

Clare has been to the party. She has done what she believes is expected. Appear. She sat in the living room. Here are her peers: The novelists look like money and even the poets seem canny, mathematical. Or maybe no one looks like money, because no one looks at ease. Almost everyone is white. No one, as far as Clare knows, is not straight. Clare does not know much. She pushed herself to attend. She read the listserv invite with a moan. It is precisely the sort of thing she does not care to do but the doing of which convinces her of her sanity. Anyway, all this makes sense, fossil fuels, gynecology, a giant bird on a plate.

She watched the winey beauty of the Midwest. She was in the living room of the poet couple and their roster of amanuenses. All are tantalizing because drunk. Everything is sex. The poet Loudermilk is propped against the mantelpiece. Clare might like to die for him, or, she thinks, perhaps she will kill him. Thank god she does not write poetry. He and his "cool, dim Easter / Basket" are so beloved. He's rewriting the rules of the poetry game with his fresh prosody, his striking neologisms. Or is it the prosody that is striking, the neologisms fresh? "These are the poems of our time," Clare overhears one besotted second-year say.

Meanwhile, there doesn't seem to be anyone resembling Halloween's Troy.

Just before midnight there is an exodus.

Clare stumbles out into the frigid grid. Lawns are spiked with frost and with detritus. The building Clare lives in has an enormous mansard roof. The whole thing is a rectangular mushroom, a brutalist mausoleum.

When Clare was in college, there had been a very few people for her, people she had known. She does not understand why now, but these people did not touch her. Or, they may have touched her in a physical sense but in no other. They were like her, even sometimes a lot. It felt like looking through a glass partition into a room in which there was a mirror. Clare danced behind the glass partition and was reflected. A friend was on the other side of the partition and danced, too. Their reflections looked similar. So they danced—together.

Clare could not tell if she was alone. Of course Clare was not alone! Just look at this dancing. But her confessions were muffled, especially if she tried to shout them through the glass. The friend gyrating in the other room, visible through the partition, leaned down and helpfully turned the music up.

"This is life," Clare told herself, and went for a walk with her notebook. Her mother called and reminded Clare that she, Clare, was definitely not having any issues. Clare was well! If Clare happened not to be well, then Clare should consider disappearing from the face of the earth, because if Clare was not well then she would be dead to her mother, who had long since had enough.

Clare pondered these entailments.

She went for another walk. She wandered for hours and did not do the assigned reading for her courses. People in the wealthy suburb raked their lawns and clambered, complaining about life's dullness or its complexity, into SUVs. Astonished, Clare watched them. Their faces coordinated perfectly with the landscape. They knew just where they were. Meanwhile, the United States wrung its hands about its war. Astonished, Clare stood in the sale section at Urban Outfitters and watched a celebrated visiting professor, a writer, shop. The visitor, caressing a cardigan with studied nonchalance, seemed to wish that Clare was not observing her.

The boyfriend at the literary magazine had determined that he preferred men. He told Clare a story about a day when, walking through a glass revolving door, he had accidentally tried to get out of the way of his own reflection.

They had almost the same problem, she and this ex-boyfriend.

But Clare was confused, because in fact the campus was all brick.

"I need to be by myself for a while," the ex-boyfriend told her, through the phone.

Clare walked calmly to the library and did not cry.

She tried to pick out a poem.

Clare was well!

Clare wrote her prize-winning story and the ex was jealous, then relieved.

Clare had a close female friend with whom she slept. The female friend liked to play a game in which she and Clare would, on separate occasions of course, sleep with the same man. They never discussed the nature of the game but played it often and maybe furiously. Perhaps it made them feel better. It was, as everyone was saying, fairly painful to be alive these days. As the news got worse, fashion's call for whittled hip bones intensified.

Clare was reading all the essays of the psychoanalyst Jacques Lacan. Clare knew that, in doing so, she flirted with hackneyed undergraduate predilection, but Lacan liked shiny things, and Clare did, too. Lacan enjoyed cybernetic suspicion. Something glinted along the horizon and you thought it was alive; you felt yourself recognized and therefore had faith in your existence.

Clare understood that according to this theory of mind she did not, strictly speaking, exist. It was just a trick done with light and air.

Clare read Lacan's early essay "Logical Time," in which three prisoners are called before a warden who must liberate one. The boon will not be given outright; instead, the warden arranges for a test in which five disks differing only in color, three white and two black, are to be handed out. Each prisoner will receive a disk, black or white, and must divine its color. Any conclusion as to the color of one's disk must be arrived at by logic. Random guessing is not permitted.

The three prisoners are each outfitted with a white disk, and, having hesitated together for a certain time, exit the room in unison.

Lacan says that he knows why.

A prisoner who looks and sees two white disks knows that he can be either a black or a white disk. This prisoner then imagines the points of view of the two others: If he were a black disk, he thinks, the others might be able to think, If I were a black disk, too, then the third person would leave immediately, because he would know, seeing two black disks, that he is a white disk. But this third person hesitates, and, indeed, we all hesitate, and, therefore, we are white.

This was neat enough, but the thing that bothered Clare, the thing that interested her, was that each prisoner must use his own allotted time only to interpret the contest as it occurs to others. If a prisoner misunderstands another's hesitation, if he allows himself to be preceded, time will lose its meaning.

Thirty

Fortune

But, truly, it's amazing! It's fully a miracle! Does Loudermilk not realize what a powerful enemy he has cultivated for himself in Anton Beans? Can this reality truly not have sifted down into the dim sedimentary stream of this individual's so-called thought? Does Loudermilk not have the faintest clue as to Anton Beans's formidable and copious resources? Either Loudermilk has a death wish, which, given his obvious taste for embodied life Anton Beans feels safe in ruling out as a factor, or, what is worse, he simply *does not know.* Loudermilk is, possibly, for some unfathomable reason, unable to sense, and therefore ignorant of, Anton Beans's abilities. That this second option is so evidently the case is beyond maddening to Anton Beans. Loudermilk fucking underestimates him! There is the rub.

If Loudermilk were, for just one moment, able to get it through his thick (admittedly unusually well-formed) Cro-Magnon skull what a dedicated adversary he has now actively nurtured for himself in Anton Beans, surely Loudermilk would never dare to repeat a stunt like the one he pulled two packets ago, submitting a poem with a title that was obviously a muted commentary on Beans's own extraordinarily natural, well-maintained *pelisse*. When Beans had graciously offered to provide a close reading, Loudermilk's response had been, "No, dude, it's chill," by which he indicated that Beans should not trouble himself. The other workshop participants found this absurd demurral at first baffling and then, distressingly for Beans, very, very funny. Beans is still trying to get their ringing giggles and guffaws out of his brain, where he fears these echoes of ignorance and folly may have permanently lodged, due to his own infallible memory.

That any of this happened at all bespeaks a towering lack of perspicuity and gross miscalculation on the part of Loudermilk. Exhibit A, Beans does not hail from Maryland. Exhibit B, Loudermilk is an obvious philistine. Loudermilk will, Beans reasons, have to pay. And not at a seasonal discount, either.

Anyway, Anton Beans has for a while been pretty sure that he knows something about young T. A. Loudermilk. He's been taking notes on Loudermilk, on this wonder stud's speech patterns. They are a mishmash of several regionalisms, dominated by the normalizing argot of American television and movies, nothing so very out of the ordinary. What is extraordinary, then, is the fact that Loudermilk should have been able to compose the poems attributed to him in the workshop packet, which, even Anton Beans cannot deny, are fairly excellent poems. These poems are written using a highly literate, if eccentric, style. It's not so much that they're full of big words, but that the lines are so exactly composed—and with so little effort, or so it appears. The writing is limpid, almost prosy. The command of contemporary syntax is breathtaking.

Loudermilk could not have composed these poems, not without a truly aggravated case of personality disorder.

This, at any rate, is Anton Beans's professional hunch, in his capacity as Doctor of Linguistics.

But Beans wants concrete proof. It is for this reason that he has renewed a conversation with one of his former Bay Area associates, a programmer with a side interest in natural language, someone with a few experimental tools. Beans has made transcriptions of Loudermilk's more coherent utterances during the course of their workshops together. He has emailed these transcriptions, along with several poems by "T. A. Loudermilk," to his contact. He wants to know, based on the contact's research so far, what the likelihood is that the author of the speech of Loudermilk is also the author of the poems attributed to T. A. Loudermilk.

The contact has just gotten back to Beans, now that the semester has concluded with an inebriated whimper. He tells Beans next time, please, more of a challenge if at all possible. Beans skims the data. It's statistically pretty unlikely, is the long and the short. It's a significant result.

Loudermilk and T. A. Loudermilk are not the same person.

Beans logs out. He lives on a hill above town in a pointy Victorian, where he rents a monastic, high-ceilinged room. Beans could afford something considerably better but, because he is a sage man, prefers to keep his true assets under wraps.

If Loudermilk is not the author of the poems of Loudermilk . . .

Anton Beans paces. He goes over to his wall chart of outstanding poetry journal submissions and updates it: one new rejection. He puts an *X* in the column for *Electronic Mail*, in the row for *Method of Reply*.

Anton Beans frowns. He needs a change of scene. There is a white-hot feeling in his gut. For some reason Beans's thoughts turn to Chelsea Clinton, who has just graduated from Stanford. He thinks of the decade of brutal magnification of what is probably in fact a very slight asymmetry in her face by candid photography. The American media, if not the world, is cruel.

Beans recalls a section from Marta Hillary's interview with the *Paris Review* of three years ago, an article he had savored and virtually memorized. Marta (b. 1957) narrates her childhood. It was peripatetic, partly continental. Installed in West Berlin with her free-spirited American mother, Marta had traveled, after 1971's Four Power Agreement, between East and West with some frequency. She made it sound like a spy novel. "It was an object lesson in contrasts: the sick glamour that seemed to have come from the Americans, the austerity of the other side. We had next to nothing so I was sometimes glad to be out of that, the Ku'damm and this aggressively good life that was pumping through the West. There is a way in which everything I've done comes out of the experience of standing at a checkpoint, feeling the presence of that faceless power. You have to have something that no one can take away from you, that you can do even if you are in prison. That is what poetry is."

Though calculated, it was adroit, nearly seamless. Marta is someone who can teach him how to move between worlds.

Anton Beans decides he will go for a walk. He sets out for the center of town, noting that he will refresh with a wheatgrass shot as necessary, but he ends up following Chapel Street all the way to its intersection with Van Veldt. It's not until he comes to the intersection itself that he stops and realizes what it is he is doing.

Beans recalls a conversation he'd overheard on the first day of workshop, when Loudermilk had admitted his allegedly strategic choice of residence to two eager members of his cohort. Beans recalls Loudermilk's slick little bad-boy prepster, nouveau Bret Easton Ellis ensemble, the haze of Axe body spray and suggestion of a scandalous succession of boarding schools that surrounded him, his bland homosocial banter and early provocation of Don Hillary.

It is getting to be dusk, and Anton Beans recognizes what must be the Loudermilkian shanty among Greek edifices. Sadly for Loudermilk, his early citation of the intersection gives him entirely away, since everything else around here is an enormous manor inhabited by upper-middle-class thugs. Beans slides into a stand of trees bordering the run-down property and approaches the shelter, such as it is, without much difficulty. There is one light on.

Obligingly, the sky continues to dim. Beans scuttles across the snowy lawn and gets below the illuminated window. He waits.

Once his breathing has slowed Beans decides to risk it. He is crouching, facing the building. Slowly, cautiously, Beans raises his eyes above the sill.

In the room before him, someone in a baggy black T-shirt is hunched over a card table. Beans gazes. Beans stares. The person is writing. Beans strains his ears and can hear dull scratches of a pen, an occasional labored breath. The person is not Loudermilk.

Anton Beans cannot believe his luck.

III

VOLTA

Thirty-One

Images

Clare Elwil has not returned to New York for the holiday interregnum. Instead, she remains in furnished midwestern rooms, combing over the past. She has come to the conclusion that—but she pauses, midtrain. It is 11:00 a.m. For the moment, Clare ignores the day of the week, the date. The sky is white, edged with orange. Clare is in bed, testing her senses with the cold against her exposed face, the chill end of her nose. The radiator whispers. *Is it OK to not be working?*

It is the same question. Clare has asked it for at least a month now. Is it OK to not be working, to be unable to work? Her mind begins to speed up and she knows that she will spend the next twenty minutes only trying to slow it enough so that it will remain with the sentence, with the dim containers that are words, so that it will willingly squeeze through, into and out of, words to produce articulation, so that the world will not end, the plane will not fall out of the sky, the officer will lay down his arm, the children may hold reasonable opinions rather than signs imploring U.S. aid; so Clare may do what is called thinking, may experience discrete thought rather than bounding through the endless black and rainbow that is the mountain-heap of images constituting the trash heap of her being. The world keeps ending, in myriad and novel, fresh and sudden, gradual, mechanized ways. It isn't quite her memory, she thinks, this ferocious slideshow. The visions aren't organized in the style of a narrative, something personal that follows a human agent from cradle to eventual grave. If she only sits here, the images cycle at a terrific rate; they clatter and swish and fold in half. They shiver and multiply. She thinks of names. It gets a little better. She thinks, hotly, of her own small success—but mostly she thinks of failure and death. She cannot find her way out of the labyrinthine enclosure, this psychotic office park. She must recall her body. She must gently alert it to the necessity of getting out of bed, of washing face and hands and stepping to the kitchenette to heat water. She must stay here, with the hands, with her face. Yes, she foresees the possibility of rising, but at a great distance, a horizon. It inspires nausea. A bunker buster is a type of bomb designed to penetrate hardened targets. She can't think. Therefore, she cannot work. And, meanwhile, the world keeps ending. Yet how can she live in the time that remains without work, or, rather, work in the paltry time that remains? For surely it is not OK to not work. This is the price that must be paid for being, for the condition of being squired around in a sentient frame. One must work to justify one's being. There is no right, otherwise. Oh, certainly, for others there is a right. Some people—the poet Loudermilk, for example—are perfect. They have appeared in the world with automatic integration. They are one and whole and true and would never engage in this sort of dialogue. For the question persists: *Is it OK to not work?*

We will all die so soon. Clare can barely breathe and the end of her nose is cold. Others are probably better than she is. With a lurching motion she forces herself out of bed. She fights up through the thicket of images. She tastes chalk. *There is nothing to be done.* She wobbles toward the kettle. Aeneas prayed to be allowed to descend to the underworld. She has hardly spoken to another human for nearly a month. The Bill Clinton head hangs by its neckhole from the knob of the closet door.

Later, with coffee, Clare sits. She will, she tells herself, begin. She breathes. Yesterday, she almost wrote. A sentence, she tries to coax herself, just one smooth sentence, please.

Clare checks her email. Her mother sends messages from South Beach where she has descended to muse out the holiday season. Each missive concludes, *Love~ Mommy,* the tilde a flourish. Clare's own words, or, rather, the little shuttles she was once pleased to drive among them, dissipate, are sucked back up into the black heaven of her nonsensical mind. *Why can she not move?* She stares at the latest tiding, a happy Christmas. Something else always comes to pass. This is not writing. There has been no new story.

Compelled to hand something in for her workshop during the semester, Clare surrendered, at the very last moment possible, the first pages of a piece she had begun that dreadful winter before the accident, a time of radical restructuring of the federal government and the spontaneous invention of new police. The story was not her best work, but it seemed, somehow, topical? Perhaps it was even an oracular vision, a warning she had attempted to relay to herself but, subsequently, failed to interpret. It was intended as a *gothic* tale and had clearly been composed by a terrifyingly industrious version of herself who was thinking about the fun of getting into genre, like how her main bag would be realism but from time to time she might dabble. This thing read:

A Killing
By Clare Elwil

Stefanie Segal was the only daughter of Harvey and Tabitha Grace Segal (now Tabitha Grace Greene). She was born in 1982 and raised on the Upper East Side of Manhattan. In the first week of January 2002 she was nineteen.

Stefanie had returned from school and was staying in the Dorchester on Park and 76th, where her mother resided with a new husband, a bankruptcy lawyer.

The lawyer, Glenn Greene, liked modern. A lot was white, and there were clean lines, minimal pottery, brutalist shelving.

Glenn was short, with a gut. He dressed well and styled his thinning hair unpretentiously. He appeared briefly, made nice.

He was always disguised by mauve corrective lenses and went straight to Stefanie's mother, caressing her hands.

Stefanie's mother was enmeshed in a social saga that had occupied her since before the time of Stefanie's birth. The liberating advent of pagers and cell phones had done little to inspire in this parent a more sanguine view of the outdoors. She stayed in until dinner, in constant dialogue with a BlackBerry. She subsisted on powders.

Stefanie felt, it being already her sophomore year of college, that she must soon devise an interim profession for herself. As her mother had once said, there was no point in kidding yourself: men always made the best money. In Stefanie's own estimation, it *was* important to think of one's gender. For this reason she had begun to reflect more seriously upon the employment opportunities offered by auction houses, particularly with reference to the slightly masculine, she felt, sector of decorative arts, earlier American antiques. She intuited this would provide the correct frame for her own mostly wholesome excellence, her patriotism. She was ready to go entrepreneurial, if need be.

Stefanie's best friend at school was Kathy Hu, who was about to become president of the college Democrats, which for Stefanie right now was perfect.

Both she and Kathy were interested in a devout wonk named Rory. Rory's issue was global debt. More than once Rory had been coaxed into a three-way over fro'yo and seasonal berries in a secluded corner of the cafeteria. Kathy preached management. Stefanie prided herself on her command of historical fact.

At any rate, Stefanie was very much caught up in work. And, actually, although she was in the city for a good stretch, she'd felt more than a little sluggish about contacting her old group. She'd worked through a new introduction to finance and done some very successful sartorial negotiation with her mother, who had been happy to be convinced of the sagacity of replacing every item of clothing Stefanie had arrived home for the holidays with with a more current and upmarket version. It was obvious, then, to both of them, what time in Stefanie's life it was getting to be. Stefanie felt cheerful. She would be restored to her field, fully armed.

Four days before Stefanie was scheduled to make her return to school, Glenn knocked on the door of the generous guest bedroom.

Stefanie switched off CNN but didn't have time to get off the king.

"Hey, *you*," Glenn said, as his face appeared.

"Hi," said Stefanie.

"Your mother and I were just about to take off, but I want you to know I got something for ya."

Stefanie smiled. She slid to her feet.

Glenn opened the door wider. "From a client. Here ya go." He was holding out a white envelope.

"Oh," said Stefanie.

"Didn't know what the hell to do with this, but I'm like, I know she likes history, right?" Glenn smiled, flicking the envelope at Stefanie.

You had to hand it to Glenn.

"Thank you."

"Don't mention it," Glenn said. He was already at the other end of the hallway.

"Bye, baby doll," she heard her mother trill.

Stefanie was halfway through an outdated documentary on Madison when she remembered Glenn's envelope. She had been giving herself a pedicure and IM'ing halfheartedly with Kathy, who was obsessing over the nomination procedure for an all-female eating club that recent alumnae in finance were setting up, when she saw it again, out of the corner of her eye.

Glenn got me something

what Kathy wanted to know.

my mom's husband

i know / what?

don't know

u like him?

of course, typed Stefanie. Then she wrote, *crap gotta run*

She closed the window rapidly, semi-rudely, as if she had been compelled.

She hauled her body across the bed and seized the envelope from the marble bedside stand, tore the top. They were membership cards, two of them. She extracted one. *MUSEUM OF THE DECORATIVE ARTS OF THE COLONIAL AMERICAS SUSTAINING MEMBER*. There was some sort of urn imprinted.

It was so perfect.

•

Stefanie was on Fifth in 7 For All Mankind jeans, Ferragamo loafers, a Theory top, a vintage peacoat from Searle, and a Longchamp bag she was borrowing even if they were so played out. She avoided the cobblestoned side where ice had been permitted to set in threatening welts. She was wearing cashmere gloves from J.Crew in "Flurry."

She thought about Kathy.

She didn't know why, come to think of it, she could never bring herself to compete with K-Hu. It was of course what made their relationship possible to begin with, and it wasn't like Kat wasn't worthy of your jealousy or like Kat didn't occasionally groom herself with the misfortunes of others, but she was just so convinced of herself in the end, and she wanted these things that made actually interesting men kind of hate you, so that was strange.

It was winter, and there was nothing on the trees, and even the blue in the sky looked damp. Salt-stained taxis hurtled by.

Stefanie was about a block away, and she resolved she would not look at her phone again until she was at least done with the museum.

She waited at the light. What she was doing right now, if she were forced to admit this to herself, which she was not sure that she was, was she was thinking about her parents' marriage. She was, if she had to describe what she was doing, trying to "see" it. What she could remember from the apparently better years wasn't much, just some brief scenes. Her father with the paper and a calculator. Her mother giving some instruction to the nanny, who in turn gave Stefanie a triangle of toast with a red layer of jam. The noise of the rapidly, and perhaps irritably, perused paper.

Her father lived in Boston now, so he was close. She was thinking, maybe in the next semester, that might be the time, once spring was fully on, she'd go by. She'd contact the offices, make an appointment. He would like that. Then she'd show up better dressed than the secretaries, turn heads. They would certainly discuss the markets. She would read up on currency, she thought. It would be a very, very good restaurant, and afterward he would ask if she would be by more often, if they could make it a monthly thing. "You know, I think sometimes I just need to hear from someone like you." Then, "It was difficult, what with your mother's condition. But now that we know she's settled . . ." His eyebrows would knit. Stefanie would silently indicate that there was no need to enter into distressing detail.

It was a small mansion, a town house, late nineteenth century. Stefanie could not recall ever having seen it. Then again, she could not recall *not* having seen it, either. It was recessed, which is to say, had been built to abut the sidewalk at a time of wider sidewalks, carriage circles. There was a revolving glass door fitted into the original entry, and Times New Roman in gold bore the legend MoDACA: MUSEUM OF THE DECORATIVE ARTS OF THE COLONIAL AMERICAS.

Stefanie pushed through into marble territory, warm halogen lighting, new-carpet smell. She removed her gloves and permitted herself to glance at her phone. Nothing doing.

Damnit, Kathy, she thought.

Now she was saying, "Hello," to a wizened bat in a maroon wig. This hag, presumably a lifelong bulimic, was ensconced in a round brochure display *cum* info desk constructed from some sort of gleaming composite.

"I have this," announced Stefanie, presenting Glenn's card.

The old woman twinkled. A lacquered talon tapped the surface of the proffered item.

Stefanie retracted the card. "Great." She collected a sticker bearing the museum's logo.

Stefanie was applying the sticker and walking. She was thinking that at the very least the museum might have contrived to create an unpaid internship for someone young and possibly economically disadvantaged.

Later, once she had viewed the re-creations of the twelve Virginia parlors the museum was apparently famous for and passed through a special exhibition of early Brazilian maps, Stefanie wanted to pee. A sign in one gallery indicated a staircase. Stefanie descended, let herself into a (surprisingly) dingy WC.

There were two stalls. Stefanie chose the left.

This was where it happened.

Stefanie was wiping with a folded square of tissue. And there was a sound. It was a scurrying. Stefanie gasped and dropped the paper into the toilet bowl. She rapidly did up her pants. Could they have *rats*?

It was too disgusting!

Stefanie exited the stall. She was searching around the floor. For some reason she wanted to see this with her own two eyes. She stood still, looking, panting.

Now it was perfectly silent. Stefanie waited. There was nothing.

Stephanie approached a basin.

She was moving her fingers through a weak stream and contemplating her own unlined forehead in the mirror when she saw, out of the corner of her eye, something.

It was behind her, and at first she could not understand how it had gotten "up there." This was her first thought, how had it gotten "up there." Though, if she had been thinking clearly at this moment, it would have occurred to her that she was not observing an animal hovering in empty space, upon, as it were, the very air, but was rather seeing a furred face that, though small, hardly larger than a grapefruit, was supported by a substantial furred neck, a neck covered in the same glossy and wavy black fur that covered this small face, this lean frame that stood approximately the same height as Stefanie herself. It was, she might have thought if she had been able to think clearly, *like* a slight woman, a woman with an abnormally small head for her height, covered all in black fur. Though she was not sure if it was a woman. The face was flat, like the end of a stump. Its eyes were round and wet and black, and whether or not it had a nose, it certainly had a mouth, for now it opened this mouth, revealing a set of short, peg-like teeth, and behind these teeth a very red throat, and Stefanie, perhaps this was where she screamed?

Stefanie regained consciousness before they were able to convey her to the hospital, and so she spent the ambulance ride chatting desperately with a paramedic named Aaron. She was doing a thing where she wanted to practice her game. (Aaron was twenty-eight and covered in small muscles, superclean, possibly gay, but perhaps just from Colorado, at any rate she was going to pretend.) They were talking about how crazy it was. That she must have slipped. But it was so lucky she had screamed. (Had she screamed? She had no memory.) Who would have found her otherwise? And was she showing any symptoms of a concussion? Her head was not tender anywhere. Just a bit tender. Well, they had called the ambulance, Glenn could cover it, might as well take her in. Just keep her a moment. Someone to come and get her.

Stefanie was asking Aaron how he felt about his job, because this was fascinating, his job. Aaron said something about never a dull minute, and Stefanie, she did this thing, it was so unlike her, she said, "But what about a month, Aaron?" She said, "What about a *year*?"

Aaron began doing something with packets, organizing them.

Stefanie tried to let her muscles go limp. Her heart was racing. She could taste blood on the inside of her mouth. She thought about Aaron's student loans. She thought about his limp dick and shaved chest, his shaved scrotum in the mirrored door of his bedroom closet, the lack of molding in a mediocre condo, drugstore toiletries, adult Ritalin and razor blades and a bong in the kitchenette. Aaron's framed photo of a childhood dog with a face like a shriveled chrysanthemum. Stefanie envisioned Aaron kneeling before her. She brought the head of a hammer down full force into the center of his dirty-blond skull.

•

In the hospital, Stefanie was saying something to her mother about how it smelled. It *stank*.

Her mother, wearing a black fox-fur vest with extra tufts of fox around the armholes, nodded. She was seated in a chair, and she wore leggings, a pair of supple Fendi over-the-knee boots, her hair in a ponytail, unhurried makeup. But it was her mother who reeked, Stefanie meant. It was her mother who reeked of steamed skim milk and rabbit turds, her faithless genitals crushed together in the elastic hammock of her legwear.

Stefanie said, "I would like to see you get raped by a pig."

Stefanie's mother had the BlackBerry out and was peddling in some crucial announcement. Her eyeballs recalibrated behind spikes of dried mascara. "What, Stef?"

"I said," said Stefanie, but at this moment a doctor in a white coat entered.

"Well, hello."

Stefanie let her head roll. She provided the doctor with what she believed was an excellent view of her upper teeth. She saw herself sever a magnificent slab of flesh from the doctor's right thigh, rub her face in the sticky heat of this thing. All its sick oils and weeping would get on her; it would dry caked on, a mask.

Stefanie gave the instruction slowly, precisely,

in order that it not be mistaken. "I. Need. A. Knife."

Later it was termed an iron deficiency.

The doctor prescribed some supplements.

Anyway, Stefanie quickly realized that she could not talk like this.

To be continued . . .

Clare thinks she knows why she had not finished. The effort necessary to the illustration of the weird carnage to come—the psychotic eros, the final sex-murder scene with the father—seems monumental, stupid, entirely crippling now.

Other students bit their lips. This is to say, in workshop. They stared at everything except Clare's face. Eventually conversation coalesced around Aaron's grooming habits. A long collective interrogation transpired regarding scrotal depilation, its pros, cons.

Possibly the strangest thing about this was that Clare had had a choice when it came to submitting a story. There was another unfinished tale from this era of intense Elwilian productivity, fairly similar to the first except it was about a girl who wasn't rich. It was, additionally, set ever so slightly in the future, describing an American summer that had not yet come to pass, a time that the real Clare was destined to spend mostly in bed. Given the story's predictive nature, Clare preferred to show it to: exactly no one. Another fragment, it read:

Alice
By Clare Elwil

Alice was not her real name. Her real name was Ali. It was not short for anything. "*Just* Ali," she had quickly realized she sounded ridiculous, not to mention potentially poor, saying.

Actually, she'd come to the city from Springfield, Massachusetts, from her mother's home, and had put herself through NYU, incurring along the way the requisite staggering debt. A pathological mistrust of others had solidified along this way, too, though perhaps it had been there for a while. In high school it had been easy enough to think of it as minor shyness, to believe that it might've had something to do with the fact that others did not recognize the finer things, that at graduation, for example, boys stapled the severed tails of freshly slaughtered squirrels to their graduation caps in one corner of the football field just before the ceremony.

In theory, she'd been wanting to major in something sexy like Italian; however, in practice she found herself mortified not just by the $800 totes favored by the spindly trust funders who attended the info session, but also by the muteness she'd experienced when so many interchangeable *i*-ending names (*Leopardi*, *Marinetti*, *Pasolini*) were presented after she'd expressed a desire to study Italian art and literature. It was something she could never quite come back from, the odd looks handed around among the participating graduate students and a youngish professor in a knotted cashmere scarf.

When she majored in English, it was not something she regretted so much as something she did not have to make an effort in. She finished in three years. Strangely, the class that made the biggest impression was a poetry workshop conducted by an elderly Polish poetess whose main response to her verse was that she "might next time try to go a little further inside [her] own head," though "Alice," as she now constantly styled herself, could never manage this to the poetess's satisfaction. She briefly dated a soft-spoken dyslexic fireman who lived on Staten Island. Then she moved to Greenpoint. Then graduated.

Alice had very little difficulty getting her first full-time job, and to some extent this shocked her. It was after the tech bubble burst and from what she heard from her few acquaintances still laboring toward degrees, she was lucky not to be posting on Craigslist for work as a dominatrix.

Alice drank as much water as she could on the train. Her biggest worry, she felt, for the next ten years, if she could just keep on doing so well as she had, would be getting anywhere near even remotely approaching fat. She kept this thought in her mind to prevent herself from thinking constantly about money.

She worked.

She rode a single train.

Every week it was her task to compose a newsletter. The newsletter updated a select list as to the activities of the office, a foundation dedicated to the preservation of historic urban architecture. Alice herself was not energized by this cause, but she found it easy enough to talk as if she were on the morning of her interview. The woman in a turquoise sweater was named Marcy. Accompanying Marcy was a flat-faced man named Coop, some sort of partially retired architect. Alice launched into a monologue on caryatids.

A little shadow crossed Coop's face.

They offered her minimum wage.

Alice shared a railroad with a much older woman who had been living there for many years. The woman, currently in the process of marrying someone in Ohio whom she had met online, was seldom present. Alice was paying more than half the rent, she knew, particularly since the woman, who in her forties had repellent forehead creases that looked incised, made some quip about this being cheaper for her than storage. However, it was still comparatively a deal and for all intents and purposes Alice lived alone.

The place was on a tree-lined street. A nearby mechanics' allowed their aged pit bull to roam free, grayish teats dangling.

Alice privately referred to this creature as Space Ghost because of its black head and white body. It was deaf, and blind in one eye, but had come to acknowledge Alice after she'd drunkenly fed it leftover pierogies from a foam shell. Sometimes Alice set a plastic-wrapped coupon circular down on the stoop and sat on it and the dog came and rested its huge decaying jaw on her shoe.

"There, there," said Alice.

Alice, it had to be admitted, was spending a lot of time alone. She was letting her health insurance lapse, which she knew could be dangerous, but she was working pretty hard and pretty soon would be able to swing a little bit more, certainly, if she played her cards right.

She had now been at the Historic Architectural Features Foundation (HAFF) for almost two months. You could feel the roiling force of New York summer heat preparing to unleash itself.

Alice wore a lot of brights. She wore coral with white, bitter yellow with white. She read an actress's advice about the dangers posed by financiers and overconsumption of salt. She avidly apprised herself as to the rise of so-and-so, designer to Mrs. Bush. It was 2002, and American morality was again ascendant, or so the press proclaimed. It was a time of stalwart renewal, faith, and swift justice. One day, walking south on West Broadway, Alice saw a man in his thirties in khakis bellowing wildly into a pay phone receiver: "WHAT YOU NEED TO UNDERSTAND IS THEY WON'T STOP UNTIL THEY DESTROY US."

Alice made a rapid turn.

She had canned olives, ketchup, and saltines for dinner.

The office was still.

Marcy was located behind a sliding-glass panel, and Coop apparently worked somewhere else and checked in remotely.

It did not occur to Alice to ask questions about HAFF's own finances, and even if it had she would not have done so. She was set up at the conference table with a whirring Dell and fed summary data via email attachments.

Alice was often idle.

At 10:31 a.m. on one Friday, Alice had already completed the newsletter for the week to follow. She was now a full five days ahead of schedule. At first she was pleased with this achievement and began typing up an account of her meager earnings and their destinies (rent, loan payment, Metrocard, utilities, credit card, food), but then she began to think of Marcy, who was as ever silent, a sweater-toned shadow behind the bluish partition. What if this was all only a test? What if Marcy was recording each of Alice's keystrokes, what if it was known that today alone she had already devoted over twenty minutes to Tara Reid's thoughts on self-realization, plus another fifteen to a search for "real cork wedges lace-up platform"? And then there were the 2.5 hours yesterday allotted to GeoCities research into the exploits of the three most popular girls from high school, clicking through eighty-eight photos of Justine Talbots superbly depilated in a cherry-red one-piece mid-jump on some frat's backyard trampoline, not to mention pages by Jamie White and Jenny Hayes, their assorted infants and corgis and stoner baby-daddies, everyone drooling in hoodies.

Or the more than two hours she had squandered Wednesday pretending she might permit herself to consider deferment of her student loans?

Alice cycled back through the week.

The drive labored.

If they fired her now, she might have to miss a payment, not to mention what would transpire in another two weeks, when rent came due.

Alice was knocking on Marcy's panel. She rapped, thrice.

Alice's heart was struggling around like a separate creature. The only thing that could save her now would be a full admission.

She tried, "Marcy?" This was a squeak.

She waited. She wanted to remember the phrase

she had just moments earlier composed: Marcy, I'm so sorry to bother you. I just wanted to let you know how much I am enjoying this position.

It reminded her of what she'd told the fireman, when he'd asked her not to leave her toothbrush in his sink-top glass, when he'd lovingly restored it to the front pocket of her backpack.

But now the panel was actually genuinely moving, and it was going to be necessary to speak.

Today's sweater was chartreuse. Marcy peered out, stifling a yawn. "Yes?"

"Marcy, I'm so—" Alice began to say, but now she could no longer remember her prepared statement. Somewhere on the street below somebody was leaning on their horn, and this was when it happened.

There was a hiss. Actually, it was a hiss followed by a sort of gurgling, whispery echo, as of wet sand sucked down a drain. It was very close to Alice's left ear. Alice heard someone mutter, "*She doesn't care.*"

At first, because it had been so long, you know, *since*, Alice concluded that it was Marcy who had done the speaking. It took a few seconds to parse Marcy's intent. Alice decided to ask, "Who doesn't?" She said this softly. She did not wish to appear out of line.

Marcy blinked. "Sorry?"

There came a slithering rustle. "*Tell hr nothing's wrong, you have cramps.*"

Marcy's lips were not moving.

"Uh," Alice was saying.

"Tell."

"S-sorry, Marcy," Alice stuttered. "I—uh—wasn't feeling very well, and I just wondered—um." She could go no further.

"Oh, wow," said Marcy. "You should take the day? I think it's fine. See you Monday." And Marcy shut the partition.

Maybe it was luck, a piece of fortune, but the thing was really did she want to return to the apartment? A downstairs neighbor was home with a troublesome pregnancy and spent many hours with the phone on speaker, updating a female relation.

Alice selected Union Square Park. It was not the cleanest but was free. She set her bag on her knees and withdrew *New York* magazine.

In the section on parties, actors and R&B singers made a few patriotic assertions. Alice stared at the silk-wrapped breasts of one reality star.

No need to think about it yet.

Alice turned the page.

It was an ad for GUESS jeans. A caption read: "FALL 2002, Death Valley, CA, *Golden*." In the ad, a couple propped each other up atop a pile of boulders in distressed denim. They had presumably been photographed just moments before they were to die of thirst after their motorcycle crash.

"They look happy."

Alice froze. The voice was to her right.

To her relief it was an actual person. Alice's eyes fell on a long thigh in over-dyed jeans.

"It's funny how that's supposed to interest someone."

Alice glanced across the crotch of the jeans to the hem of a striped polo in shades of peach, squash, and carmine. There were ropy arms attached to this affair and a handsome grinning head.

"Sorry if I startled you," the head pronounced. "I don't normally talk to strangers."

"Oh," said Alice, squinting.

A black fly zoomed.

The male body laughed for no apparent reason. "What's your name?"

"I'm Alice," Alice immediately replied. She felt better, if dizzy. What a relief; he was just trying to pick her up.

"Ha," said the body. He wanted to know what she was doing. He said that they should go somewhere if she felt like it.

It had only been a very minor incident. And now there was only a very minor incident, again. But this was to be expected. They were crossing the street, and in the wind produced by a taxi flashing across an intersection, there came a kind of crinkling, a puffiness in the depths of Alice's left ear, and there it was once more, It said, "*Fun.*" Just that. *Fun.*

•

They drank wheat beers, and he was not weird.

"I just really liked your outfit," he said. "I could tell it said something about you. Like how you *carried* yourself."

He said, "Don't think I'm weird."

She was like, "Oh my god of course not!"

His name was Alan, and they talked for an hour about having nearly identical *A* names. It was a subject since it affected one's sense of self. One frequently came first, because of the letter. If your name was Alan or, say, Alice.

Alice adopted Alan's tone. He was casual but seemed to have standards. He was from the city, duh.

Alice glanced around the room. They were below street level, and there was a sweet and aged light dribbling in through the windows.

Alan was at Stern.

He was interested in sustainability.

He was examining her and wanting to know something or other about her "roots."

Alice said, "Like where I'm from?"

"Sure." Alan crossed his arms over his chest. "Since you know I'm from here."

"Oh, yeah," Alice said.

"So? Yeah?" Alan grinned. He revealed very straight, but also very narrow and weak-looking, teeth.

Alice got up and told Alan that she needed to use the bathroom.

In the "bathroom," which was in fact an alcove with a sink and toilet stashed behind a pair of cabinet doors that attached to each other with Velcro, Alice began washing her hands.

She gazed into a spotted mirror that hung from a wire.

Because there had already been two minor incidents.

This was why they were, in hindsight, so very clear. They were minor, as yet. Just practical nothings. If she ever remembered this, this would be the day on which it would have started again, if it did, which it might not.

The voice was distinct.

It was low and intelligent. No, it was not *precisely* female. Not precisely. No. It could have been the voice of a girl, that was not impossible, but *was* it, *really*?

Alice held still.

Only if she didn't_ _ _NO.

Only if was it the voice was **it it it it it it it** the one doing the talking. YOU REMEMBER. No, ? OHYes you do?\ SO fun pretending to ty[e oo shit, I ~~mean T~~YPE when I use your SHIT.

•

It seemed to end.

Alice held her head. She dug her knuckles into her eyelids, scrubbed.

She was alone.

Sort of.

No, she was not alone. She could feel it waiting in the wings, as it were, there, ready to *take* a word from her, *take* it to say it again, back, back again, as *you*.

That was the thing, the words appeared, to hang, as, in, *thin* air

TIMES T1ME STIMETIM3SSSESS

Time withered. It exploded whitely across the sink

SSSSSSSSSSSSSSSSSSSSSSSSSSSSSSSSSSSSSSSSSSSSSSSS
SSSSSSSSSSSSSSSSSSSSSSSSSSSSSSSSSSSSSSSSSSSSSSSS
SSSSSSSSSSSSSSSSSSSSSSSSSSSSSSSSSSSSSSSSSSSSSSSS
SSSSSSSSSSSSSSSSSSSSSSSSSSSSSSSSSSSSSSSSSSSSSSSS
SSSSSSSSSSSSSSSSSSSSSSSSSSSSSSSSSSSSSSSSSSSSSSSS
SSSSSSSSSSSSSSSSSSSSSSSSSSSSSSSSSSSSSSSSSSSSSSSS
SSSSSSSSSSSSSSSSSSSSSSSSSSSSSSSSSSSSSSSSSSSSSSSS
SSSSSSSSSSSSSSSSSSSSSSSSSSSSSSSSSSSSSSSSSSSSSSSS
SSSSSSSSSSSSSSSSSSSSSSSSSSSSSSSSSSSSSSSSSSSSSSSS
SSSSSSSSSSSSSSSSSSSSSSSSSSSSSSSSSSSSSSSSSSSSSSSS
SSSSSSSSSSSSSSSSSSSSSSSSSSSSSSSSSSSSSSSSSSSSSSSS
SSSSSSSSSSSSSSSSSSSSSSSSSSSSSSSS

ssssssssssssssssssssssssssssssssssssssssss
ssssssssssssssssssssssssssssssssssssssssss
ssssssssssssssssssssssssssssssssssssssssss
ssssssssssssssssssssssssssssssssssssssssss
ssssssssssssssssssssssssssssssssssssssssss
ssssssssssssssssssssssssssssssssssssssssss
ssssssssssssssssssssssssssssssssssssssssss
ssssssssssssssssssssssssssssssssssssssssss
ssssssssssssssssssssssssssssssssssssssssss
ssssssssssssssssssssssssssssssssssssssssss
ssssssssssssssssssssssssssssssssssssssssss
ssssssssssssssssssssssssssss

ssssssssssssssssssssssssssssssssssssssssss
ssssssssssssssssssssssssssssssssssssssssss
ssssssssssssssssssssssssssssssssssssssssss
ssssssssssssssssssssssssssssssssssssssssss
ssssssssssssssssssssssssssssssssssssssssss
ssssssssssssssssssssssssssssssssssssssssss
ssssssssssssssssssssssssssssssssssssssssss
ssssssssssssssssssssssssssssssssssssssssss
ssssssssssssssssssssssssssssssssssssssssss
ssssssssssssssssssssssssssssssssssssssssss
ssssssssssssssssssssssssssssssssssssssssss
sssssssssssssssssssssssssssss

ssssssssssssssssssssssssssssssssssssssssss
ssssssssssssssssssssssssssssssssssssssssss
ssssssssssssssssssssssssssssssssssssssssss

*SSSSSSSSSSSSSSSSSSSSSSSSSSSSSSSSSSSSSSSSSS
SSSSSSSSSSSSSSSSSSSSSSSSSSSSSSSSSSSSSSSSSS
SSSSSSSSSSSSSSSSSSSSSSSSSSSSSSSSSSSSSSSSSS
SSSSSSSSSSSSSSSSSSSSSSSSSSSSSSSSSSSSSSSSSS
SSSSSSSSSSSSSSSSSSSSSSSSSSSSSSSSSSSSSSSSSS
SSSSSSSSSSSSSSSSSSSSSSSSSSSSSSSSSSSSSSSSSS
SSSSSSSSSSSSSSSSSSSSSSSSSSSSSSSSSSSSSSSSSS
SSSSSSSSSSSSSSSSSSSSSSSSSSSSSSSSSSSSSSSSSS
SSSSSSSSSSSSSSSSSSSSSSSSSSSSS*

*SSSSSSSSSSSSSSSSSSSSSSSSSSSSSSSSSSSSSSSSSS
SSSSSSSSSSSSSSSSSSSSSSSSSSSSSSSSSSSSSSSSSS
SSSSSSSSSSSSSSSSSSSSSSSSSSSSSSSSSS$SSSSSSS
SSSSSSSSSSSSSSSSSSSSSSSSSSSSSSSSSSSSSSSSSS
SSSSSSSSSSSSSSSSSSSSSSSSSSSSSSSSSSSSSSSSSS
SSSSSSSSSSSSSSSSSSSSSSSSSSSSSSSSSSSSSSSSSS
SSSSSSSSSSSSSSSSSSSSSSSSSSSSSSSSSSSSSSSSSS
SSSSSSSSSSSSSSSSSSSSSSSSSSSSSSSSSSSSSSSSSS
SSSSSSSSSSSSSSSSSSSSSSSSSSSSSSSSSSSSSSSSSS
SSSSSSSSSSSSSSSSSSSSSSSSSSSSSSSSSSSSSSSSSS
SSSSSSSSSSSSSSSSSSSSSSSSSSSSSSSSSSSSSSSSSS
SSSSSSSSSSSSSSSSSSSSSSSSSSSS*

*SSSSSSSSSSSSSSSSSSSSSSSSSSSSSSSSSSSSSSSSSS
SSSSSSSSSSSSSSSSSSSSSSSSSSS$$$SSSSSSSSSSSS
SSSSSSSSSSSSSSSSSSSSSSSSSSSSSSSSSSSSSSSSSS
SSSSSSSSSSSSSSSSSSSSSSSSSSSSSSSSSSSSSSSSSS
SSSSSSSSSSSSSSSSSSSSSSSSSSSSSSSSSSSSSSSSSS
SSSSSSSSSSSSSSSSSSSSSSSSSSSSSSSSSSSSSSSSSS*

SSSSSSSSSSSSSSSSSSSSSSSSSSSSSSSSSSSSSSSS
SSSSSSSSSSSSSSSSSSSSSSSSSSSSSSSSSSSSSSSS
SSSSSSSSSSSSSSSSSSSSSSSSSSSSSSSSSSSSSSSS
SSSSSSSSSSSSSSSSSSSSSSSSSSSSSSSSSSSSSSSS
SSSSSSSSSSSSSSSSSSSSSSSSSSSSSSSSSSSSSSSS
SSSSSSSSSSSSSSSSSSSSSSSSS

SSSSSSSSSSSSSSSSSSSSSSSSSSSSSSSSSSSSSSSS
SSSSSSSSSSS$$$$$$$$$$$$$$$$$$$$$$SSSSSSS
SSSSSSSSSSSSSSSSSSSSSSSSSSSSSSSSSSSSSSSS
SSSSSSSSSSSSSSSSSSSSSSSSSSSSSSSSSSSSSSSS
SSSSSSSSSSSSSSSSSSSSSSSSSSSSSSSSSSSSSSSS
SSSSSSSSSSSSSSSSSSSSSSSSSSSSSSSSSSSSSSSS
SSSSSSSSSSSSSSSSSSSSSSSSSSSSSSSSSSSSSSSS
SSSSSSSSSSSSSSSSSSSSSSSSSSSSSSSSSSSSSSSS
SSSSSSSSSSSSSSSSSSSSSSSSSSSSSSSSSSSSSSSS
SSSSSSSSSSSSSSSSSSSSSSSSSSSSSSSSSSSSSSSS
SSSSSSSSSSSSSSSSSSSSSSSSSSSSSSSSSSSSSSSS
SSSSSSSSSSSSSSSSSSSSSSSSSSSSSSSS$$$$$

SSSSSSSSSSSSSSSSSSSSSSSSSSSSSSSSSSSSSSSS
SSSSSSSSSSSSSSSSSSSSSSSSSSSSSSSSSSSSSSSS
SSSSSSSSSSSSSSSSSSSSSSSSSSSSSSSSSSSSSSSS
SSSSSSSSSSSSSSSSSSSSSSSSSSSSSSSSSSSSSSSS
SSSSSSSSSSSSSSSSSSSSSSSSSSSSSSSSSSSSSSSS
SSSSSSSSSSSSSSSSSSSSSSSSSSSSSSSSSSSSSSSS
SSSSSSSSSSSSSSSSSSSSSSSSSSSSSSSSSSSSSSSS
SSSSSSSSSSSSSSSSSSSSSSSSSSSSSSSSSSSSSSSS
SSSSSSSSSSSSSSSSSSSSSSSSSSSSSSSSSSSSSSSS
SSSSSSSSSSSSSSSSSSSSSSSSSSSSSSSSSSSSSSSS

*ssssssssssssssssssssssssssssssssssssssssss
sssssssssssssssssssssssssssss*

*ssssssssssssssssssssssssssssssssssssssssss
ssssssssssssssssssssssssssssssssssssssssss
ssssssssssssssssssssssssssssssssssssssssss
ssssssssssssssssssssssssssssssssssssssssss
ssssssssssssssssssssssssssssssssssssssssss
ssssssssssssssssssssssssssssssssssssssssss
ssssssssssssssssssssssssssssssssssssssssss
ssssssssssssssssssssssssssssssssssssssssss
ssssssssssssssssssssssssssssssssssssssssss
ssssssssssssssssssssssssssssssssssssssssss
ssssssssssssssssssssssssssssssssssssssssss
sssssssssssssssssssssssssssss ssssssssssss
ssssssssssssssssssssssssssssssssssssssssss
ssssssssssssssssssssssssss*

*ssssssssssssssssssssssssssssssssssssssssss
sssssssssssssssssssssssssssssssssssssss$*

*ssssssssssssssssssssssssssssssssssssssssss
sssssssssssssssssssssssssssssssssssss*

*ssssssssssssssssssssssssssssssssssssssssss
sssssssssssssssssssssss*

Alice swiped ineffectually at this lattice.

U LIKE ME NOW/? it wondered.

"I like you very much," Alice whispered. "Tell me what you want."

WHAT W4NT?

U KNOW

"No," Alice said aloud. She tried to be conciliatory. "Or, just, not now. Later."

TH+N WH=N

"When?"

W H EN

"S-soon," Alice stuttered. "Soon, soon, soon."

U PROMIS

"Yes," Alice said. "Promise."

When she was a little girl, Alice, or Ali, as she was at this time called, had learned she had a special gift. This gift was the ability to play with time.

The way the game went was like this: You had to choose a point and stare at it, and at a certain moment you had to think, I've got you, Time!

It was like catching an animal by its tail. Time pulled you through the loop, after.

And it only lasted a minute, because of the difficulty of holding on to time's tail, but during the period during which you held on to time's tail, nothing else could happen. This meant that nothing happened to you, and that nothing happened to anyone anywhere else in the world. And nothing happened. Nothing. Happened.

Time's tail was burning hot. It was sharp as glass but never left a mark.

It was best if you chose something bright to

stare at, something bright and very small, like the head of a screw or someone's jewelry.

Ali sat on the driveway while her mother's lawn mower was repaired by [. . .]

There it ends. Clare rolls her eyes. The story is—the *stories are*—ridiculous, and yet: they are analogues for each other, foils if not twins. They each describe vital, ineluctable forces. Monstrous entities, furred and fanged and made of words, obscure themselves by means of their enormity. They are images we cannot quite look at, glimpses of a catastrophe we convince ourselves comes from another country, another way of life; not our own. Clare's father, Clare thinks, had he been a careless man?

It chills Clare and chills her hotly.

Today is Christmas.

She did not die.

Thirty-Two

A Very Interesting Young Man

On the first day of the year, there is a foot and a half of snow in Crete and Harry has, uncharacteristically, left the house. Loudermilk went home to The Cleaner a week ago.

Crete is a bright vault at 3:00 p.m.; air very fresh. Harry follows a squeaky path dug between banks to the downtown. He hopes he won't encounter anyone he'll be compelled to speak to. The few residents he sees are either over the age of thirty or under the age of ten. Everyone moves with caution.

Harry means to stretch his legs and then return to the place, get back to his notebook, but for some reason in spite of the holiday the Ground House at the center of town is open, and Harry is suddenly aware that coffee prepared by someone other than himself, for himself, though eminently affordable, would be an amazing luxury.

Harry goes in. He mutters his order to a girl with reddish dreadlocks. He receives a small coffee and pays with a twenty. Now he goes to the vacant bar along the window, lowers himself onto a stool. The snow is amber, or it is cornflower blue.

"Hi."

Harry turns. The poetry woman Marta Hillary is standing just a foot or so away.

"Hi there," Marta Hillary repeats. She is a *poet*, Harry corrects himself. She wears a black parka. The tip of her narrow nose is pink. This is an event.

Harry manages to nod. He struggles to prevent himself from losing his balance on the stool.

"I know we've met. Where was that, exactly? You're not in my class?"

Harry knows that sentences exist, but currently they hover somewhere out of reach, spinning.

Marta is unperturbed. "It's nice to see you again." She studies Harry's face. "I see that you, like me, have decided not to leave town." She smiles. "It's very beautiful here in winter, don't you think? I couldn't bear to leave. One simply has so much room, and on a day like this, I think you have to say that it's like a prism out there." Marta fusses with the top of her parka. She sips tea from a paper cup. "Don and Lizzie, my husband and daughter, are skiing. They're out west. I just let them go. Just like that. Strange of me, don't you think?"

Harry has no idea why his opinion should have any bearing on Marta Hillary's relationship with her husband or child.

Marta continues, "So I've decided to stay put for the moment." She pauses. "Oh, now I remember! You're that psychologist, the one who knows our new star, Troy. I was sorry we were not able to speak more, the other night perhaps, or last month? I believe you are a very interesting young man." Marta

Hillary seems to press something into Harry's gaze, and for several seconds he cannot look away from her. "Yes, *now* I remember," Marta intones. "I remember I was very glad to see you. At our *home*."

Marta Hillary has a paper napkin and is writing something down on it. "Here," she says.

Marta Hillary goes out the door.

Harry forces himself to stay and consume coffee. He sits and touches the cup. He carefully folds the napkin Marta Hillary has given him and puts it in his coat pocket. The napkin has writing on it Harry does not want, for the moment at least, to read.

Harry leaves the Ground House. He walks to the library, where he checks his email. There is just one email from a real human. Predictably it is from Loudermilk. Loudermilk—also predictably—doesn't say much. He tells Harry he hopes he's still alive and, if so, there's a little something that Harry could please do if Harry wouldn't mind, and this thing is, of all things, to write to Loudermilk's great new conquest. A log-in for an account Loudermilk has independently invented, prufrock69@hotmail.com, and an institutional address for the mark are provided. Loudermilk says Harry should make what he writes *as good as a poem*. Loudermilk also says, *So she knows I'm thinking about her. We're in her class next semester and need to initiate ass-kiss pronto! I'd do it myself but you know my, uh, anthropological history. Now get spastic with it, you Amish pirate you, thanks dude.* There is, in addition, a brief and enigmatic P.S.: *Why do farts smell? (it's a joke).*

Thirty-Three

Letters

Thu, 8 Jan 2004 22:30:32
To: mjhl12@gsas.ui.edu
From: prufrock69@hotmail.com
Subject: Happy New Year

Dear Professor Hillary,

Please excuse this email address. I hope you are very well. Happy New Year's Greeting and looking forward to working with you next semester.

Sincerely,
Troy Loudermilk

Fri, 9 Jan 2004 17:36:05
To: prufrock69@hotmail.com
From: mjhl12@gsas.ui.edu
Subject: Re: Happy New Year

I won't comment on the address.

I, too, look forward to our work.

Regards,
MH

Sat, 10 Jan 2004 10:01:20
To: mjhl12@gsas.ui.edu
From: prufrock69@hotmail.com
Subject: Re: Re: Happy New Year

Dear Professor Hillary,

Thank you for your message. That is great news.

I wanted to say I am already getting started on some poems and cannot wait to share them with you.

Sincerely,
Troy

Sat, 10 Jan 2004 13:41:08
To: prufrock69@hotmail.com
From: whytnoise <louderme@aol.com>
Subject: Re: Fwd: Re: Re: Happy New Year

Dude, I can't believe you didn't get this one, such a classic. Answer: so that deaf people CAN STILL ENJOY THEM

anyway i like what U R doing??

don't see LORD OF THE RINGS til I'm bakc

Sat, 10 Jan 2004 14:10:15
To: prufrock69@hotmail.com
From: mjhl12@gsas.ui.edu
Subject: Re: Re: Re: Happy New Year

I'm always here to read your work. You don't say anything about when you plan to grace Crete with your presence again . . .

Sun, 11 Jan 2004 19:56:12
To: whytnoise <louderme@aol.com>
From: prufrock69@hotmail.com
Subject: Re: Re: Fwd: Re: Re: Happy New Year

She likes you for some reason, I guess. I actually really don't have anything for you to give her right now as far as poems go, so tell me when you're coming back? I'll be working till then. I'm a little confused about why I need to start doing things as you from this point of view, like with her. I guess see you.

Sun, 11 Jan 2004 20:01:11
To: prufrock69@hotmail.com
From: whytnoise <louderme@aol.com>
Subject: Re: Re: Re: Fwd: Re: Re: Happy New Year

dude chill. i'll be back in a day. then we can talk. its really weird basically writing email to yourself, by the way . you should try it sometimes

Sun, 11 Jan 2004 20:01:31
To: prufrock69@hotmail.com
From: whytnoise <louderme@aol.com>
Subject: Re: Re: Re: Re: Fwd: Re: Re: Happy New Year

also DO NOT NEGLECT THY HILLARY

super super important

do not pass go do not collect 4100 lick butt now

Sun, 11 Jan 2004 20:21:59
To: mjhl12@gsas.ui.edu
From: prufrock69@hotmail.com
Subject: Re: Re: Re: Re: Happy New Year

That is fantastic, Marta. You'll hear from me in a few days provided weather doesn't screw flying up.

Mon, 12 Jan 2004 12:48:02
To: prufrock69@hotmail.com
From: whytnoise <louderme@aol.com>
Subject: Re: Re: Re: Re: Re: Fwd: Re: Re: Re: Re: Happy New Year

Haha. nice. good thing my dick is as big as you make it sound

Mon, 12 Jan 2004 12:50:01
To: whytnoise <louderme@aol.com>
From: prufrock69@hotmail.com
Subject: Re: Re: Re: Re: Re: Re: Fwd: Re: Re: Re: Re: Happy New Year

I'm pretending you didn't just make me read that.

Mon, 12 Jan 2004 13:10:41
To: prufrock69@hotmail.com
From: whytnoise <louderme@aol.com>
Subject: Re: Re: Re: Re: Re: Re: Re: Fwd: Re: Re: Re: Re: Happy New Year

pretend all u want

Thirty-Four

We Prefer to See Ourselves Living

Harry is starting to comprehend what he wants a poem to be, what a poem is for. He recognizes, too, that he might do this work anyway, even if he had zero readers. It's convenient that there is an audience, since this means there is a manner in which he can function, relative to society. (As if he wanted to! Still, the thought is not without its comforts.) This is identifiable behavior, the composition of poems, not nothing. Harry trots over to the library. He encounters the silty, electrified images of Apollinaire. He thinks about the various tortured ambitions of modernists to represent the present. Harry thinks how words are objects. People make use of them without seeing them, without tasting them, without attempting to feel their hard and glossy limits.

Harry knows he wants to create a long poem. *Write* is, by the way, not the correct verb. He wants to *assemble* the poem, like a staircase. It should be a perfect and purposeless machine and it should depict the world, what has become of the world, through its intelligent arrangement of word-objects Harry has unearthed, a reporter writing about "ops tempo" or someone saying the phrase "Connecticut friends." He doesn't know why certain groups of words appear to him with a lasso around them, a magic circle alerting him to their pertinence. Some words mean so much more than they mean to mean.

Anyone could write the poem he wants to write, Harry thinks, if only they were willing to see what he sees. But they aren't, and it isn't even personal.

For now the major fact of his existence is the change in his place of residence. At first he'd been beyond irritated by Loudermilk's suggestion that he think about getting some kind of part-time job. Loudermilk had barely been back from the East Coast for three days before it seemed like he couldn't shut up about it. Loudermilk was pretending to see things about Harry, like that Harry wasn't showering with much frequency and was maybe subject to twitches and tremors and that Harry was, Loudermilk had on one occasion observed, at this point not beyond relieving himself in a Mountain Dew bottle taped under the card table in his room at a convenient angle, and so on. To which Harry had replied that the problem was not so much his as the house's, the lack of properly secreted bathroom facilities, in case this wasn't already sufficiently obvious to an all-knowing virtuoso of life like Loudermilk. Which remark Loudermilk had parried to the effect that this wasn't really stopping Loudermilk, in case Harry hadn't noticed, which, what with Loudermilk having been back for at least thirty-six hours at that point, Harry had to admit that, yes, fine, he'd definitely had a chance to admire Loudermilk's enthusiastic employ of the plumbing and had Loudermilk been feeding on a constant diet of asparagus and decomposing horse flesh for the last week?

Loudermilk had very calmly and sweetly requested that Harry consider shutting the fuck up. Loudermilk said that he had an idea. He said that he had something that he wanted to show Harry. He dug around in his backpack and extracted a folded printout, which was revealed to be a poster:

WANTED
Janitor
Get paid $$$$ and get an awesome,
awesome place to live at!!!
Delta Psi Kappa needs a janitor now!

There was below this a drawing of what appeared to be a plantation manor surrounded by a heart in pink highlighter, and there was a phone number.

Loudermilk was gazing calmly over at Harry, who by then was holding the poster. "I called them, dude," Loudermilk was saying. "The Seminars rents their shit out for functions all the goddamn time. This place is a known quantity."

Harry was examining Loudermilk's face.

"I really," Loudermilk was saying, "think that you shouldn't get weird about this. I think it could be an opportunity for you, Harrison. I would really think you could get into this, if you know what I mean."

Harry demurred.

"Harry? Pussy, and I am not talking about felines, OK? Ya heard of it?"

Harry said, "Thanks for being disgusting and, as ever, super literal."

"Except, dude, that I am not being literal and would you listen to me for one half a second, please? I called them, right? And it sounds like nobody answered the ad at all so they're totally desperate, basically, plus, like, bethonged? And I got you an interview. It'll be easy, I swear to god. I know it's something you can do. I mean, I feel partially responsible for the fact that you never get laid and this is, like, my Christmas present to you this year, you know? I feel totally guilty, man. I mean, *look* at you."

Harry asked what Loudermilk planned to do without him.

"Without you? Don't you worry about me! Dude, for one I'm not going to constantly obsess over the possibility of offending your intense-crazy paranoid-schizoid sense of smell every time I fucking have to unleash a totally normal, healthy, and respectable duke or dukes here in the free-form *cuarto de baño* de Evelyn. And I'm also totally going to finally be able to stop bothering you while you're at work writing something epic and being an insane genius, by the way?"

The very next day Harry went. He'd very compliantly let Loudermilk walk him over to the Delta Psi Kappa HQ, and then as usual he'd let Loudermilk do the talking. The girls did not bat an eye. Two of them were blondes who seemed to have recently had the opportunity to cook their hides in the full heat of the equatorial sun, while the third was a speckled redhead with a fat if well-shaped face who kept touching her narrow mouth, as if to reassure herself of its persistence between nose and chin. All three of them kept nodding at whatever anyone said, and the shorter blonde was all, "I totally bet he would so be at home up there, oh my god! My cousin is kind of sad or whatever and he lived in an attic for a while and it totally worked for him."

"Nice," the redhead told her.

There was some whispering, and then the three of them brought Harry up the back stairs while Loudermilk loitered, examining the nap, or so he claimed, of a pool table in a bookless room with a very big bar and a creepy coffered ceiling they apparently liked to call the Library.

Harry didn't know what else to do, so he let them guide him. To be honest, he didn't feel that weird. He either said nothing or made a motion with his head if it was absolutely necessary. They took him up to a small suite of rooms rank with mildew and said some things about when trash had to be moved and where it went. They were smiling at him a lot, blinking and staring as if he were a baby animal. Mostly, he felt like they were harmless enough.

Harry was looking around the space. It was a room under an eave, and it had a sink on top of a janky-looking cabinet and there was a toilet down the hall, but it was a place where he could supposedly exist in solitude, without Loudermilk and without everything that Loudermilk had begun to stand for in Harry's mind, which included not just violent early-morning shits, but also a weird kind of authority Harry wasn't sure, suddenly, looking around, that he so much wanted or even required anymore.

Harry wished he could say something like they did on television, where they shouted, "I'll take it!" but his stomach froze and he had to wait until the "ladies" had gone back downstairs again and he could follow and then indicate to Loudermilk by means of one of his signature meaningful looks that he was into the proposition.

Loudermilk hammered out the details and they went home to pack Harry up.

Now, in the middle of the day sometimes, the whole house will just be still, and Harry will know that everyone, down to the last sorority sister, is out, and he will descend to the main level and dust and straighten and empty trash cans. He does whatever it seems to him like a good idea to do and then returns to his own quarters. Sorority girls really like sex toys: This is something that he didn't know before he took this position. Anything even vaguely penis-shaped he finds lying around he's made it a rule to leave perfectly undisturbed. So far no one's said boo. An envelope of cash appears under his door every other week.

Harry guesses they must be relatively OK with his job performance, uncertain though he still is of the exact nature of the task.

More important is what is happening to the writing. Sometimes he'll write a poem that he doesn't even give to Loudermilk. He's using a typewriter to make drafts and clean copies. The narrow window over the counter he uses as a desk has a view out onto the blue tops of a pair of pines. Today's result, a two-fer, is as follows:

Rush Job

I was a member of a firm of twins,
A single box that could be blamed
For rising unilateralism, the crime-
Genius connection, not to mention
Any trail of long ionic air. In truth,
I kind of flunked the interview . . .

A preponderance of green dots here
Indicates the so-called Westerner
Crossing a laconic California coast
At 15,000 MPH, absolutely no re-
Guard for overhangs of debt or
Breaking no news to one's vendors.

Not the shuttle itself but the sheath.
I guess it comes down to intangibles.

—T. A. LOUDERMILK

We Will Bury You

It was Death, aptly enough, that brought me
  back to
A distant, looming ceiling red with coffered
  gold,
Among other environmental bona fides.

I was somebody I wished I'd met,
As the cult of martyrs developed in the West;
You get the impression SUVs are decadent,
  somehow.

Brandishing a phallic wand, an archaeologist
  with clear blond eyes, a Bob,
I guess I'll woo these impolitic wonks
At the necropolis, ha!

Striding among them,
A charioteer, I watch as some are wrapped
In spotted pelts and set alight like dogs. This
  post-flight ritual

Stands as a contemporary analogue.
Military leaders lead themselves.

—T. A. LOUDERMILK

Thirty-Five

Love

Clare is, even, writing.

She knows the story is fake and sounds nothing like her, but she has discovered that one way a person can write is *not to*. Clare shouldn't write, because Clare cannot. However, Clare can write something that someone else would write, no problem. And there happen to be a lot of prototypes floating around.

Clare thinks, for example, about what other students are producing: the tale of the demise, by compression van and obstructed rearview, of a hapless young husband on Rollerblades in an icy moonlit parking lot; the legend of the conflicted political allegiances of an entrepreneurial DJ and former child chess prodigy in Buenos Aires; a prose ballad concerning the mystery of one incommunicative mother and her real-estate addiction. What these well-crafted works share is an overweening dedication to both psychological *and* empirical detail; their authors seem to believe in the existence of an actual, real world subject to capitalism but also, and more significantly, to the laws of attachment and causality. Romantic and/or familial love is the eternal cultural dynamo to end all cultural dynamos and/or mediating entities. They fuck you up, your mum and dad. It makes some sense.

Too much sense, if you're asking Clare, which, let us check for one brief moment—ah, yes, no one is!

Clare, having descended into solipsistic obsession regarding the story she has not yet written, missed the university's registration deadline. She had been thinking, before she lost track of the calendar year, about enrolling in a Sanskrit reading course or maybe something on documentary film, but now she's come up against a virtual barricade in the online catalogue. No amount of refreshing can save her. She has been forced to turn herself over to the administrators in Building 109, who have pertly informed Clare that her options are few but luckily there is more than one way to skin a cat and there does happen to be a seminar—if Clare will condescend to take a class in the department from which she is receiving her degree—with some availability.

This is how Clare manages to become the unique pupil in poet Don Hillary's Spring 2004 offering. This seminar bears the extremely disheartening one-word title "Love." Thanks to Clare, it will now not be canceled.

Clare wants to consider this misbegotten sequence of events as little as possible. She is, additionally, almost certain now that Hillary, formerly a character in her one good story, knew her father when they were both in the Seminars together, *how bizarre*. And, as Clare apprehends on day one, Hillary's class is not just distressingly unpopular, given the universalist topic, but more than slightly unbalanced and very, very verbose. Hillary gallops around a sonnet by Keats for approximately 135 percent of the allotted class time and then, spent, summarily dismisses her. It is a routine, if not intentional.

Hillary will say, "I guess we're going to get started."

"Am I sitting too far away?" Clare, at the other end of the table, will foolishly inquire.

"Too far away for *what*?"

Clare will change the subject. "Are we going to wait for anyone?"

"I'm not going to." It's a now-breezy Hillary, shuffling papers.

Clare reminds him that she is in fiction.

"Why's that?"

"That I'm in fiction?"

"That you should mention it."

"This is a poetry class?"

"I told you I have no prerequisites. Neither should you." Hillary's voice is treacly, lascivious, but his eyes are dead. Clare thinks he may have forgotten her name.

"This is about living, about writing and living," Hillary seems helpless to prevent himself from insisting. "Real things. How people *live*," he repeats, "in writing, and how they write. What is true. It's about great poetry, the great themes. This is about how—" Hillary trembles.

Clare bites her lip. "I didn't do the reading," she announces.

"No one here does the reading," Hillary tells her.

It is even stranger than the fiction Clare must laud and eviscerate on a weekly basis.

However, Hillary's shaky pedagogy is having one salutary effect: it has caused Clare to recognize that, in spite of her own difficulties and loneliness, she is, at least, not the one in charge.

Even if she must give up the old dream of flawless self-expression, even if that is no longer possible, given the mess that is/are the channels via which her feeling circulates, yet she *can do* other things. She can imitate. She can become someone she is not. She can mimic and she can compete. And the reason she can do this is that there really is no other means of expression, speaking of what is true.

Clare remembers reading somewhere that when the mind is like a passageway where someone is talking, the voice belongs to someone else. Was it an academic poet who said this? Maybe Heraclitus? Virginia Woolf?

In any case, it's a notion she can reverse-engineer.

Because Clare *can* write, as long as she does not do it.

And she's been thinking, for example, about what others in her fiction cohort *would* write, were they her. She deliberates in a casual fashion regarding the timeline of her existence. She scouts out appropriate stopping places—places/stages/days/events on or at which a prose portraitist of the human condition could linger, gently stroking in stirring, and romantic, and uplifting, and potentially emotionally devastating, touches.

Clare considers her childhood. It encompasses the brief period during which her parents were to be regularly found on the same continent and, at times, within the same open-plan loft space, if not the very same room. There might be some sort of symbolism one could use to indicate that, despite their best attempts to sacrifice their child on the altar of their arbitrary decision to couple, the child's imaginary death and (very) real emotional suffering were not sufficient tribute. Clare imagines the story that a fiction writer named Dev O'Shaughnessy might compose. Dev has lately turned in a tremendous narrative about suburban front yards and what they meant to wicked, soulful tweens of the male persuasion in 1987. It is couched as the report of an imaginary anthropologist. Dev's tale made a splash and Dev now has an agent and, apparently, a book deal. It happened in two weeks. Dev, if he were Clare or she he, could compose an edgy and prismatic short story about parents who observe their child knocking a cup off the edge of a table. The parents start talking about suicide. The story could be just their dialogue. It would be an allegory for the slow death of the republic, the narcissism of semi-elites. It would be a well-made mirror. It would make D. H. Lawrence's corpse roll over and shed a tiny tear. Dev would surely garner another book deal from it.

But Dev and Clare are not the same person, and this is why the idea of writing a story *by* him so fascinates her. As long as she doesn't care too much, the task amuses. And she will not write about being a child or being a cup on a table. She won't write about the most obvious subject, as far as she is concerned: the long string of failures to either kill herself or be abruptly destroyed that have made up her triangulation within her mother's sense of modern love. Clare won't talk about this, because she doesn't have to. No one can force her to do it.

Not the incident with the ice-skate blade she somehow fell on in a wet elevator one winter afternoon, ripping open the interior of her left cheek, staining her white gloves brown. Not the other unforced injuries to her face, the broken teeth and split lips, the black eyes and cut cheeks and lumps to the forehead, though she's never broken a bone and has barely had so much as a cut anywhere else on her body. Not the year of shoplifting nor the year of dealing speed. Not the week of the gentle busboy she'd had unprotected sex with against a boulder in Central Park. Not the hellish lethargy she'd fallen into late freshman year of college, when she'd begun sending manic emails to professors she suspected of wanting to bed her, emails she later saw in her outbox but could not recall typing, nor the unsuccessful attempts to fail out of school, when her mother had called off plans for a third marriage because of her daughter's "instability," when Clare's mother had wetly sobbed late one night in her newest loft that Clare was ruining Trudy Elwil's renowned existence but that over Trudy's dead body would Clare start seeing a psychiatrist. None of this. And certainly not the road trip Clare had taken alone at the end of sophomore year, when she'd briefly shared a hotel room with an electronics salesman in Las Vegas. None of these times. Not the stories of all the airplanes Clare has missed because of hearing voices, long before the accident, not that day at the Orsay, long before anything went wrong. Not the unforeseen accident itself. Clare does not care about the accident, and it will be far better to write about things that she does care about, at least a little, while pretending not to care about them, because in these cases you *can* pretend not to care. What you write has to be a choice, Clare thinks. You have to choose. You have to have something to do. It has to be work. It cannot be the truth.

Thirty-Six

The Iceberg

Lizzie tells herself for the umpteenth time that she's only practicing using binoculars, because what they never show you in movies is that it's actually kind of hard to do! They don't go into focus all that easily, and you never know when you could be invited to go on some sort of bird-watching safari by some very advanced boy you are likely to meet in college and then look like a total scrub when you can't even make out whatever rare plover it is you're meant to be stalking. In 2004, it is all about being well-rounded!

Lizzie keeps a diary of her observations. This makes it a little classier. It's the first thing she does when she gets home from school, or home from whatever: pick up the binoculars, check out what it is that's going on at the moment. She has a pretty good view of the snow-filled yard and pool house and neighbors' places, and just between Lizzie and Lizzie's diary, Lizzie has seen some things! Anyway, it's not like there's that much going on in this town. It's not like Lizzie's a perv. Everyone should just be grateful that she doesn't try to date frat boys like every other underage girl!

It's late afternoon, and Lizzie is sitting by her beloved window, her best friend. She has a bowl of Pirate's Booty and the binoculars to her eyes, but then she hears something below her, on her very own lawn. She sets down her accessories. It's just her mother, of course, stalking the whiteness of the yard, cell phone jammed to face. Her mother has nice legs and decent hair, Lizzie thinks, which is good because you can always go to the salon, and her mom does look pretty good for her age. She watches her mother draw a figure eight with one hand. Her mother pauses, tucks phone to chin. She lights a cigarette, untucks phone.

Her mother never used to smoke like this. But she also never used to stand in one place in the freezing cold for over an hour, listening to somebody talk, interjecting various adamant things in German.

Lizzie scratches her elbow. She wonders if she should say something to her dad about this. Like maybe this would be a good opportunity to find out what's up. She could test her dad, say something like, "Oh, I think mom has a pretty serious friend or something now," and see what her dad's reaction is. Not that Lizzie even wants to know, because she doesn't. If her father is fully aware of what's going on with her mom, Lizzie doesn't know if she could take it. She doesn't know if she would be incredibly sad or really, really angry, or some combination. She doesn't even want to find out how she would feel, to be honest, which is why she hasn't said anything. Plus, they haven't talked about splitting up for a while, so maybe they've changed their minds.

Lizzie touches the binoculars but leaves them on the sill. She presses her nose against the cold glass.

Now her mom is sitting in the snow. This should technically be prohibitively uncomfortable, even with her mom's Moncler parka, which Lizzie is likely to steal. Breath and smoke rise as wraiths, degenerate. Lizzie is trying to observe the look on her mother's face, because she's noticed that it changes. She's made some notes on this fact in her diary, about how her mother looks so much younger sometimes now, about how she looks kind of worried, too, but not exactly worried. It's difficult to explain.

Lizzie has seen the movie *Titanic* three times now. Once really stoned, once sober, and one time kind of stoned, plus hungover. She feels there is this instructive continuum between Billy Zane and Leonardo DiCaprio, both of whom are obviously gay in real life but whatever. Leonardo is really nice the whole movie long, and he's sexy, but there's nothing quite as sexy as when Billy Zane is near the lifeboats being evil. The look on Billy Zane's face when he is near the lifeboats, Lizzie can't quite explain, but it is like the epitome of sex. So, therefore, what *Titanic* teaches you is that the best person to try to get to fall in love with you is someone who is somewhat outside of your natural social group. When you find this person, this gives you a lot of power. Then people who are within your social group (the Billy Zane character, for example, in the case of the Kate Winslet character) have to give you a lot more respect, because they recognize that you don't depend exclusively on your born social group to give your life meaning. You know how to have adventures. It's very American to be like this, which is why *Titanic* is one of the powerful movies of all time right now, being that they have come to the end of the greatest American century and now it's apparently time to set fire to a certain mostly non-Christian sector of the planet.

Lizzie thinks that maybe every adult in America has seen *Titanic* and realized they need to hurry and find their Leonardo DiCaprio before the total flowering of the apocalypse. The way her mother is looking into the air now as the sun begins to set makes Lizzie think of how Kate Winslet looks when she takes off all her clothes to pose for Leonardo DiCaprio, even though Billy Zane could show up at any second. In that moment, when she's naked, posing, Kate Winslet doesn't give a fuck if Billy Zane suddenly shows up, because she's busy making herself truly vulnerable to another human being for the very first time in her life, and there is something strong in that, and this is something that Billy Zane's character could never take away from her. Anyway, it's like this is, weirdly, what her mother is doing, even though she's not naked and is only talking on the phone while flirting with pneumonia.

She kind of looks vulnerable. It is intense.

It's particularly weird because when Lizzie's mom first started telling Lizzie about how maybe two people can love each other very much but still not be right for each other in the long run, Lizzie didn't want to believe it, and she was probably kind of mean to her mom for saying that at the time. Lizzie thought that her parents really loved each other and were happy. This shows how much Lizzie knows.

Lizzie still sometimes, though, when she is in her room, can't help thinking about Thanksgiving when Harry was up there with her and she tried to make him tell her about Loudermilk. Harry, Lizzie reflects, would have been perfect to be her Leonardo DiCaprio, but obviously she is not lucky enough to be into that. Lizzie is cursed with liking guys like Loudermilk, the Billy Zanes of this world. She's cursed with stalking them at the mall and downtown, then calling them up constantly until they agree to see her. And then she's cursed with needing to bend them to her will, which in Loudermilk's case has included a lot of agonized grunts and blue balls in semi-public places. Anyway, Harry is kind of a weirdo, even if he is a Leonardo, what with him being in such proximity to her bedroom in the first place and obviously right in the middle of perpetrating some kind of freaky voyeur thing on her mom. It felt, speaking of voyeurs, very French, very New Wave, for a second there, and perhaps Lizzie had been somehow reacting to that. Lizzie sighs. Now her mother is getting exercised about something or other and the smoke is coming out heavy and she's starting to cough. Actually, it looks for a second like she's choking, but then she's waving a hand in front of her face or even laughing, and she hangs up and flicks away the cigarette and goes indoors, and it turns out CPR is not necessary, for which thank the freaking Lord.

Anyway, it's Saturday, the worst day of the week. Not to mention that today happens to be the worst day of the second week of February and also the worst day of the entire year.

Lizzie is supposed to call some people she knows to do something, but honestly she doesn't feel that much like it. She thinks about working some more on her art project, still shoved to the back of her desk drawer and now additionally sequestered inside an old Christmas card, a churchyard drowning in iridescent snow.

Lizzie puts the binoculars down. She's done with her Pirate's Booty, which will be doubling as a low-calorie dinner.

She goes into her bathroom to wash her hands and spends a little time primping in front of the mirror. Lizzie reflects on the fact that she's way too good for this stupid town. Even her mother knows it, which is why she feels so guilty all the time about them having to live here.

Maybe they will go to Switzerland. Lizzie can meet some new men there.

Lizzie is making a photogenic face at herself in the mirror.

She stops making the face.

She washes her hands again, and then starts putting on light makeup because she has decided that she is going to go out. She's just going to go and see what this Loudermilk is up to. She's going to make herself do it. When she's in college in a couple years or in Switzerland or wherever next year she'll probably tell someone a hysterically funny story about how she threw herself at this much older guy who barely gave her the time of day, in spite of his rampant sex addiction, and all the unconsummated hard-ons she inspired in him, who was this stupid jock poet who at the time seemed intensely talented, and it will be a pretty good story.

Lizzie is done with her makeup and is rolling herself a j. She makes it strong and smokes half of it out her window. Then she goes downstairs and yells for whoever's listening's benefit that she'll be back later on.

On the sidewalk she smokes the other half.

Lizzie thinks, In thirty seconds I shall be super fucked up!

She reminds herself that what she needs to do is navigate toward the Common Lot, then position herself so as to be able to intercept her Billy Zane.

Lizzie is delighted by the beauty of frozen nature around

her. The world is so cold. She has no idea how long she spends on the sidewalk, staring up at an early star.

Later she is downtown, and even later she and Loudermilk are standing together in the alley behind the Common Lot, and Loudermilk is saying, "I can't fucking do this," and he's holding the back of her head and crushing it to his breastplate, to the center of his chest.

Lizzie might mainly be thinking about how incredibly high she is or even how many times a nearly identical scene has played out before, but that doesn't mean—even when Loudermilk departs abruptly with some shitty excuse about needing to go back inside so it doesn't look like there's anything between them—that it totally takes away from this epic moment.

IV

YOUR BEST READER

Aboulomania

They were brilliant, and they were fools, with
Their relentless on-message responses and
Pan-gender upper-middle-class perfectionism,
Playing the role of rationalists in the extreme.
However bright the scenarios of birdsong and
Bells, forest-green winter wheat, silver-green
Ornaments, spasms of doubt and blame, they
Kept to the agreed-upon ops tempo with
Admirable sangfroid. Creating mass affluence
With windfalls for the fortunate few, they went
On "research binges," only pausing to regroup
When a small, hassled woman appeared with
Afternoon treats of scotch and RingDings.
Reporters pounced, even as soldiers quietly
Applauded, in sudden graceful fits. They were
Very big in personal hygiene after devouring
A small alp of food. Their recommendations
Were quirky—ask any yeoman worth his fat.
Taped to the receiver was a sign in neat calligraphy
That read, Leave the country within 48 hours or
Suffer the consequences. It looked like a frail,
Frail piece of fragrant cake, hanging there like
A Marxist terrorist or euphoric business text.
In 21st-century woodcuts, for example, and recent
Pulse-pounding frescoes, pets become the new
Children, even as a sadist and a nincompoop
Embrace the nation-building challenge of the
Decade, along with its infamous synthetic turf,

Frozen potato products, a much reviled gigantic
Concrete bowl, and lots and lots of sofas. I had
A five-day hypomanic episode in the pampered,
Perfect grass to catch a drop of solitude. But it
Was frustrating to watch myself unconsciously
Ad-libbing an extra hop into the movement. Or the
Note of personal rancor—my own "Suez" moment.
They were ibis eggcups! They were the behemoth
Who snaps the ball, the multiple choices of a Scan-
tron test, invisible celestial interlocutors, doctrinal
Voids, economically independent soul mates! They
Possessed hundreds of pictures of women giving
Head and understood the weird drafts of freezer
bags.
Their displeasure over one CIA exercise was quite
Outlandish and crashed emptily to earth. Here
The laurels seem equally distributable . . .
They were virtual Frenchmen; their limited public
Visibility allowed them to practice head-shrinking
In Oregon. They were domestic paragons! They
Were, of course, pillaged almost immediately
Afterward. Like some mild and generally useless
Tips or misspelled figures from Celtic myths,
They took the death of love as their special
Premonition. They had to backtrack elegantly,
Performing immediate dances with recyclables in
Hot plastic ponchos, enduring everything from
Laborious negotiations to painful rock music.
They were lubricious and empty-headed robots by
The time they got to me. It was a delicate day.

I tried to think of a more à la mode shade for
Operational flexibility and social bravado. The
Old ways had taught cadets to be bullies, and I
Fought the team's traditional kelly green with the
Knucklebones of saints, not to mention at least one
Passive-aggressive screed. We're talking about
Post-hostilities control and embrace of uncertainty,
A lack of curiosity about significant details. There's
A lot of money to pay for this and the absence of
A president. There's the residual anxiety. The rest
Of it is assembled from surgical tubing and a
Leather coin purse. It's a *Fragebogen*, or question-
naire. P.S. the aroma of mugwort is also v. nice here:
You're not going to tell me if it's in the mail?
(A) Yes. (B) No. (C) I could shave my head and
Weave you a bracelet out of my hair? He looks
Soft. He's a resolute nonconductor of electricity.
In spite of this, I still didn't think the planned flow
Was right. All the A-Team guys wanted to be in on
Phase III, and now Georgia was the world's only
Consumption superpower, leaving decapitation
Attacks and coulis-of-heirloom tomato appetizers
As our last resort. I called it, "Operation Provide
Comfort," once unemployment reached 70 percent.
The power vacuum led to looting and Disneyesque
Water jets that bent. Those looking for detail said
This would make some "things" more like "events."
Revenge killings, crime, chaos—all this was so
Foreseeable, a result of changing the occupational
Structure scattered over an ever-messier world.

In elementary school we called it "playing."
We thought of it as standing on a banana peel,
Awaiting our date with implosion, whether we
Are to be a two-planet species or not. No "fee
Simple" properties, no oranges or seed potatoes,
No sixty-billion-dollar hemp or sunny jellied after-
Life. We'll dance but we won't touch. We'll touch
But we won't shop. The only way out is to make
Foreigners more like us, which was when U.S.
Marshals stopped being vague and started getting
Recondite. This was the much-touted civilian-
Military difference. We were persuading the
Public to foot the bill for robot dogs and mice. We
Lived in a period that disdains bold colors but
Still, nearly every working group said, "Be like
Us," with a destructive self-confidence, from
Her Connecticut friends to the least mercurial
Son on the roster. We each appeared in an info-
mercial astride a roll of polyethylene. What, then,
Is the American, this new man, if all his powers
Must be wielded through others? The solutions
Will be centuries in coming, and I pant for life.

—T. A. LOUDERMILK

Thirty-Seven

A Novelist

Anton Beans pants. He sighs. He attempts to still his heart. Right now he is doing a kind of thing he has never done before. He is lying under Loudermilk's bed and there is something sticky and probably chemically unstable affixed to his neck/skull base, just below his right ear. He is fairly certain it will turn out to be a used condom. Either that, or a mutant tapeworm parthenogenetically forged in the crucible of filth Loudermilk cultivates in all areas pertaining to his physical person, if not his very soul—if, for example, Anton Beans were a dualist, which Anton Beans is not.

The main thing distracting Beans from his bacteria-stocked misery is his sense of sight, and his sense of sight is unfortunately filled with Loudermilk's manically tapping heels, sheathed in hunter-green Ralph Lauren Polo socks. In addition to damage to his immune system and spinal alignment, Beans has suffered an in-depth intro to the private fantasia that is the mind of Loudermilk, his bizarre machinations plus inordinately well-developed self-regard. This exposure is likely to be permanently traumatizing in a way Beans had previously believed only the mishandling of infants during breastfeeding could be.

Loudermilk is seated, hunched over what appears to be the discarded top of a water-warped Ping-Pong table, which is awkwardly supported by a stool and a cardboard box balanced on a plastic crate—though, Beans notes, there's a perfectly serviceable card table shoved off to the side of the room. For hours now, Loudermilk has been reliving, via recorded audio, the secret history of his own inhumanity. Anton Beans now knows well what it sounds like not just to be made love to by Loudermilk but to be surveilled by him, and it's starting to be difficult, most distressing of all, not to take Loudermilk just the littlest bit seriously, particularly given the fact that among the horde of anonymous co-eds, Beans thinks he can make out the whimpers and obscene requests of one or two female poets whose unthreatening competence in sestina and pantoum composition had previously led him to consider them as potential reviewers for his next book. There's been some maniacal laughter from the desk, too, some cries of, "Stellar!" and "Fuck, yes!" which presumably indicate moments at which Loudermilk has astonished himself with his own intellectual prowess, or maybe the activities of his own dick, it's so tragically challenging to tell the two apart. Beans isn't, by the way, sure what Loudermilk is getting up to here, but the athletic lout does actually appear to be writing, drafting something Beans is afraid may well be a Loudermilkian take on the Great American Novel, which Beans supposes is probably just what the Great American Novel is supposed to be, anyhow.

Now Loudermilk mutters, "'A golden statue with long, swift arms; cheeks like beaten metal, gleaming and enticing, since expensive. Her braless tits were plums.'" He pauses. "No, fuck me. 'Her sweet, tart tang was . . . plum'? Fuck."

Beans begins dry heaving.

Loudermilk shakes his head. He is crossing some things out, chuckling and sighing. He replays a recent visit to Marta Hillary's office hours.

"You may sit." Marta is alert, formal.

There's the sound of a zipper, movement of stuffs. The recorder is relocated.

"So," Marta says. "'Aboulomania'?" She laughs dryly, as if she had months ago privately predicted that Loudermilk would write this very poem. Beans reflects, not without a snap of rage, that she does not seem entirely displeased—though whether Marta is in larger part satisfied with her own prognostication or with Loudermilk is by no means certain. She has not, after all, secured her current status through self-abnegation. "Otherwise known as pathological indecisiveness. A disorder in which the patient is beset with anxiety and mental anguish, overwhelmed by the possibility that all decisions lead to uncertain ends. See also, paralysis by analysis. A terrible thing, to be sure, but also, one must imagine, fairly common, given the diversity of choice in the postindustrial world." Marta pauses. "I thought the conversation in class was fine. It was a bit limited but essentially fine. I wanted to offer a few mechanical remarks."

Something happens.

"Oh," Marta continues, none too impressed by whatever the something is, "I'll take that as a sign of your approval." She sighs. Possibly she's stretching. Her jewelry makes a sound. "Obviously, there is much to recommend this poem.

It shows a staggering mastery of contemporary idiomatic speech and the many styles of lie in which we indulge, perhaps through a strange sort of necessity, to 'get by,' as it were, in the present-day U.S. Formally, if not thematically, it cites 'The Waste Land,' I suppose, the obsessive use of quotation. In a way there's something a bit cynical about this—but you do take it somewhere else. I feel—exhaustion. Maybe a kind of dissociation? Maybe I prefer to think of the whole thing as a sort of golden bough, the poem as an offering for my entry into hell? Some late republican context for you! In any case, I love the language, the sick mania. The images! The thing about 'sofas,' yes, the banality but also the very *scale* of crimes of contemporary culture. Government as endlessly prognosticating talking head. Who are 'they'? Who is 'he'? Who is 'I'? It's a great treatment of the notion of propaganda and the mystification of agency that is so necessary to it. Now—" Marta coughs once, sharply, and then, with far too much warmth for Beans's comfort, sighs again. "I *do* think there are a few points at which the lines sort of lag. For example, when we come to 'Operational flexibility and social bravado,' I think there's a weak sort of vagueness and you aren't doing yourself any favors. But you cut those two phrases and bring up 'The / Old ways.' You'll have to change 'had' to 'that,' 'taught cadets to be bullies, and I fought the team's traditional kelly green,' etc., but you get to keep the original sense. It's even clearer, tauter, firmer."

There's some silence.

Marta asks, "Don't you agree?"

Loudermilk comes in: "I just wonder if what I'm writing is something that you or, uh, like, *people* can understand. Like, generally? I mean, this is all so good to know, not to mention, *deep*."

Marta does not take the bait. "Generally?"

"I mean, uh, the, uh, creative side of this, you know? Like, are people going to actually *care* about my poem? I mean, outside of this place. Which of course is so wonderful."

"'Are people going to actually *care*?'" Marta repeats. "People are—" she begins, but does not to know how to complete her sentence. "You are writing at a very high level, Troy," she says.

"*Loudermilk*," Loudermilk corrects her.

"I prefer Troy, if you don't mind? It seems fitting somehow, for our age. Anyway, you can't write for every reader. That's not the point. You can only write for your *best* reader."

"Who's that?"

"A vital question."

"So, like, do you think you can help me find out?"

"I'm already doing that for you, Troy."

"Oh, certainly!" Loudermilk is quick to agree.

But Marta does not feel the same way Loudermilk feels about whatever it is they are currently supposed to be unpacking. "That is the point—of what, if anything at all, I am attempting to get across to you. Writing cannot be taught, and here is the reason why: You write, not to address the world as it is, but to *create* the world, all over again. Truly great writing does that. Truly great writing is not about the expectations or needs of contemporary readers. It's not even really addressed to its own time. It shouldn't be! It doesn't need to be. This is the mistake so many of your classmates make, and I wonder if it's not somehow encoded into the DNA of the workshop setting. Students come to this place expecting this, they think I can hold their hands, but this is not how things *are*. We do not write for one another—as or however much we may think that we are doing so. We're not here to address one another. We're here to confront something *about* humanity, to confront the fact that, as humans, we are fated to make things, and we are, meanwhile, the subjects of history. We each have two hands and this is, quite simply, what culture is! It's where all the tragedies come from, but it's also the source of great joy and mystery. I expect my students to be able to see past whoever's sitting across the seminar table in front of them on a given day. We have to imagine that writing is an act of transhistorical communication, not a mere performance, and that's what I most want you to understand! I need you for poetry, Troy. That's why I summoned you here."

"You mean today?"

"I mean today but also long before. I know you felt my call. It awakened something in you."

"I love it when you ladies take initiative."

But Marta keeps talking, saying something about measures of feeling, about excavating them, how the poet has to get a sense for something that she calls "mahss," which she says is a German word, which she says does not mean the same thing as "mass" in English; that when making word selections, the poet has to weigh the "thingliness" of the word, the word's "itness," whatever this is, which is where Loudermilk switches off the MP3 recorder.

Loudermilk gets up from his "desk" and strides around. He goes back to the desk.

He begins to write something.

Beans is, meanwhile, still processing Marta's various

pronouncements. An irrational thought keeps presenting itself: that it has been *she* all along who has been writing Loudermilk's poems, in some not-insignificant sense—that she and she alone has willed all this into being, that Loudermilk, and the minion, and even Beans himself are mere sock puppets for some dialogic impulse the great Marta Hillary is attempting to work out.

"Your boy Loudermilk has a sick, *sick* Land Cruiser," Loudermilk intones, interrupting Beans's despair. Loudermilk scribbles on. "*THE JERKSHOP: A Novel*," he whispers reverently.

But moving on from this anointed idiot: Beans is still here and sort of shakes himself awake and another excellent question is—not entirely a non sequitur, this—how did Anton Beans end up in this predicament? For Anton Beans has been working hard. Setting aside for the moment the matter of whether the institution truly deserves his heroism, Beans must ensure the Seminars are defended, that the program won't become a breeding ground for unserious dabblers like yonder Loudermilk, who clearly want to dilute American literary art to so viscid and anodyne a consistency that it may at last be profitably branded, bottled, and purveyed via America's proliferating upmarket health-food emporia, if not the soda machines at Panera Bread. Beans is, or so he believes, the only individual conscious enough to recognize the necessity of standing in the way of this eventuality, and it is for this reason that he has elected to take on the far-from-undemanding task of unmasking devious and captivating Loudermilk. And to accomplish this much-needed reveal, Beans must discover the diminutive minion.

The minion is not in the place where the minion used to

be, which is to say, within the confines of this surely condemnable shed where both Beans and lothario Loudermilk now find themselves, though of course mythomaniac Loudermilk can have no suspicion of the presence of a sleuthing Beans. Beans was surprised mid-snoop by the precipitous return of his devious colleague. The place isn't really safe enough to have multiple exits. Beans had hoped—foolishly, he now sees—that by venturing into Loudermilk's man lair he'd be able to find some trace indicating where it is Loudermilk has sequestered his little friend, who is clearly the true author within their arrangement. Loudermilk's own bizarre, noisy attempts to "write" have convinced Beans that Loudermilk is, very definitely, not the poet. And not only this: he is impure. He's writing, the philistine!, *prose*. Though of course Beans hasn't found any material proof of the former presence of the minion. There have been no clues, no letters with forwarding addresses, no farewell notes, no forgotten belongings, nothing that appears to have touched the little guy. It's tabula rasa. Loudermilk, for all his campy bro displays, is no fool. His cleverness may mostly be unconscious but it is, sadly, very, very real. This won't be an easy case.

Beans is about to sigh, but instead of sighing he catches his breath. Loudermilk's heels have stopped tapping. The laughing and the whispers and the scratching of the pen have ceased. Beans hears what Loudermilk hears, which is a rapping, as of someone gently tapping, tapping at the shack's front door.

"Harumph!" says Loudermilk, in an anachronistic sonic frown. He shoves back his chair, pads off.

Beans recognizes that this is his chance. Could he crawl

out a window? Beans reflects gloomily that if he departs now he will do so without the information he has come to this cramped den of ambiguous iniquity to obtain. Also, he will exit with an antique prophylactic cemented to his head by what is surely the nonmetaphorical cement of Loudermilk's spermatozoa. It will be, to say the least, demoralizing. Beans may never again have the emotional wherewithal to probe Loudermilk's treachery. Loudermilk may—if Beans leaves him to his project now—get away with it.

This cannot be permitted. Certainly not at Marta's school.

Anton Beans mentally reassumes the position.

He hears another voice. It isn't, all too predictably for what seems to be Beans's inordinately poor luck regarding all things Loudermilk, the minion. It's a female. At first Beans hears tone rather than discrete words. It seems like she's building up to something? They draw nigh to the door of Loudermilk's boudoir/writing atelier.

A girl says, "It's very you."

"That's not so unusual. Now what was it you wanted?"

"Oh my god, Loudermilk, testy much? Let's just take a moment to celebrate the fact that we're here, together and alone? I notice, by the way, that you have a bed."

"No."

Beans initiates a secular prayer. It seems that this is the voice of Marta and Don's teenage daughter. Beans either has primary information or is about to learn more about this young woman than he has ever wanted to know. Perhaps both. Also, his right side is entirely numb.

"Loudermilk, you're very shy today."

"I am not *shy*."

"No offense, but given our track record, you do seem pretty shy."

"This is a house I happen to *share*, Lizzie."

"Since when is sharing a thing you do? Also, what happened to Harry?"

"He'll be right back."

"I totally believe you."

"OK, great, well, I'm glad we got that settled. Let me know how your art project goes. Or better yet, don't."

"Loudermilk, I know you're not really this mean. I came over because I want to tell you something. Don't you want to hear what it is?"

"No."

"No? It's really important. I have this idea, and I was thinking, like, maybe you want in?"

"Hmm, let me check. Nope!"

"You haven't even heard what it is!"

"Do I need to?"

"Yes, because it's totally amazing and I promise you will be sorry if you miss out."

"Thanks for letting me know!"

"Loudermilk, I'm serious. Like, because"—this girl Lizzie is whispering now—"you're a great artist and I for one happen to really know this. I *know.* I'm sorry but I know about you and Harry. I've been around a lot of poets, I mean, *really* a lot, and I know what you guys are doing. I mean, unlike a lot of people I've *talked* to Harry. I *know* who he is. I know who you are! And I don't care! Honestly! You're an artist, too! A great artist. Like I'm an artist, a great artist, I hope, and I thought we—"

"I don't know what you're talking about." Loudermilk is

impassive. "You and I are not going to collaborate on your latest papier-mâché princess crown. You saw this house, where I do my important writing, and now—"

"But you don't *do* any writing, Loudermilk."

Beans is not able to help himself. He's lost track of his body and even where he is, in the sponge cake of this saga. And, quite simply, he farts.

It might be audible.

"*What* was that?" Loudermilk demands.

Beans clenches up.

"Ew," says Lizzie Hillary. "You farted, Loudermilk. And, FYI, *you* didn't write those poems."

Beans silently exalts the random benevolence of the universe.

"I heard that, too, and yes, yes, I did."

"No, no, you didn't, Loudie-Lou. Harry's the one who writes those poems. I know that. Listen, anyways, it really doesn't matter to me who does what. It's like my mom always says: 'It doesn't matter *who's* writing the poems. It's that they get written.' And, I think, I mean, you're an artist."

"I'm a poet, Lizzie. I'm a very good poet. I'm about to change the entire game."

"Stop it! This is so dumb, Loudermilk. I mean, maybe you'll change the game, but don't forget the fact that I *get* you. I totally get all of this. We're like peas in a pod, you'll see."

"That's nice, but no one's going to see anything, because you're leaving right now. Actually, both of us are leaving. A rotten egg just shat itself."

"Actually, I'm not."

"Yes, yes, you are."

"No, no, I'm not. Loudermilk, don't you get it? You made me do this. You're the artist, like, the artist *and* the muse! You make me *do* things. That's what artists do. I can't stop now. I've never been this inspired. I'm so totally, I don't even know, I mean, everything you *do* is amazing. Who even cares about poetry? Loudermilk, I'm *in love* with you."

"YOU'RE NOT IN LOVE WITH ME!" Loudermilk screams.

The front door bangs.

Then it bangs again, softly.

Which leaves Anton Beans alone.

Thirty-Eight

In Advance of the Broken Arm

Never let it be said that Anton Beans is not persistent. What Beans realizes next is not that he needs to get out of the house, because this is something that he already knows. He needs to get out, and also he grasps, with the same monomaniacal swiftness native to the well-tuned Beansian brain, that Loudermilk has not departed with the aim of leading his lady friend in an elaborate high-impact LARP. No, though indeed Loudermilk may live his life as if each new day dawns upon an ever more outlandish and arbitrary improv scenario, Loudermilk is not under any illusion that his life is either a game or a show—or, for that matter, a realist novel. Loudermilk does what he does because he has to, and not because he believes, at base, that any of this is fun.

Beans, currently dissimulating himself behind a set of mildew-infested laurel bushes, is about to benefit. And the reason Beans is about to benefit is that Loudermilk, whom he can perceive striding off into the near distance on long, khaki-encased legs, has a very serious bee in his bonnet and the name of this bee has got to be Harry, the minion, the little friend. Beans pops back out from behind one particularly spotty shrub and sprints up the block, taking cover again on the south side of a mailbox. His heart pounds and his stomach sloshes. Loudermilk, and Beans, are fast approaching the heart of the Grecian quarter.

Loudermilk apparently finds a certain solid-looking sorority to his liking. He stops at the edge of its lawn, pivots. Beans creeps closer. Beans gets behind a white Focus. He observes, across the Focus's back seat, Loudermilk's steely progress. Loudermilk is, from what Beans can discern, the opposite of delighted.

Though, to be fair, Beans reflects, it is difficult to say just what it is that the minion has done wrong. Is it that the minion has committed unspeakable carnal acts with somebody living on the inside of this sex-segregated mansion? Given the minion's previously observed proclivities, not to mention the kid's obviously crippling anxiety disorder, that seems unlikely. Beans's eyes narrow. Loudermilk is going around the back of the building. Beans skips out from behind the budget vehicle, skitters across the lawn, throws himself behind the tumescent trunk of a convenient oak.

Beans observes from beside this helpful quercus as something relatively, though not entirely, unexpected occurs. Loudermilk, with the assistance of a rusty fire escape that whinnies with his weight as if alive, is scaling the rear of the sorority. Beans curses himself for having neglected to provision himself with a camera on this particular fact-finding mission. Surely this act on Loudermilk's part is the epitome of what is forbidden in this intransigent social sphere!

Anton Beans recognizes that it will not be possible to imitate Loudermilk's choice of route without running an inordinately high risk of being observed, as well as of having the fire escape collapse under the weight of Beans's hypermasculine, if pleasingly rounded, physique. Loudermilk continues to ascend. Anton Beans grits his teeth. He recalls third-grade gym class, when he had made a name for himself as a wall-climber to be reckoned with, an inspired negotiator of ceiling ropes and ramparts. Though this was a long time ago, and though the Beansian corpus has met with a certain amount of expansion over the intervening years, Beans believes that the ability to convey your body weight vertically by means of your own arms and legs has to be enough like riding a bicycle that, once learned, it's something you never forget.

Thirty-Nine

Their Penultimate Encounter

Harry is having better days these days than he has in a long time. It may have something to do with the solitude. Or maybe it has something to do with the contrast between the new solitude and what he can recall now of the minor hell that was the experience of living constantly in Loudermilk's shadow.

Loudermilk's shadow was long and reeked of stale semen.

Which is why Harry's metaphorical soul descends drearily into the literal soles of his Converse when Loudermilk's face abruptly appears in his window this unseasonably warm March afternoon, interrupting Harry's view of the two pines.

Harry's first instinct is to ignore his best friend/fiend, but given that they are several stories up in the air and that Loudermilk is furiously tapping on the none-too-stable window five inches from the end of Harry's nose, Harry is obliged to respond. He raises the pane and Loudermilk clambers in.

Loudermilk wastes no time. "I'm none too pleased, Harrison," he says.

"Hello to you, too."

"Whatever." Loudermilk has no time for pleasantries. Then, "You've never actually been in a relationship so I won't dazzle you with details but something very unusual has taken place and you and I, Harrison, we need to chat about it."

Harry is not sure what to say. The afternoon had seemed to be going so well. Now it is Loudermilk's property.

"I hope you're not sighing at me!"

Harry stares hard at the blue industrial carpeting of his attic floor.

"I came here to let your numb ass know that we are having a problem. And that problem has to do with *your* writing, Harry. Because I'm starting to get the feeling that people are beginning to believe that it doesn't *come* from me and that, as you know, is not really going to fly around here, here in the land of the author-as-hero. We are getting into some serious T-minus-one dookie."

Harry shifts his eyeballs a few inches to the right. There's an interesting snag in the carpet. The window is open and unseasonable birdsong wafts in along a gentle, earth-scented chill.

Loudermilk presses his lips together. "And it's these *females*," Loudermilk says. "That's where all this weakness is coming from. Marta thinks she controls me, and meanwhile turns out her daughter won't leave me alone, even though I've told that crazy little dick-straddler a million times desperate estrus is only hot for so long. It's like it makes that head case *happy* to see somebody playing the game like this! But not Marta. This delusional tease isn't finding me convenient enough for the next dynasty of her poetry popedom. She needs someone she can 'mold' or whatever, like the world's most genius zombie. And these poems are getting *too* good—"

Harry raises his hand. "I'm confused. Does this lady not lap milk out of saucers or something?"

"What?"

Harry realizes his mistake. He recalibrates meekly. "I just thought this was the plan."

"No! This was not the plan. And, P.S., you, Harrison, do not even know what the plan is! The plan was for us to live our simple lives and wet our simple dicks and get our simple cash and now look at what's happening!"

Harry shrugs.

"Whatever, fucknuts, I've been pretty successful in this life thus far. I know a problem when I see one and I'm saying maybe you better beware!"

Harry feels like he might really like to go lie down. He feels dizzy. His face is hermetically sealed.

"This is all your fucking fault!" Loudermilk pauses. Blood is in his face. "You aren't supposed to let this happen! People are starting to *see* me."

Harry wants to say something about how of course people are seeing Loudermilk, because Loudermilk has a corporeal form and he is walking around on the surface of planet Earth, but he realizes that this is not what Loudermilk means. And he also remembers something he read a long time ago about how the devil is the emperor of the air, but he isn't sure what that has to do with anything.

Loudermilk is currently not doing much more than breathing, and even this seems like a challenge. He hisses, "I *need* you to do better."

Harry is about to nod, but at this moment there is an astonishing cracking sound like a gunshot, then a rustling and a long wail and a crashing and a thud.

Loudermilk and Harry lean out of the window.

On the lawn below someone dressed as an abstract expressionist painter is gingerly picking himself up off a tree limb it appears he has been riding astride as if the limb were a tame orca and their current tatty environs were instead the tatty environs known as SeaWorld. The expressionist is cradling one arm and talking to himself as he staggers away.

Loudermilk pulls his head violently back in and yanks Harry back, too.

"You catch that?" Loudermilk barks. "Even that precious ball of bird shits is onto us."

"At least he doesn't have a vagina."

"What?"

Harry smiles.

"Laugh it up, Harrison! What you don't seem to realize is that we are on very, *very* thin ice. Everything could fall apart. We could be left with nothing, I'm telling you. We could be totally fucked. They're *watching* now," Loudermilk pronounces in a voice starched with ancient paranoia.

Harry can't understand why he's as calm as he indubitably is. Maybe it has something to do with how he, unlike Loudermilk, doesn't have anything to lose.

Forty

Détente

It's now been a little while since Harry has seen Loudermilk. Loudermilk did not show up for his regular poetry pickup, and since that day, which was approximately three days ago—although Harry barely keeps track of the day of the week, much less the date—there's been nothing, not a crudely misspelled note slipped under his door by one of his housemates/employers, nary an email nor a distant sighting. The line has gone dead. Not to mention that Harry now has a couple of poems standing by.

Today, which is probably a Friday, which Harry could find out for sure if he went outside and looked at a newspaper, already feels pretty long. The hours are growing and it is nearly noon. A calm light is making an appearance in the backyard and in the tops of the twin pines. Harry is deliberating about maybe paying a visit to the shack. He's trying to imagine the likely conversation:

Harry: [greets Loudermilk]

Loudermilk: [unlatching multiple bimbos from his virile

person, wiping whipped cream and cherry lube from face and chest] The fuck you want, dude?

Harry: [incoherent mumbling regarding poems]

Loudermilk: Excuse me?

Harry: [further incoherent mumbling]

Loudermilk: Dude, did I not tell you not to interrupt me in the middle of my existence that is so infinitely better than yours? It irritates me when you appear here, reminding me of the fact that I'm somewhat dependent on you for my lifestyle.

Harry: [silence]

Loudermilk: I take it I did not make myself clear. Kindly leave?

Harry: [something about how he does not know where else to go]

Loudermilk: [suddenly able to understand what Harry says] But, Harrison, is that *my* problem, that you don't know where else to go? I can't be responsible for everything that's wrong with you. I'm not, you know, *you*. Not in reality. I've been helping, I've been over here helping and being an altruist, you know, but let's not take things too far. There comes a time when even the closest friendships have to end, and I know I've been pretty damn patient with you, pretty *damn* giving, if I do say so myself. So this is hurting me more than it hurts you. I'm just going to come right out here and say it: It's over between us. I don't need your poems anymore.

This imaginary conversation stands forth in Harry's mind. It's prominent and it gleams. It's very clear and hard for Harry to avoid. It's possibly constructed from finely etched crystal. It emits a high-pitched noise.

Thus there is no point in going over and talking to Loudermilk because Loudermilk is just going to formalize whatever break Harry believes has already taken place at some misty, symbolic level. Loudermilk will repay Harry's curiosity by making something currently uncertain into something very determined and very, very real.

Harry is not sure what you're supposed to do if you end up in a relationship with someone who may at once be a sociopath and/or pathological liar, plus situational narcissist, and/or suffering from a personality disorder, and then you also feel like they are the only person in the world who's ever understood you. Harry had enough problems to begin with, and now he has to wonder why he chose to exacerbate things. Not that he felt he had a choice at the time. On the one hand, now he's basically trapped in a sorority in the Midwest in a town where almost no one knows of his existence; on the other, at least he feels calm enough to actually contemplate what the hell is going on. Are there any healthy people in this world? And, if Harry were to find them, would they accept him? Since Harry, if benign, yet has a certain amount of difficulty with the idea that he is not pretty sick himself.

Harry is about to get up and fix some instant coffee when there is a small noise. It's a brief clacking sound, and it sounds like "*Pack!*" It's at the edge of his window. It happens again: "*Pack, pack, pack!*" in quick succession. It takes Harry a second to realize that someone in the backyard is bombarding his retreat with bottle caps from the sorority's lawn.

Harry looks down at the page in front of him. He has been toying with a couple of abstract remarks that may or may not become lines in his next poem:

You might need handles—just handles of a different sort

Some of his military credibility will rub off

He likes the line about handles. It's definitely weird; it offers itself up strangely, with a single concrete term. It's all Harry can do to sever his attention from the page to heed the missiles. The cap-thrower might, Harry reminds himself, be Loudermilk, in which case, he should go to the trouble of poking his head out, perhaps ask what in the hell is going on.

The caps continue.

Harry leans awkwardly over the counter to open the window.

A cap sails into the room and lands on the floor behind Harry.

Harry waits a moment, puts his head out.

Standing in the yard is someone who is, very definitely, not Loudermilk. The person has made a collection of bottle caps in the front of his shirt, employing the garment as a cap hammock. It's no small feat, given that the person is also carrying a sheaf of papers, while additionally having a broken arm.

Harry supposes that he shouldn't be surprised at the return of Anton Beans. And, when he reflects on it, what actually surprises him isn't Beans's presence, but rather his own reaction to it. Harry finds himself completely unperturbed.

Beans's face, indistinct since distant, appears mild. The mouth is turned down. He isn't saying anything. He just stares up at Harry's window. And then, with the hand of the unbroken arm, Beans points at the papers tucked between cast and sling. Beans advances, still indicating papers, plus broken arm.

Now Beans beckons. Harry understands that he is meant to come downstairs. As if to confirm the comprehension slowly dawning on Harry, Beans, magically, nods. Beans is solemn, maybe calm. Maybe this is OK.

Harry removes himself from his room and begins making his way down the back staircase, the building's sole acknowledgment of fire code. He thinks about how, if he goes slowly enough, Beans may just leave on his own. Harry numbly exits onto thawing sod.

Beans is still there and seems to prefer to maintain a distance. Perhaps it has something to do with his injury. "Greetings," Beans says.

Harry feels like an astronaut who has just clicked open his polycarbonate visor to discover that it is possible to breathe the atmosphere of an unknown planet.

"Thank you for coming down from your, um, *hermitage*." Beans frowns more deeply. "I understand that that is not a simple matter for a person like—" Beans pauses. "Like *yourself*," he concludes. "However, I have something that may make your psychosomatic risk-taking worth your while."

Beans is wearing gray today. He has on gray pants and a gray shirt and, somehow, what appears to be a gray jean jacket. His sneakers and socks are also gray. The ensemble gives him a somewhat gentle, avuncular look, lessening the severity produced by the bushy chinstrap.

It must be that Harry has to acknowledge or encourage Beans, but Harry cannot, for the life of him, fathom how. Harry remains planted where he is, as meanwhile Beans approaches, stiffly bearing his broken arm. Beans removes the papers from their secure spot, passes them, with a flourish, to Harry.

It is a new packet.

"I thought," Beans is saying, "that this might interest you."

Harry pages through. It's all almost as usual. There's the name of the spring workshop on the cover, and the packet has the customary heft. There are a few sonnets and a few experimental things written on typewriters that sprawl across the page. There isn't anything by him in here. He can somehow sense this, just by touching the pages.

Perhaps concerned that Harry is not picking up on his intended message, Beans, in his capacity as world-altering Hermes, snatches the pages back.

Part of Harry's mind, the part that is not struggling to work through the non-presence of a poem attributed to T. A. Loudermilk among the verses of the stapled Xerox, reflects that this is becoming quite the interesting pantomime.

"Look at this," Beans is saying, holding the packet open against his cast. "*This,*" Beans, hissing, repeats. Beans flicks the page, producing a sound.

It's a short poem, attributed to someone named "Troy Loudermilk." It reads:

The CNN Blues (Persona Poem)

Watching CNN in the bar gets me down.
You realize how stagnant humanity is.
Extraterrestrial radio signals are wound
On the same spool as Oscar dress choices.

Watching CNN in the bar just gets me down.
It makes me wish for a dictator.
Citizens are supposed to act as the neurons
In a massive cognitive web of terror.

Watching CNN in the bar truly gets me down.
Democracy now does seem so baseless.
I'm a stupid fear-based monkey man
And celebrities turn me genocidistic.

We're chitchatting ourselves into oblivion.
Watching CNN in the bar gets me down.

Forty-One

Worlds

Lizzie is the tiniest bit nostalgic. The mood usually comes on when she ponders the fact that in a matter of years—*one* year, to be precise—she will be exiting this absurd Podunk, never to return. Often the feeling arrives in late afternoon, when she is wandering her parents' sizable house. No one else is home; it's just Lizzie, plus whatever ghosts of her parents' codependent misery happen to be available.

Lizzie is in Marta's closet. This isn't the closet in the master bedroom. Rather, it's the closet in Marta's study, where Marta stores her version of the Seminars' institutional memory, along with the institutional memory of her marriage. Lizzie is, if not exactly equivalent to the poems written by Marta's students, then pretty much analogous. Which is why, Lizzie believes, Marta stacks and sorts and stows all the packets from her workshops next to her library of family photo albums, filled with images of various Lizzies. It's all of a piece, as far as Marta is concerned, no difference between the job and the home, the people she teaches and someone she might have given birth to, the stress of marriage, and striving after academic success. Marta has it all, and here is the proof.

Lizzie's hunting for evidence of her own juvenilia, the time in the first grade she composed a poem for a school-wide writing contest and—as a semi-illiterate and thus extreme underdog—won. The poem rhymes and it somehow means something to Lizzie. It indicates Lizzie's sophistication, even previous to schooling, previous to actual human culture, and proves that Lizzie's life will be confined neither to Crete nor to the vicissitudes of her parents' alliance. In photos, a diminutive Lizzie accepts a bouquet. She is a very young artist.

Lizzie wonders if maybe this event could become the basis of a college application essay. It could be a preview of her current efforts.

Lizzie drags a side chair into the closet. She tests the chair's stability, steps up. It brings her to eye level with the shelf supporting packets plus photo albums, side by side. Lizzie peruses the row of photo albums, their irregular shapes and spines. She decides to push these volumes aside for some reason, peering into the remote closet dark. She notes that an errant packet has been placed, not along with the nominally organized packet archive, but behind the albums. And this rogue packet seems to have been conveyed to its current resting place in haste, if not anger. Lizzie takes hold of it, descends. She drops down into her mother's wicker desk chair to read.

This packet isn't a packet from Marta's class, and it isn't even a poetry packet. It's a packet from a fiction workshop taught this semester by a visiting instructor. The visiting instructor is youngish—though, when Lizzie pauses to think about it, not really so, *so* young. The visitor has an air of arrested development, favors bright dresses. Her yellow hair is cut into a bob.

Internally, Lizzie sneers. There is a parrot on the cover of the visitor's first novel, a meandering parable regarding an adorable postmodern stowaway. It's a book for nerds. Lizzie has been forced to attend related events. Publicly, at least, the Hillarys move *en famille*.

Lizzie attempts, with middling success, to force the aberrant rage she feels into her stomach.

She is looking at the story. The story is titled "The Origin of the World." It's by someone named Clare Elwil. Because Marta, strictly speaking, does not pay much attention to what occurs on the fiction side of things, Lizzie decides she will read it. Marta has gone so far as to circle the story's title, penciling in a cryptic note:

> The hinge of writing allows the author to connect her two unknowns. We see in both worlds.

Forty-Two

Recognition

Workshop is over, and Clare is alone in her room. She experiences what has transpired as a shifting pool of ease, a gentle affective estuary. The room has few hard edges. Even austerity is a pleasure. Downtown, a siren wails.

They read her story. The class did. She does not want to characterize this event, but it has not gone poorly. It was, at any rate, an event. Things are different.

Clare thinks about the game she has played with herself. She has told herself that she is not the one writing. She has given herself permission not to write. She might be anyone; who cares who is doing the writing. And yet, they praised her—and they have praised her unique style, her surprising lack of compromise.

The visiting instructor nodded and said that risks are good. Risks are, the visitor maintained, the "salt of life." She looked at Clare. "Our shared human tragedy is, historically, that in order to have power, you must exercise power. I can see how this story understands that."

Clare's colleagues, meanwhile, had discovered a new

substance. They blew on it and sniffed. They examined its color. They applied it tentatively to their lips, providing detailed commentary.

Later, in the hall, Clare stood near the sign-up sheets for meetings with agents; these were an offering to the fiction students, who were meant to begin peddling their wares by proxy. Clare had something now. And she entered her name in small caps, trying to make it look as if it had been printed by machine.

At the center of one particularly crowded schedule pertaining to Alex Levendorff, who was presumably able to make his or her clients into instant thousandaires, Clare noted the name LOUDERMILK slashed across two time slots and enclosed in a heavily inked-in rectangle. Clare had never heard of a poet having an agent, but then again Loudermilk seems entirely unlike other poets. That long poem of his from earlier in the semester had made the rounds even with the fiction students, and Clare still can't get the part about "lots and lots of sofas" out of her head. Sofas across America, Clare thinks.

But Clare does not want to think. If she thinks too concertedly about Loudermilk's enviable situation—his two perfect bodies, the one literary, the other flesh and blood—the bubble generated by her own small success may burst, the image fade. She reminds herself that she does, more than in the past, seem to have a future today.

Instead of thinking, Clare goes over to the narrow fridge. Inside is a single food item, an enormous plastic vat of pickled peppers she purchased across the train tracks at the Aldi. They have a strange, dull, dusty taste and she has stopped eating them but does not know how to dispose of a bulk amount of yellow brine. But perhaps the pickles taste fine.

Clare tastes the pickles.

They do not taste fine.

Clare is going out tonight.

It is something the Seminars calls its "prom."

Forty-Three

Persistence

Lizzie has never been to the Seminars prom. She's underage, but it's more than this: Her *dad* is usually in attendance. It's kind of his thing. Therefore, it's, like, incest taboo, much? Not to mention that Marta has historically seemed to sanction her father's grossness on this particular evening.

Lizzie gags a little. Though no one is watching her, she pretends to vomit delicately into her own mouth.

What is freaky, though, is that tonight of all nights, night of PROM '04 CONSPICUOUS, surely destined to be one unshy soiree, Lizzie has just moments ago observed her father crawl from the dinner table with a tumbler of whiskey to ensconce himself in his leathery man cave with the supposedly subversive pabulum of Comedy Central. Until his enrollment numbers improve, he's in the doghouse, big-time. Her mom is pointedly addressing herself to dishes.

Lizzie takes one brief look at this scenario and hops upstairs. She's rapidly in her room and considers her television along with her computer. Maybe one of these devices can save her from herself! But the prospect of re-watching *Clueless* or messaging with Des Moines skaters only further convinces her of the need to execute her cherished plan. There's just this undeniable matter of a certain boy whose name rhymes with "powder ilk," or "chowder silk," and kind of also with "redder elk," along with other variants? (Lizzie is not the child of two poets for nothing.) He really needs to know what she's all about. *O Loudermilk, who are currently probably already slammed and grinding in public*, Lizzie silently prays, *hear my call!*

Lizzie whirls to her closet. She burrows through to locate a garment that was her size at the turning of the millennium and that has now, given changes wrought by developmental hormones, become rather more bandage-like. It is, Lizzie reflects, tugging it down over her boobs and butt, perfect. Lizzie adds a platinum-blond bob-shaped wig and sunglasses. Yes, she reflects, this all makes her look old. She is ready, she thinks, to execute her plan. Tonight she will show everyone who is really an artist, not to mention what a real artist is. Good thing Lizzie cares enough to snoop. Without this propensity she would have zero material, plus it is past being time to let inspiration strike. And, because Lizzie is super aggravated as far as her mother is concerned on this particular evening, she takes her shoes in hand and jumps out the second-story window, a practice her mother has for years been on her case about.

Forty-Four

And Then

Anton Beans is achieving something rare: he's attending a party with enthusiasm. He has on bleached-out denim, a color more festive, to his mind, than cold, cool white or onyx. He wears black sneakers, having decided, uncharacteristically, not to match his footgear to the rest of the ensemble. He has combed and scented his beard.

Anton Beans moves without haste. He is savoring this moment. Around him, members of his Seminars cohort pogo and wiggle. They're slick with perspiration. Mascara is migrating and dark disks of sweat have begun to emerge. The DJ throws on anti-folk party anthem "Blister in the Sun" by the Violent Femmes, and the floor loses its collective shit. Anton Beans nods.

At last Beans sees. There amid the lashing, thrusting bodies is the golden head of Loudermilk. Loudermilk is frowning with eyes shut, engrossed in absorbing the pelvic attention lavished on him by two female fiction first-years, who have made of their Adonis a human sandwich meat. It is distressingly typical, but Beans wills himself not to focus on this aspect of the situation. It's important to keep his mind on political task, not to be distracted by taste. What amazes Beans is how negligible the effect of Loudermilk's public humiliation in workshop has been. Nobody seems to care that everyone's idol has been brought low. Marta said something shockingly vapid about how we all have "our days," and no one else appears to be reflecting on what has happened—*at all*. And this is why Beans must take action.

He has made inroads with the minion. Harry, he believes this person's name is. So far, so good, but nothing will be settled as far as Beans is concerned without a full reveal—

Forty-Five

Mingling

Clare has arrived at "prom" and things already look fairly debauched, with a strong chance of "meat stink plus portable bidets" before midnight.

Clare squeezes through the vestibule, which is crowded with Seminars people deliberating about how best to walk outside to have a smoke, an undertaking rendered somewhat more complex by quantities of Everclear plus Kool-Aid dwelling redly in translucent cups. People are sloppy, and in her radical sobriety Clare is anxious.

A Chicagolander named Zach—famed for his father's unusual career as first a stand-up comedian, then state senator, a trajectory explored to withering ends in Zach's own short fiction—seizes Clare's shoulder. His eyes have this diagonal softness. He wants to take this opportunity, i.e., intoxication, to convey to Clare his newfound respect for her writing. "The Origin of the World" was really something and he's sorry not to have acknowledged her earlier. She should feel free to share her work with him outside of class.

Clare uses her eyes to convey that she so very much gets it. In spite of herself, she's flattered.

Zach manifests relief. He is about to say something about his difficult childhood but is abruptly pulled outside by two bigger men Clare recognizes as second-year poets. She hears the phrase "local talent."

Clare moves on.

She will bear witness to whatever the center of this thing is. This will be close enough to having had a "good time" to justify the trip.

She goes down a hallway that is half rotting wood and half moldering paper printed with a design of interlocking spools of thread. Music increases in volume.

Clare enters the room with dancing. It is a confusing chamber—she exits quickly.

She wants a bathroom. On the second floor of this alarmingly ornamental sorority, she discovers one. She finds herself looking down at a tarnished and possibly mold-dressed faucet knob. It is in the shape of a pair of bull's horns.

Clare examines her reflection in the chipped mirror. She looks thin, meeker than usual. She pinches her cheeks. She wonders, briefly, if Zach had been intimating that he might be willing to date her. She considers what that might be like, fondue parties and lectures on blow-job technique, before doing away with the notion by rinsing her hands.

Exiting the WC with its bovine fixtures, Clare is surprised to discover a smallish male form observing the goings-on downstairs from the relatively safe vantage of the second-floor balcony. The rear of the room where the Seminars people are dancing gives out onto a two-story atrium with elaborate double stair. The voyeur appears fixated on the activities under way in the dance-designated zone.

Clare wonders if she knows who this is. Though she does not have time to meditate on the matter, she does find it strange that someone like this individual has somehow found his way to a party. However, it's as if this person has not come *to* the party, but rather emerged from the depths of this excessively complex house. She wants to approach him but something holds her back. He seems, how can she put this, *psychologically feral*, if that is even an expression? He has the appearance somehow, in outline and from the rear, of being a creature able to approach others only in their dreams, a kind of humanoid lemur or gentle bat-boy hybrid.

Clare wonders if she's come upon him here because she is in need of a message. Maybe he knows the way out.

However, Clare's reverie is abruptly pierced by an individual in pale double denim who is bounding up the stairs. It is a manchild with a significant black beard, a second-year poet.

"There you *are*," the bearded one pants.

Clare notes that the bearded one is also in possession of a broken arm, the sleeve of his pale denim jacket having been tailored to sit neatly above the cast.

"I need you!" the Canadian tuxedo wearer informs Clare's weirdo, entirely ignoring her.

Clare watches with a mix of disappointment and shock as this odd, slight person is dragged away, down the stairs and into the dance.

Forty-Six

You

Harry has made an error. He has ventured out of the secure zone of his upstairs enclosure with the more or less idiotic idea of viewing the inanities of his audience, those professional readers he has served lo these many days and months.

This was not a prudent move.

Harry was laboring under the delusion that it might be possible to sneak up on the setting, eye the fauna, blend. The thought of descrying Loudermilk in his natural milieu hadn't been entirely un-intriguing, either. What did it look like when Loudermilk was "out there"? How great was the liberty of Loudermilk these days, really?

Harry is willing to bet that it is pretty great.

However, now Harry's arm is clamped in the clammy clamp of Anton Beans's good hand, and more than this, Harry seems to have been fully apprehended by the thought and belief of Anton Beans, meaning that Harry has become a sort of literal and material idée fixe as far as Beans is concerned.

Beans drags Harry—aka, the concept of Harry, plus Harry's body, to which said concept is attached—downstairs.

It's all Harry can do to keep himself upright, not to mention his teeth in his face rather than knocked out by the dowels of the intricate banister.

Music surges and thuds. Harry's vision is striated, a confusing mist. The music is louder and louder. "*I'm. In. Hea-eaven*," sings Mariah Carey. Harry allows himself to go limp. Moist bodies brush revoltingly against him.

Somewhere, perhaps even very near to him, Anton Beans is instructing people to get out of his way. Beans seems to know where he is going. Beans is bellowing something about turn off the music. Beans is possibly roaring himself hoarse. He keeps yelling this command regarding the music until other writers on the floor, believing that something of actual import may be going on, take up the chant, too.

The music dies.

Harry is a faded flower, a dried squid. He is draped limply across the somewhat-more-solid form of Anton Beans. He is tiny and sans volume and awaits oblivion.

"*You,*" Anton Beans is saying, by which Harry assumes Anton Beans means Harry. "Yes, *you*," Anton Beans repeats.

Harry's eyes are closed. He imagines himself stretched out upon a sacrificial altar.

"*Moi?*" inquires someone.

"Yes, as a matter of fact. I'm talking to you."

"No offense, dude, but *moi* is a little indisposed. What up with the jams?"

It is, as it was always going to be, him. It's Loudermilk. Harry wills himself to shrivel further. His eyes are sealed and he pretends that he is, in addition, dead.

"*Shut up*," Beans rumbles. The room, if it was not

particularly noisy before, becomes pristinely still. "I've *brought* you something."

"Thanks, man! What exactly might that be?"

"You know," says Beans, "what I'm talking about. You know who this is."

"I'm sorry, what?"

"You know what's about to happen here."

Loudermilk gives this a beat. "Uh, you're going to get the fuck out of my grill?"

There is a smattering of giggles from the crowd. Loudermilk has his adherents.

Beans is unfazed. "I'd like to do that, I really would," he says, "but unfortunate circumstances prevent me from being able to do so. Instead of getting, as you put it, 'the fuck out of' your 'grill,' I'm going, instead, to get further and far more intimately 'up' into it, because I and everyone else here tonight require an explanation. For example"—Beans begins shaking Harry loose from his shoulder—"who *this* is. Who is this person, Troy Loudermilk? You can't honestly say that you've never seen him before."

Harry hears the mutters of the crowd. They remark upon this person's familiarity, though really he is difficult to place. And so pale!

"I don't really—" Loudermilk begins to say.

"Oh yes you do." Beans gives Harry a more pronounced shake, causing Harry's eyes to pop inadvertently open.

"I have no idea who—" Loudermilk avers, as his face comes, as ever, gorgeously into focus. Harry finds himself staring into the copper eyes of his life's great frenemy.

"Hi," Harry whispers.

Loudermilk does not say anything.

Forty-Seven

Persona

Lizzie knows she is late. She has been, after all, just the littlest tiny bit busy. She's a creative type, and one can't be everywhere at once, and when inspiration strikes, as they say. And she's proud to have at last completed her artwork. However, there is no way she was prepared for the party to have already *ended* before she arrived! There is what seems at first like complete silence inside the Delta Psi Kappa house. Lizzie very nearly begins to cry. Then she hears a voice. The voice is coming from farther back inside the building, and Lizzie decides that she will walk toward it. This is how Lizzie comes upon a scene that she will later describe to herself as the supreme all-time competition of the world.

Everyone in the Seminars, all the current students, are gathered in this room Lizzie thinks was originally intended for something more serious and elegant than the use (party rentals) to which it is currently being applied. It has all this carved stuff and seems kind of, how can Lizzie put this, evil? But the Seminars people are at this point behaving in potentially surprising ways. Like, they aren't awkwardly rubbing up against one another but are rather standing in this sort of shocked formation, like they are anticipating witnessing an impromptu execution. The little hairs at the back of Lizzie's neck come to attention. Also, and perhaps more important, at the center of the circle are Loudermilk and this asshole self-promoter second-year poet Lizzie thinks is named Anton and then, in a final shocker, there is a very wan Harry.

Harry! Lizzie thinks.

Everyone is looking at Harry, but Asshole Anton is the one speaking. Lizzie attempts to appear nonchalant yet somehow purposeful, as if she's supposed to be there, especially given the wig. She hopes Loudermilk hasn't seen her, though, of course, who is she kidding, she also really hopes that Loudermilk did see her, that he is contemplating her superhot dress among other worthwhile reflections.

Anton is hissing something triumphant about how he's been waiting for this moment. Lizzie tries not to roll her eyes. If Anton the Poet knew how obvious and predictable his resentment is, he'd probably die on the spot, not that Lizzie is wishing for anyone to become deceased this evening or anytime soon!

She tries to give Anton the benefit of the doubt. Anton's broken arm does make him look slightly more sincere, like a general in a movie.

But there's Loudermilk. He's very distracting. He's standing so his face is in profile from her point of view. This makes it a little harder to see his expression. Loudermilk looks—and how to put this with the correct delicacy—like he's been flash-frozen. He's as suave as ever, but it's like his outlines have become just a little too congealed, too straight and thick and real? He resembles a cardboard cutout of himself. If he sways, he may fall to the floor with a little slap.

Lizzie kind of wants to rush up to him, to stroke his perfect satin face and moisten his lips with hers and reassure herself that he's still breathing, but she also kind of, very briefly, feels like she wants to never touch him again, which is just so weird. It's hard to believe that a being such as Loudermilk is capable of inspiring total revulsion but apparently this is how it is when he, like, does that. He doesn't really look any older, but the thing is, he looks so incredibly old? Like a massive shimmering mummy, someone who's been freshly embalmed and set up in state.

But Lizzie has to remember that what's crucial at this stage is that she listen to the words of Anton Beans. It's not easy, considering the fascinating visuals.

Anton Beans is clearing his throat. "You all know," he says, "the poet Troy Loudermilk. But I'm willing to bet not a single one of you remembers this specimen." Anton Beans indicates Harry, who is growing more bloodless by the minute and looks as if he may spontaneously shoot upward through the ceiling, propelled by his own ill ease. "The weirdest thing is that you've all seen him before. You had the opportunity to recognize him, but you ignored it. And the reason you ignored him is he was inconvenient to your vision. You had a hero in your midst, or so you all believed. A great poet! Why bother with this puling freak!"

Lizzie isn't sure what a "puling freak" is, but she's willing to bet it's not a very good thing to be, plus Anton Beans is currently pointing at Harry, so unfortunately it probably has something to do with him.

People in the crowd seem to want to know what the hell is going on. Like Anton Beans has done a pretty good job of lathering them up, but now it's time to drive the point home, because even if Anton Beans temporarily has their attention, they used to be having this pretty excellent party.

"Loudermilk!" some incoherent person screams. It's a girl, but Lizzie isn't big on reinforcing gender-based behavioral stereotypes.

A few other unfortunates put up some wails.

Loudermilk is, after all, their king.

Loudermilk isn't doing anything. His goose appears, for some reason, to be momentarily cooked? Lizzie is so incredibly weirded out.

"Lou-Der-Milk. Lou-Der-Milk. Lou-Der-Milk," the crowd is chanting. The room begins to sway.

"OK, OK!" comes a piercing cry from rival poet Anton Beans. "You want Loudermilk? I'll give you Loudermilk! I challenge Loudermilk and this other bizarre person over here"—indicating Harry—"to a poetry contest. That's right! A poetry showdown. You all know what this means. Even though we live in a scriptural society in which silent, private, so-called lyric reading is thought to be the order of the day, these two lucky individuals are going to have to recite out loud, from memory or extemporaneously, the very best poem that they can. And even though none of our training here at ye olde Harvard of poetry prepares us to do this sort of thing, we're going to judge them on the quality of whatever it is that they manage to do. And we're going to judge them harshly and eternally and you're going to see what I mean about what all of you have been missing."

There is crazy energy coming out of Anton Beans's face and it is visible even from across the sweat-clouded room.

Everyone, it seems, cannot stop staring.

"Well"—this is Anton Beans again—"what are you going to do?" Maybe at this moment he is only talking to Loudermilk. That seems possible.

And is there a pearlescent column of light that has descended to encase Loudermilk's body? Maybe there is. And is it this column of light that is making it so obvious that Loudermilk is at this point in time completely and utterly incapable of speech? It might be. And is this incapacity manifesting itself as a series of gurgling noises that are emerging incoherently from Loudermilk's mouth? Yes, perhaps this is so. Loudermilk gurgles. He opens his mouth and pants. Nothing happens. Loudermilk gasps. He touches his throat as if to reassure himself of its existence.

Loudermilk swallows. He says, "'The CNN Blues,'" and he pauses. "'*Persona poem*,'" he diligently specifies, as if this is the sixth-grade debate society. And Loudermilk proceeds to recite what is by far the worst poem that Lizzie has ever heard.

"Interesting!" Anton Beans all but screams, once his foe's performance, such as it has been, is complete. "I'm so curious about that poem! Now, OK," Anton Beans is fully screaming, "NOW YOU."

He means Harry. Lizzie at last understands the meaning of the performance.

Harry is, for the first time, and how can this be put into words, *someone*. Anton Beans has succeeded in performing a form of spiritual surgery, a psychic transplant. Instead of curling into himself or spontaneously expiring or even just falling down, Harry takes a shivering step forward and says, in clipped and semi-robotic tones, "'Mount Weather.'"

Lizzie realizes he means, like, as in mountain.

Harry's voice is not so bad when you come down to it. It's high and low both at once and it's functional, but beyond this it has this sort of superwavy tonal filling that makes you feel it really hard, right at the center of your body?

Mount Weather

I preceded this deluge: the phenomenon
of a pseudo-president; experimental
marriages; cavernous, red, dusty-red, gilded,
red, polysyllabic words (red, gilded, red-dusty, *der*).
Otherwise, I might be doin' something
better, eating a paste of mashed bananas
in an unpadded, wooden saddle;
coddled, if chemically enhanced. A
majority of my sainted hours are now prosthetic
fingers, important fathers, lots of feathers,
and strange oaths. People had a certain
humility, a contentious style and booming voice.
They were one Immortalization Committee,
a collective yawn; white stars, though flabby.
I'm slow but I passed. I preceded this deluge:
earned media; vast aromatic plants; "stop
loss" policies; a database of fans; the so-called boffo
scoop. I remember the frisson I felt. Yes,
yes; and yes. A female supplicant
wore a creamy sheepskin mustache.
I stared back, uncomprehending,
as the full flowering of the middle classes
commenced in a Napoleonic burst.
Viewing that oppression as a central part
of our liberation, bogged down by
diaper bags, we were hamstrung by sullen
bureaucracy, aka, the world's one mono-spoof.
We did not have enough soldiers, even if their wives

were in the dark. The premise of our exotic
exercises
was a floating island or a layer cake; some
mellifluous middle names; well-intentioned but
sloppy thinking; heavily subsidized corn.
There came a giant sucking sound. It just sat
there, oh ye fatty cold cuts! The white-collar hustle
and hideous furniture were a collateral benefit,
leavened with occasional doses of nostalgia, swarms
of finches, ruddy drakes, black-tailed gazelle.
Any vague, platitudinous quotation could
absorb me well. My face was rather badly singed,
so we applied a bleaching gel. Everything
was deliberate, meticulous, red, very red. And yes,
yes; very yes, too. There was a lot of esprit.
Our team stayed aloft in a plane for three
days straight, much as crimes, in the end, are
overwhelmed by personality. It's a quiet,
seething understatement to say the public
will survive the current plague of zeros.
I preceded this deluge: I will try to keep
my argument strictly precolonial, with
heavily bulleted sections: "1. Experience,"
"2. Lessons Learned," and "18. Action Plan."
Though in my haste I have been heard to say
there is no richer subject than the 2001
anthrax mailer (or *mailers*). "I know not *how* to
hurt other people," I also say. I stay low key and
crank out patients. You are patient
when you find beers, yes? Austere and dyspeptic,

I just thrive there, collecting endorsements
from the entertainment world, Clintonian
masks. I preceded this deluge.
I preceded this deluge. A superb antagonist,
a high-water mark, dingy with clarity, bathed
in top-secret fluid, I went boar-hunting
occasionally. It was the greatest time of our lives.

Forty-Eight

Est et Non

Directly after the accident, everything was shuttered. Then, slowly, and perhaps also abruptly, it wasn't. Or, it wasn't, and it was. It felt to Clare like a monstrous task. All things were open. But all things were things. There was nothing in the way of anything else. But it was all only real. It didn't make "sense." Clare stood at the top of an enormous tower. The tower was round and tapered like the world's tallest chimney and constructed from stone. The weather was extraordinary. The tower was located in the middle of an ocean. Wisps of cloud dangled in its environs, but most of everything everywhere was blue. There was the dense sky, so thick it was a sound. There was the water, dark navy. Clare could discern the curvature of the earth. Mostly she tried not to look down.

No one had spoken to Clare for a very long time, if ever. Clare was, nevertheless, aware it was imperative that she descend. She seemed able to recall having been told that the tower was of such a height that it would take her around six hours to go down it, a full day's work if she kept constantly in motion and took a leisurely lunch. Among the difficulties inherent to this venture were the facts that 1. There was no place anywhere on the tower, once one began to descend, at which it was possible to rest; 2. Clare was afraid of heights; and 3. The stairs that ran in a spiral around the exterior had stone treads that were at most five inches at their widest, by a meager ten inches across, meaning that to walk down, one had to dispense entirely with the idea of leaning against the side of the tower with one's right shoulder, staring down at the steps, moving forward in one's descent, and instead one had to face outward, pressing one's back against the tower and taking the stairs one by one, placing one's feet in an awkward sideways shuffle, progressing haltingly while staring into the cerulean void. So maybe it would take eight hours. Or twelve. Clare knew this was all rather specific, given she was hallucinating. The tower seemed to have no interior at all. Clare stood looking at a pile of crushed glass and rubbish tips at the tower's mossy circular top. There was nothing to sustain her.

So Clare had begun. But beginning had not been enough.

After the eighth or ninth day of sideways walking, Clare had come to the conclusion that she had either misunderstood the messages about the time required or that these messages were incorrect to begin with. It continued. It continues. It reminds her sometimes of the time she went to hear her father read at the Poetry Project when she was fourteen and he was in town and was reading with the famous poet John Ashbery, and John Ashbery read a long poem in sentences and the sentences were such that Clare is unsure if later anyone remembered the poems her father read. And after, Clare had sat in a bar on 8th Street and it was balmy spring and she hadn't said anything to anyone until she had gone home. And years later when she had mentioned this to her mother, her mother had said, "But you never went to his reading, don't you remember? That was the night Alain was here and I made you stay in. I don't think you know what you're talking about."

However, today it is April, and Clare is older and walking toward Building 109 so that she can collect the last packet of the semester. The air is like bathwater. It gives an amniotic feel. Time is buoyant. It rocks. It vibrates eerily backward every once in a while.

Everyone else, Clare thinks, is hungover. They have feted Loudermilk's demise. They are presently sorting through their own recent ethanol-soaked pasts and will arrive at provisional conclusions before they exit their dwellings to drag themselves toward the site of acquiescence to packet protocol. They are heavy with the previous night's disclosures. Next week they are likely to demand administrative justice. Clare keeps thinking that there must be a story in this, but she can't quite make it out. She recalls again what a beautiful voice the real poet had, his line about Clintonian masks. It's been a while, too, since she thought so directly about her tower. She looks down at her feet, but it's just the Cretan sidewalk. *Troy* Loudermilk, Loudermilk's full name is—as Anton Beans had said. *Troy*, whom Clare has briefly met. God, the trip is taking a while.

She is expecting Building 109 to be deserted. However, when she opens the door there is chatter and a lot of it. Everyone is standing in the front room, pressed together, as if they're witnessing a new contest. Clare has just made the decision to attempt to sneak by, when what is/are the actual object(s) of fascination catch(es) Clare's eye, which is, it must be said, the verb-related understatement of the year, since Clare is well-nigh frozen.

Someone has xeroxed her vagina.

Not *Clare*'s vagina, but someone's. Actually, maybe Clare means "vulva"? Someone has presumably clambered atop one of the trusty Seminars machines, dropped trou, pressed lips to plate.

This person—enterprising and biologically female, not to mention well versed in the intricacies of desktop printing—has subsequently taken the step of scanning said genital copy and converting it to a PDF of sizable dimensions, such that she has been able to print it out on some nine—Clare is not at the moment one for counting—eight-and-a-half-by-eleven sheets of paper, taking advantage of the office's impressive laser printer. The original Xerox has been reconstituted, rectangle by eight-and-a-half-by-eleven rectangle, on the wall of the Seminars HQ front parlor in a prominent location, one normally occupied by an oil portrait of dopey old Rainer Dodds, kindly patriarch, shaking hands with Henry Ford as out the window behind them horticulture and industry glowingly coexist, invisible music sailing over the land.

The original portrait lies facedown on the rug. It appears, somehow, to be sleeping.

It's a nice vulva, too. It appears friendly.

It is also, Clare realizes, a materialization of the title of her recent story.

Clare has not gone unperceived.

The origin of the world, Clare is thinking.

The room is full and no one is really saying anything. They all mill around gazing up at this veil-free desktop rendition of Courbet's much more modestly sized masterpiece. It's like they're standing in the studio of some artist, but they don't know who. The only sound arises from someone who, seated on a sofa, scrubs away at a scratch-off ticket, oblivious to artistic value.

The others begin to notice Clare, and their pointed looks suggest they are waiting for her to tell them something. From underneath their carefully crafted hangovers, they wordlessly implore her. Is this her message? They do not want to return to their rented places of dwelling without a word. They want to know what this thing is, why it appears, if the author is at last coming to take full command.

And the author is born again.

Clare remembers the tower, its final steps, which she takes in a single bound, landing with ease.

She will figure out what it means later.

"I guess it's spring," she says to no one.

Forty-Nine

The Author

There is a prone body facedown at the edge of her lawn. Meanwhile, Lizzie Hillary is not alarmed. Birds warble, and Lizzie is wearing cutoffs and a T-shirt that fit her best when she was eleven. The T-shirt was acquired outside the francophone world and yet for some reason it reads MAÎTRE-CHIEN. Lizzie throws herself across the lawn. She nearly barks and howls. Her parents have joined a delegation of concerned academics protesting President George W. Bush's speaking engagement at a local community college, and good for them, and particularly good for them in that they are not here with her and the birds. No one can prevent what is now very much about to go down.

Lizzie is moving with a mixture of terror and joy, and she can imagine it is fascinating to see. Too bad no one is watching. Too bad so few recognize the greatness of her artistry. Too bad she can't take credit where credit is due.

Lizzie comes to a standstill, squats.

"Troy, Troy, Troy," Lizzie says. "Loudermilk, Loudermilk, Loudermilk." She pats the back of his head, her poor destroyed man. She knew he was going to figure out how much he needed her one day, and here he is, sultry from sun and slightly foul. Lizzie pats harder. She flicks Loudermilk's left ear.

There is a moan.

Lizzie, a true artist, turns and sits and maneuvers Loudermilk's heavy, hot cranium onto her bare thigh.

"MPHHphlfg," Loudermilk is saying.

"I know," says Lizzie. "So true! Are you ready to wake up now?"

"Beans," mutters Loudermilk.

"What? I don't have any beans, OK? Loudermilk, I think maybe it's time for you to wake up. My parents' lawn is probably not so super comfortable. Um, Loudermilk?"

Loudermilk wriggles. He rolls his head back and forth on Lizzie's thigh. He is mashing his face against her. He gets his hands under him, opens one eye.

"Hi there," Lizzie tells him. "Rough night?"

"Shit," Loudermilk says. He rolls over onto his back. "The fuck?"

"Um, *well*, I think you were sleeping on my lawn for, like, a while. And you smell really bad? So that's what. It's kind of rude, Loudermilk."

Loudermilk closes his eyes. "Yes," he says, frowning.

"But anyway I'm not really mad." Lizzie touches Loudermilk's face. "See?" she says, leaning over to kiss him on the mouth. "See how not really mad I am, the poet Troy Loudermilk?"

"Uhngg," Loudermilk says.

Lizzie kisses Loudermilk again. Lizzie removes her thigh from underneath Loudermilk's shoulder where it has become trapped and gets on top of Loudermilk's abdomen from which vantage she continues to kiss him. This is something she's seen in movies.

"Uhngghmm," says Loudermilk. His legs stir and his arms encircle Lizzie's back. "You taste like toothpaste."

"You taste like dead butthole."

"Thank you."

Lizzie sits up. "Is it always going to be like this, Loudermilk?"

"Like what?" Loudermilk wants to know.

Lizzie is looking across her parents' lawn. She is staring at the fence there. She feels like she could just keep looking at this fence forever. She doesn't know how to progress from this moment, how to make something else happen, what she should say next to make it be how she really wants it to be in her life, and this is how she knows that she is young. Lizzie says, "I'm not really so stupid, you know."

"I know."

"No, you don't. You think I think you're going to change my life, but I don't and you're not."

"You're young, Lizzie-Liz."

"Right, I'm like seven years younger than you, which is basically five. And pretty soon this won't be illegal, but who's counting."

Loudermilk doesn't say anything.

Lizzie puts her hands on Loudermilk's chest. "Loudermilk," she says, "get up."

Loudermilk is staring at Lizzie but doesn't move.

Lizzie makes a fist and pounds on Loudermilk's chest. "Loudermilk!" she hollers, "I want you up on your feet right now!"

Loudermilk is motionless, staring, a human stick.

"Loudermilk! Loudermilk! Loudermilk!" Lizzie is yelling, "Get up! Get up! Get up! Get up right now, piece of shit! Get up off my lawn! Get up! Get up on your own two feet!" Lizzie slaps Loudermilk in the face. "I hate you! Why won't you ever *do* anything?!" Lizzie is crying. Lizzie gets tears on Loudermilk. Lizzie is sobbing, she bends over Loudermilk, she puts her arms around Loudermilk's head, puts her face on his wet face. "Loudermilk, oh my Loudermilk," she whispers, "*leave me alone.*"

Epilogue

Sat, 1 May 2004 23:10:02
To: prufrock69@hotmail.com
From: prufrock69@hotmail.com
Subject: The Jerkshop

What up H-Bag,

bet you're thinking I'm pretty slick. I'm writing you from me, as me. Or you as me and me as me and therefore it's me. Pretty genius, if I do say so myself. the perfect closed system!

Anyways, if you didn't have a massive coronary you realized by now I skipped town and you're sitting around pondering me ending my semester a little early. But what you _need_ to know is I got an incredible offer, Harrison me boy, and there's no place for me but the BIG apple. I feel like I couldn't even have planned this, like how amazing things worked out but, hey, when you've got extreme talent haha ;)

Apologies for the silence. I want you to know that getting an agent has been good but maybe somehow subconsciously I did plan it all? I can't wait for you to see teh novel when it comes out. Don't worry broham: I totally changed your name ;) ;) :))

We both got ours!

I'm attaching a scan for you, because your becoming a genuine Seminars person and you need 2 know what's ↑. This is a just little something something, the secret to the special sause. You being you *might* have missed it. Enjoy your times, man. Get that degree! Hey workshop worked for me so who knows what it would do for you.

Here's to hoping some day our paths do cross but not too soon.

Your sincerely,
LOUDERMILK

Metadata: 1 file attached, originovdapussy.pdf

The Origin of the World

By Clare Elwil

"You're telling me I have to choose?" the writing teacher wants to know.

They are in his office and the student has placed a sheet of paper on his desk.

"It's—it's," the student stammers, becoming paler and more shapeless. "I'm just not"—she pauses—"*sure.*" She touches her prim eyewear.

The writing teacher knows that all personality is, at the end of the day, a performance. The student is waiting. The writing teacher examines the page she has placed before him. On the page are three paragraphs he has not yet read with any sort of concentration. After he has selected one of them, the student has told him, she will know how to begin her story.

The student is saying very respectfully, very softly and crisply, that she needs his help. She needs his help because she does not understand beginnings. She says that she understands everything else, it's just where things begin that trips her up. This is her expression, "trips [her] up."

The writing teacher is not sure if he's heard of this sort of problem before. If a piece of writing does not begin, then does it even exist—or, for that matter, *matter*? It annoys him because this isn't a problem pertaining to writing; this is a problem pertaining to a particular kind of person and he's sick of these kinds of problems as well as these people, not least of all because he'd like to leave his wife.

But the student is not leaving, and her proffered writing is also still here.

The writing teacher scoots the paper closer to his side of the desk.

He reads:

A. While I was still in Paris, I dreamed about my father for the first time in years. And then, through the eeriest of coincidences, I actually saw him, though at no point had I sought him out. It was in the Musée d'Orsay. It was my last day in town. I was standing in Room 20, on the rez-de-chaussée, staring, as my repulsively ill luck would have it, into the pinkish cleft of L'Origine du monde, *Courbet's idealized depiction of a female crotch. Then, as my eyes moved across the surface of the painting to the frame, and as I took a step back, I turned to see, exiting the room, a man I hadn't noticed previously. It was him, unmistakably him, though we hadn't spoken in years. He passed through the doorway in a white scarf.*

B. *While I was still in Paris, I dreamed about my father for the first time in years. And then, through the eeriest of coincidences, I actually saw him, though at no point had I sought him out. It was in the Musée d'Orsay. It was my last day in town. I was standing in* Room *20, on the rez-de-chaussée, staring, as my repulsively ill luck would have it, into the pinkish cleft of* L'Origine du monde, *Courbet's idealized depiction of a female crotch. Then, as my eyes moved across the surface of the painting to the frame, and as I took a step back, I turned to see, exiting the room, a man I hadn't noticed previously. It was him, unmistakably him, though we hadn't spoken in years. He passed through the doorway in a black scarf.*

C. *While I was still in Paris, I dreamed about my father for the first time in years. And then, through the eeriest of coincidences, I actually saw him, though at no point had I sought him out. It was in the Musée d'Orsay. It was my last day in town. I was standing in* Room *20, on the rez-de-chaussée, staring, as my repulsively ill luck would have it, into the pinkish cleft of* L'Origine du monde, *Courbet's idealized depiction of a female crotch. Then, as my eyes moved across the surface of the painting to the frame, and as I took a step back, I turned to see, exiting the room, a man I hadn't noticed previously. It was him, unmistakably him, though we hadn't spoken in years. He passed through the doorway in a red scarf.*

The writing teacher looks up. "Are these different?" he wants to know.

The student's demeanor hasn't changed. Maybe she looks surprised, but mostly she looks exactly the same as she looked before.

"What exactly are you trying to get me to tell you?" the writing teacher demands, more frankly than he means to. He's spoken without much foresight or control.

"I need help. Like I said. I don't know how the story is supposed to begin."

"I'm supposed to choose"—he pauses—"on your *behalf*?"

"Yes."

"OK. Then I choose red, the last one. How's that?" The writing teacher realizes he is trembling.

"Oh."

"*Oh?*" he parrots.

"No, no," she reassures him. "I think it's a great choice! I always think it's best to choose what you really want." And here she adds, "*Consequences be damned.*"

The student reaches across the desk and, producing a pen the writing teacher has not seen before, circles the passage he has chosen. The pen makes a squeaking sound.

Then the student rises from her chair. Taking the paper with her, she exits the writing teacher's office.

•

That night, in his large and comfortable bed, the writing teacher dreams a dream. In the dream, the writing teacher is in a bare room, watching as a strange game unfolds. The game is played using round black and white tokens. These tokens—large cardboard dots—are affixed to the backs of three faceless prisoners. A prison warden (also faceless) has been tasked with freeing a single prisoner and, for reasons not elaborated in the dream, wishes to employ a rational system to make his selection. In the game there are a total of five cardboard dots, two black and three white. The prisoners are aware of the number of dots and their respective colors. Each prisoner is to have a single dot taped to his back. The first prisoner to identify the color of his dot for logical reasons, without recourse to his reflection or direct communication with the other two prisoners, will be freed. And presumably go on to lead a full and liberated life.

In the dream game, the faceless warden decides to affix white dots to all three of the prisoners' backs. This removes the scenario, the dreaming writing teacher observes, in which one prisoner sees two black dots (he will immediately conclude that his dot is white) and introduces uncertainty. Each of the prisoners sees two white dots. Therefore, they must conclude that the warden has either assigned three white dots—which is the case—or that the warden has assigned two white dots and one black dot. It is, at first glance, equally unclear to each of the prisoners whether they have been assigned a white or a black dot.

This first glance is a moment in which nothing regarding the dream game has so far been resolved, except that the distribution of dots is not immediately knowable.

Each of the prisoners recognizes that the other two prisoners, like him, hesitate to act. They also recognize the meaning of this hesitation. They slowly come to understand that the hesitation means that everyone is seeing the same thing. Each of the three prisoners sees two white dots, and no one sees either: A. two black dots, or B. a white dot and a black dot. The prisoner seeing scenario A would immediately come to a conclusion about the color of his dot (= white) and rush off. Prisoners seeing scenario B would immediately recognize that they are not black dots because the prisoner they see wearing a white dot continues to hesitate, rather than rushing off to share his conclusion, and those seeing scenario B would in turn rush off, having used induction to conclude. Everyone is hesitating. This inertia is meaningful. Since it is a kind of inertia that is recognizable, the writing teacher thinks, it is useful.

The prisoners each reach a conclusion, or so

it seems to the writing teacher in his dream, by interpreting the inertia they have perceived. They successfully rule out both scenario A and scenario B. Each jogs joyfully forward to attempt to be the first to tell the warden the tale of how they came to their shared conclusion. As only one prisoner can be released, each must hope to be the sole individual to benefit from this collaboratively established realization. They are all running now . . .

The writing teacher wakes up the next day puzzled by what he has seen. How can anyone win if all three of the prisoners share the same conclusion? Yet, all the same, he feels pretty good.

He stares at his wife, who is already on her feet and moving around their room.

Five days pass. Then another day. Maybe a week flows by. During this time, the writing teacher does not see the student who did not know how to begin her story. Then it is time for class again. The class meets and the student is there. They are going to discuss a story written by a different student, a fact that brings the writing teacher a modicum of relief, a certain sense of safety. They discuss this new story, which is a well-crafted tale about disappointment in college. The writing teacher is pleased.

Forgetting his recent history with the student who did not know how to begin her story, the writing teacher throws caution to the wind and recounts his recent interesting dream regarding the black-and-white-circle game played among prisoners. He describes the dream, just as it occurred to him.

The students listen. The writing teacher has the distinct impression that they find him to be a gifted raconteur. It's a fairly cerebral set of events all in all, and yet they do not look bored.

"I woke up," the writing teacher concludes, "feeling mystified. It's amazing the little things the unconscious brain can produce!"

The students are nodding. This is to say, the students are all nodding except for the student who did not know how to begin her story. There she is in a striped sweater.

The student who did not know how to begin her story raises her hand.

"Yes?" says the writing teacher.

"I have a question," the student says. "Maybe it's an observation, I'm not sure."

"Shoot!" says the writing teacher, with what he hopes will pass for breezy enthusiasm.

"So, I'm thinking about your dream. Though distributed across this weird imaginary time, it's not really a story. It sounds deceptively like a story, but it's not actually a dynamic arrangement of events. Rather, it's a discrete series of what I'd call entailments? It's like an elaborate, folding scaffold."

"Hmm," says the writing teacher.

The student's eyes narrow but she continues. "When expanded and considered at length, it will point to a specific kind of datum related to human social experience. I would call this scaffold a 'sophism,' which is to say, a deliberately erroneous argument. This scaffold consists of events of looking and thinking and, eventually, walking. It is produced via the medium of a room. It is also produced through the medium of others. The scaffold, once unfolded, is a piece of persuasion. It suggests that information in human social life is mostly generated not through deception or confession but rather (and ironically) through the act of recognizing that other people do not know what you also do not know."

Now everyone in the room is staring at the student. The writing teacher realizes that it is possible that she has never spoken in class before.

"But I can poke holes in this sophism. It's not very hard to do. Most fucked-up and ersatz of all is the warden, who is in fact unable to assign any combination of dots other than the three white dots, if he values the notion of a fair game. In distributing three dots of the same color, the warden renders the puzzle equally challenging, which is to say, equally time consuming but *artificially so*, for all three contestants. Had he distributed the dots differently, for example at random handing out two black dots and one white dot, the wearer of the white dot would have been the instant winner.

This is similarly true for a situation in which one black dot is present, for its wearer would be at an immediate temporal disadvantage in the reasoning process. Any scenario the three wearers of dots could contemplate other than the one that they in fact encounter is an impossibility, given the need for a game. This has nothing to do with real life. Simply put, a warden who behaves differently cannot exist within the game. Therefore, there was also, ironically, never a game, never a contest here, and never a warden with the will to choose. I knew the solution even before the dots were distributed, which is, by the way, the real test of logic."

No one says anything.

The writing teacher looks down at his watch. He looks up again and lets everyone know that the class has ended.

All semester long the writing teacher waits to see the story to which he has, or so he believes, supplied the beginning. He reads other stories, but the student who said she did not know how to begin her story never hands anything in.

The semester ends.

The day before winter break, the writing teacher sees the student in the hallway of the building in which his class is held and decides that he will approach her.

"You really know how to make a guy wait,"

he jovially informs her. It seems like a good way to break the ice, and the double entendre nicely masks any actual eagerness on his part to read her work, he thinks. She'll have to puzzle through what it seems like he really means before she can get to the fact that he's just asking her to hand in some work. There's no way she can know that he only considers her another writer—and a worthy competitor, at that. She'll never know that he's completely uninterested in her physically.

The student stares at him. "Oh, I already stopped writing! Isn't that what you wanted?"

It's very strange, because it seems so matter-of-fact. The writing teacher wonders for a moment if he is still dreaming.

"You stopped writing?" he repeats.

"Yes. Yes, I did." The student smiles. She turns back to her acquaintances.

The writing teacher walks slowly back to his office. He'd be lying if he said he wasn't totally elated by this turn of events. He hears laughter in the hallway behind him and stops for a moment to listen. He can't hear what they are saying, but he reflects that it must be nice to still be so young.

Afterword

The Libertine

> The state of society and the Constitution in America are democratic, but there has been no democratic revolution. They were pretty well as they are now when they first arrived in the land. That is a very important point.
>
> —ALEXIS DE TOCQUEVILLE, *Democracy in America*

When I began writing this novel, I was, mostly without knowing it, reproducing a trope from the libertine canon. I was rehearsing an archaic situation-comedy format I had first learned about by watching the 1987 film *Roxanne*, in which Steve Martin attempts to seduce Daryl Hannah, the titular Roxanne, by way of a hunky proxy played by Rick Rossovich, an actor I don't think I saw anywhere else ever again but who apparently had an important role in *Top Gun*. Martin's character, C. D. Bales, is a philosophically inclined fireman with a very (unbelievably) large nose. I don't need to explain why this proboscis presents a problem in mid-1980s America, though of course today we'd probably just think of it as an additional genital. Through a series of mishaps and happy coincidences, Martin/Bales woos Hannah/Roxanne, and true love conquers all, forestalling forever the false promise of a nose job looming, in true eighties-fantasy fashion, on an earlier horizon.

Roxanne is a retelling of Edmond Rostand's popular 1897 play, *Cyrano de Bergerac*, itself a fanciful version of the life of Savinien de Cyrano de Bergerac (1619–1655), a real person and early instance of that paradigmatic literary figure, the libertine. The libertine, recognizable since the seventeenth century, if not before, is usually thought to be a symptom of the emergence of democracy in France. This character hates society's laws and loves the roiling dynamics of nature. Not content to acquiesce to the supposedly civilizing influence of Christian systems for the orderly reproduction of humanity (marriage, chastity, prohibition of crime), the libertine transgresses in the service of freedom—a freedom the libertine believes is perfectly natural and therefore good.

Cyrano is less overtly sexual and violent in his fictions than his eighteenth-century inheritors—Choderlos de Laclos, the Marquis de Sade, Crébillon fils, et al. A guy who wrote under a pseudonym, i.e., a shortened version of his own name, he poked fun at a degenerate aristocracy, adored the picaresque mode. His libertine tales are designed to convince readers of the beauty of intellectual and social independence; atheism, too, perhaps. He was an early science fiction writer and legendary with a sword. His best-known novel, *Comical History of the States and Empires of the Moon*, an autofictional account of travels to outer space, is said to have influenced Jonathan Swift. It was published two years after his death.

As I was saying, when I began writing this novel, I thought of him or, rather, sort of thought of him. I thought of the fictional Cyrano invented by Rostand and of his need for a proxy to speak words of love, all of which I managed to associate with Steve Martin. But I wasn't thinking about love, exactly, or, for that matter, Steve Martin. I was really only thinking about the proxy part of the situation, about writing, about a world in which it might be convenient not just to have such a proxy, but to *be* that proxy. That is the world I have created in *Loudermilk*, in which a proxy is not an accessory to a comedic plot resulting in happy marriage but rather the main event, the hollow hero we can't look away from, though in truth we know little enough about him.

Loudermilk is a libertine. That much I can tell you. We encounter him during the academic year that leads up to the Swift Boat controversy of summer 2004, a mythological ruse that seems either to have altered American politics forever or to be the symptom of some other transformative event more difficult to name. This gambit followed, as we know, on the heels of a war waged to rid a foreign nation of a three-letter acronym.

Loudermilk is a figure of numbness, bravura, and excess, a fabulist who has appeared late enough in modernity and the history of democracy to be less at odds with the civilizing influence than, for example, Sade. Loudermilk has flirted with student government. He's not, on the whole, terribly opposed to institutions. Loudermilk enjoys a good court battle and a nice contract. He likes to play with serious, bureaucratic stuff—and email. He's friendly with administrators.

Indeed, Loudermilk's self-generated status as a fake poet and fake person, with a name that seems like a joke, could be explained by the need to have easy access to sex and cash. However, if we take a closer look at Loudermilk, this explanation hardly seems sufficient. First, we know that Loudermilk is already rich; second, his carnal successes and apparent familiarity with socially acceptable forms of violence are unavoidably his own. Thus, Loudermilk's wish to exist as a proxy for Harry's writing, for Harry's "voice," cannot be explained with recourse to the well-known story about vice and the satisfaction of worldly needs. I emphasize this point because Loudermilk does so very much to make us believe that this is what he is up to. He makes us dream—fantasize, even—that he is taking advantage of Harry's writing in order to "get" something, in order to obtain some freedom that he could not otherwise access.

But Loudermilk doesn't need Harry to obtain pleasure or even power. Rather, Loudermilk does what he does because he can do it. He does what he does because the stakes of his chosen school are so bathetically low. He does what he does because of the existence of institutional structures that produce the illusion of self-expression, along with the related illusions of self-determination and liberty. Loudermilk does what he does in a society in which there is, allegedly, no "natural" audience for poetry—in which poetry and its audience must, necessarily, be invented by the institution. Loudermilk decides to participate in this game of invention on his own terms. If the institution wants to render Loudermilk's self-expression false, a gesture accomplished merely in order to obtain a fellowship, then so be it! Loudermilk will go one step further: he will be already false, already a pastiche, already a construction.

Loudermilk, c'est moi.

But that is not all I have to say to you; otherwise, I would have written an opinion piece instead of a novel. The reason that this is a novel instead of an essay has to do with the nature of the libertine and what the libertine—always a fictional entity—makes possible. As I've attempted to suggest, the libertine is not just enticing and law-breaking; the libertine is a sort of philosophical construct. I've put him before you here precisely because he does not live in the sense in which you or I do. He is a figment of democracy, an ever-flourishing side effect of its ideals, a ghost whistling through databases and hovering over staff meetings. But although the libertine is not real, the entities that give rise to him (institutions, the law) have a vital and domineering reality. Far from being crushed by these, Loudermilk thrives on their banal hypocrisy, attempting to make it his own, an engine that drives him, a weird form of sex. Loudermilk comes after Sade and has gone one infinitesimally small step further than that great master of our pleasures. Loudermilk is an American and thus takes great pride in seeking petty advantage. He is also—and here is his greatest achievement—normal rather than perverse and, most perverse of all, on the whole, fairly average.

LUCY IVES

2018

Acknowledgments

This novel was something like a decade in the writing (I'm afraid it may even have been more). My first thanks go to college friends at the *Harvard Advocate* for Sunday-morning conversations regarding poetry that somehow came to form the basis of this book. You all know who you are; I wrote this for you. I also want to thank Andrew Durbin and Katy Lederer, who read very early versions of the manuscript during a time when I was struggling to understand it. What is here is different, and that is partly because of you. Thank you both for so kindly reading and listening to me. Thanks, too, to Eliot House, the Headlands Center for the Arts, and the Millay Colony for offering much-needed space and time as I pieced together a final draft. I would like to note that the writers and editors of *The Atlantic* of 2003 and 2004 furnished detailed and indelible language I mined to create Harry's poems—and that Abraham Adams heroically watched *Roxanne*. Special thanks to the i-Vigilante/Subaru Wars club-band for a certain beautiful holiday.

I am very grateful to Chris Clemans, who is a literary

agent, yes, but also a sort of kindred spirit and one of the best readers I have ever encountered.

Lastly, I would like to thank the inspired Yuka Igarashi and everyone at Soft Skull Press for their clarity, thoroughness, and enthusiasm for this project, which was born of a strange rage to tell a story about poetry and deception. Yuka: Thank you for helping me see how to do what I had for so long wanted to do. It seems like a miracle, but I have the sense that this is what you do every day.